The
WIND
IN THE
WOODS

THE
WIND
IN THE
WOODS

Rose Senehi (signature)

Rose Senehi

KIM

K.I.M. Publishing, LLC
Chimney Rock, NC

2015

Published by

K.I.M. PUBLISHING, LLC
Post Office Box 132
Chimney Rock, NC 28720-0132

PUBLISHING HISTORY
Canterbury House Publishing, Ltd., March 2010
K.I.M. Publishing, LLC / May 2015

Published in the United States of America.

PUBLISHER'S NOTE
This is a work of fiction. The names, places, characters, dialogue, incidents and plot either are the products of the author's imagination or are used fictitiously, and any resemblance to actual persons, living or dead, companies, places or events is entirely coincidental.

Library of Congress Cataloging-in-Publication Data
Senehi, Rose.
    The Wind in the Woods / by Rose Senehi
       p. cm.
    ISBN-13: 978-0-9962571-4-5 (trade pbk. : alk.paper)

1. Summer Camps—Fiction. 2. Serial murderers—Fiction. 3 Blue Ridge Mountains—Fiction. 4. Appalachian Region, Southern— Fiction. 5 Real estate development—Fiction. 1. Title.

    PS3619.E659W562010
    813'.6—dc22
               2009047077

For Hali Calcutt, a true North Carolina heroine

PROFOUND THINGS, AFFECTING THE LIVES and character of thousands of people, can occur when a unique combination of circumstances fuse like they have in North Carolina's Green River Valley. This dramatically rugged section of the Blue Ridge Mountains captured the hearts of this nation's earliest settlers. For generations they clung to their land as tenaciously as the massive hardwood trees had to the monolithic granite mountains rising from the rich bottomlands of the Green River that runs through it— thus protecting large tracts of primeval forests from development.

At the beginning of the twentieth century when the wilderness movement gave impetus to the concept of summer youth camps, a new influx of rugged individualists were drawn to this valley, and they in turn, clung to and preserved this hauntingly beautiful place with the same fervor. But these new guardians went one step further. Since 1910 they have imbued hundreds of thousands of eager, inquisitive young minds with the same passion and respect for this magical place and all the creatures that roam it.

CHAPTER ONE

Among those who rose with the sun were three to whom it spoke caution.

The seal of the state of North Carolina sat at the top of the letter like a threat. But for Gary Skinner it was a dare. He wadded it up and tossed it across the room, then swiped the greasy paper plates and runny fast food containers off the table. *Once they get their hands on you, the bastards don't want to let go.*

He went over to the fridge searching for breakfast and took out a beer. He couldn't let them catch him for anything before the social security checks started rolling in. All that bar fight bought him was two months on a stinking cot in the Buncombe County jail. A slight smile tugged at one corner of his mouth. *If they only knew who they ushered out of that cell.*

He set his beer on the counter and rifled through the cardboard carton from the food bank. A dog poked its nose through a hole in the screen door. "You'll get your turn," he snapped at the golden retriever tied up outside. He pulled out a loaf of bread and slapped it on the counter, then opened the peanut butter and spread it on a piece of spongy white bread.

He took a couple of gulps of beer, thinking about the smug little probation officer barely able to keep her baby fat from oozing out of her tight jacket. She had handed him a list of soup kitchens like she figured the only way he was going to get anything to eat was to beg for it.

If everything went the way he planned, by the end of the week he'd have enough cash to head back down to Satellite Beach. Things in Florida should be cooled off by now. Good thing he lit out of there before the sheriff brought him in for questioning about Melissa Hunt. Every time they come up with a murder victim, sooner or later they round up all the drifters. His name was already floating around in too many investigation folders.

He rifled through the carton again, this time noting the contents. Nothing but beans and rice. Not worth the energy it took to paste a grateful expression on his face. He grabbed the box, kicked open the screen door and tossed it on the heap outside.

Leaning against the threshold, he scanned the barren foothills dotted with broken down trailers rented out by the old couple who ran the gas station at the foot of the mountain. They only let him stay in one to make sure they had someone handy for all their dirty jobs. He had wanted to puke when he phoned the old hag from the jail and sweet-talked her into bringing his van back to the trailer, certain she was too lazy to nose around.

He couldn't quite figure out what kind of day it would turn out to be. North Carolina clouds differed from the sudsy white billows that ballooned up into the atmosphere along the Florida coast. There was no telling if the bizarre clouds lit by the sun hiding behind the mountains would forecast rain and keep people off the trails. Damn. He'd spent two days scoping out that park.

A bony cat licked itself on an abandoned toilet bowl leaning up against a shed. He picked up a can and threw it, sending the critter flying under a junked car. Noticing the dog pawing at the pile of garbage, he went into the house and came out with a bag of dog food. "Here, boy. Gotta keep you fed. Don't want any of them damn nosey bitches thinkin' you ain't being takin' care of."

The dog wolfed down the food and looked up at him. Discipline would be easier if he kept it a little hungry. "Come here, boy." He bent down and untied the rope, careful not to be too rough and have it act afraid of him on the trail. He fastened the collar he'd picked up at

Walmart, snapped on the leash and led it to the van. Once the door opened, the animal jumped in just like it had when he spotted it two days ago on a country road beyond a farm. It couldn't be but a couple years old.

He went to the back of the minivan and looked around before unlocking it. He got in and checked once more to make doubly sure no one was watching before closing the doors. Crouched on a knee, he pulled the blanket off a trunk pushed up against one side and unlocked it. He wrestled it forward so the lid would stay open. A pack of 14" zip ties lay on top of a hooded jacket. He took out two, wound them into small loops and secured each with a rubber band, then unbuttoned his back pocket, slipped them in and refastened the flap.

Next, he reached for the scabbard tucked in a pouch, pulled out the U.S. Marine Corps bayonet and ran his thumb along the eight-inch blade. Satisfied it was still sharp, he put it back in the scabbard, pulled up a pant leg and fastened it just below the calf. Deftly, like he'd done it a million times.

He slid a black chrome baton from a case he retrieved from another pouch and quickly expanded it to a couple of feet. It would come in handy to teach the dog to obey. He pounded the tip of the baton on the floor and collapsed it, then returned it to the case. He pulled up his other pant leg and strapped it on with wide strips of Velcro fished out of the trunk.

A lot of the survival methods he'd learned in Vietnam had been put to use over the past forty years while trespassing in backwoods, parks and abandoned mountain roads, living mostly out of a van or a tent. He'd already discovered that a closed off side trail led from the lookout point at the nature trail just outside Lake Lure and circled back to Route 9, a hundred yards from the main entrance. That's where he planned to make contact.

He'd checked his supplies yesterday, but now he had to get everything properly laid out. A box with enough survival food to last at least five days was pushed up against the wall next to the trunk. He reached for the sleeping bag, made some room and unrolled it, then took two blankets from the trunk and spread them on top. After taking the hooded jacket out and hanging it up on a wall hook, he dug out a large roll of duct tape and stuffed it in his backpack. A whiny whimper made him look up. The dog stared at him from the front seat. "You better shut up yellow dog, or you're gonna get a beating you won't forget."

He got out, made sure the doors were secure and climbed behind the wheel. It would take a good half-hour to get to the park. He had picked it out because it was an easy trail. The last thing he felt like dealing with right now was some bitch used to running up and down steep mountain trails who'd put up a fight. The last time, he had scratches all over his face and had to hole up in a swamp for a couple of weeks.

ANNIE WINSLOW LISTENED TO THE SOFT wheezing of her old calico cat asleep at the foot of the bed when a sudden screech from an owl snapped her mind back to the noise in the night. Must have been a raccoon falling off the wood pile, or maybe a stray cat knocking something over in the shed.

She remembered lying awake, transfixed like prey hiding in a hole, convinced she was a breath away from being caught. I'm too darn old for such crazy thoughts, she told herself. Serves me right. When am I going to learn not to watch the eleven o'clock news. Must have dreamt all night about that poor old thing beaten to death in her trailer. Melancholia settled on her like a layer of ash. She fought it off. Self-pity was eating her alive. If she could only stop reaching over in the night to touch her husband. The shocking feel of cold sheets stung like a razor slash.

The waking day peeked through the crack in the curtains. Had to be close to six. She had better get up and get going or be late picking up Ruth for their hike. She slipped out of bed, went over to the window and pulled the curtain aside. Vivid strips of fuchsia clouds streaking across the rising sun's golden glow reminded her of the yellow caution tape zigzagging around the old woman's trailer.

Ice cubes dropped with a thud from their form in the fridge. She eyed her cat. Not the slightest twitch. Why am I so jumpy? The stares of grinning grandchildren in gilded frames followed her around the dimly lit room as she dressed in a pair of shorts and a tee shirt. She quickly pulled on a pair of socks, scooped up the cat and let it out on her way into the kitchen, getting a whiff of the sweet honeysuckle climbing up the porch post.

She sank down on a chair by the door and put on her hiking boots tucked underneath. Traces of North Carolina red clay peeked at her from the seams. Her glance followed along her legs. Still looked shapely; if only her face and neck had held up as well. She picked up her watch lying on the windowsill over the sink and strapped it on as she waited for the coffee to brew.

Now that light was streaming in the window, she could see she'd put on the same tee shirt she was wearing the day Cal died. She started to peel it off, then stopped. *This is nuts. I've got to shake off these heebie-jeebies.* She poured herself a cup of coffee and remembered the last time she felt like this. It had started the same way in the morning, and by sunset she was sitting in a funeral parlor ordering Cal's casket.

Maybe she should phone Ruth and call off the hike. *No. If I cancel my plans every time I get a premonition, I'll end up a basket case.* She swept the gloomy memory from her head and checked her watch. Plenty of time to pick up Ruth and get to the Tate Nature Trail in Lake Lure by eight.

Excitement rippled through her. *That's better.* How she loved early morning hikes. It was as if she were stealing the mountains from the sweaty grip of July when the woods still sparkled like a freshly cleaned room and the sweet musty smells of the night lingered on the velvety mountain air. She shook off the fears and loneliness of the night. *That's right,* she told herself, *life is good.*

She stuffed a bottle of water and a peanut butter and jelly sandwich in her backpack along with her wallet and cell phone, then went through the laundry room to the garage. She opened the door to her sedan and stood there holding it for a moment. Instead of getting in, she turned, opened the door of her husband's SUV and climbed up.

A statuette of the Virgin sat on the dashboard, and his prescription sunglasses jutted upright from the cup holder. She swore she smelled the aftershave lotion he always splashed on in the morning. The notepad and pen under the rubber bands wrapped around the visor caught her eye. She pictured him writing down his mileage and what he paid for gas, and wondered if he was shaking his head about how few miles per gallon he was getting as his left ventricle exploded on the way into the kitchen.

She scolded herself for dwelling on morbid thoughts and focused on the hike. She took one last look around the SUV before sliding down and getting into her Chevy.

In the spring, she'd hit on the idea that day hiking would be a good way to get Ruth and her out of their rut. She'd played tennis up until the time she hit sixty when her knees couldn't take the impact of an extra fifteen pounds, but Ruth had spent most of her life either perched in front of a computer in the hospital's billing department or lying exhausted on the couch every night watching TV and munching on popcorn.

The Chevy swung onto a narrow paved road and began to slow. It rolled to a stop in front of a neatly landscaped bungalow, and a woman rushed down the steep driveway with her hefty breasts bouncing like a jalopy on a bumpy road. Annie reached over and swung the door open.

"Look at that sky. It's going to be a glorious day," Ruth Rodman breathlessly pronounced as she threw her backpack and trekking poles in the back and flounced onto the front seat. "The sunrise had me a bit worried, but look at it now."

The cheerful greeting convinced Annie this wasn't the time to bring up the sense of danger that took hold of her last night. Ruth would accuse her of being paranoid.

The vehicle continued along the mountain road that would eventually spill into Hendersonville. Bordered by the kind of stridently maintained homes that spring up in the affluent suburbs, the view filled Annie with a rush of joy—the special kind one gets when setting off on a journey of discovery on a sunshiny morning. Thank God she'd found a friend who was going through the same anguish and could share her struggle to make a new life.

She had stopped barging in on her daughter's hectic life every time grief grabbed her from behind. The last time she phoned Marcie, she was in the middle of serving her two boys a rushed dinner with her husband bellyaching about something from the next room. On the bad days, she turned to Ruth to keep from shattering into a million bits.

"You're gonna like this one," Annie said, tossing over a pile of papers she'd pulled off her printer the night before. "Their trails range from easy to strenuous. I've marked about two miles of the moderate ones. We should be done before it gets too muggy."

"Are you sure you got that moderate part right?"

Annie laughed. Poor Ruthie hated these hikes. The only reason she resigned herself to them was she knew she had to do something other than sit in her kitchen and stare a hundred miles into space thinking about her dead husband. "I'm sorry about last week. I thought you were ready for something a little more challenging."

"Challenging? Life-threatening was more like it."

The two women sat alone with their thoughts as the vehicle cruised through Hendersonville, already alive with traffic, then onto Route 64 toward Chimney Rock. The car weaved its way up and down the twisting mountain road and turned east onto Route 74 at Bat Cave and started its decent down the Hickory Nut Gorge.

Ruth stared out the window at the craggy mountains looming up on either side. "Tell me. Why is it that I'm already looking forward to coming back home to my pillow-top mattress?"

Annie laughed even though she felt a little guilty. Last week's trek to the Walnut Cover Overlook had been a big mistake. The short trail on mile marker 431 off the Blue Ridge Parkway might have been a better choice for today, but someone had mentioned the nature trail park in Lake Lure was an easy trek and usually deserted. After last week's disaster, Annie didn't want to take any chances.

Up ahead, they almost passed the trailhead set back over a knoll. A lone grocery complex sat across the isolated mountain road. Annie pulled in and looked around. No one but a man walking a dog. A van was parked on the edge of the lot twenty-five yards away. Annie got out the gear and locked the car while Ruth checked out the trail map posted up ahead.

Ruth came back, slung on her backpack and grabbed her trekking poles. "Looks doable. Let's go."

Annie smiled at her somber determination.

The trail quickly swallowed them into its swarthy world. Every once in a while the sun broke through the canopy, giving the wide park-like trail a dewy glade look. The two women climbed the gradual ascent on their way to the overlook on the Mountain Vista Trail.

Ruth plodded steadily along, pleasing Annie. She had picked the right spot after all. The overlook was just ahead. A good place to let Ruth rest up a bit. The two women sat down on a rock and looked out at the granite-faced Rumbling Bald Mountain. Ruth unsnapped her backpack, pulled out a bandana and wiped the sweat dripping down her face from her short silver curls.

Annie listened to the utter quiet. The moment was timeless. Except for the edge of a golf course spread out below, it struck her that this same scene could have been spread before a Cherokee brave on a hunt for the bear they called by the name, Yan-e'gwa. Annie was more convinced than ever that these hikes connected them to the ancient people who respected the land; it felt good to be among their spirits. The moment captured Ruth, too. She was leaning forward, her forearms braced on her knees, staring out over the valley. Annie knew what was running through her friend's head, and she leaned forward and put an arm around her shoulders and squeezed. "Don't worry. We're going to make it, Ruthie."

A golden retriever suddenly appeared, panting and wagging its tail as it feverishly licked Ruth. She covered her face with her hands and laughed and screamed at the same time. The dog quickly acknowledged Annie with a slurp across her face. The animal pranced in front of them, waiting for an appreciative response. Ruth gave in and unzipped her pack, pulled out some jerky and offered it a piece.

Annie reached over and petted the dog, thinking the man who had been walking it in the lot must be making his way up the trail. She rose and turned to see him coming toward them. He was tall and thin in the kind of way that made him look like he'd given up on life. His shallow, grizzled face broke into a randomly toothed smile that struck her as insincere.

The dog sat calmly at Ruth's feet, begging for another treat with his eyes. Ruth, who had taken no notice of the man, rigorously ruffled the dog's head with both hands.

Annie's muscles tightened. Something was wrong with this picture. What was this vivacious dog doing with this vapid, scruffy looking man? Why didn't the dog run to greet him? Repulsion rose in her chest as he neared. She backed up. Her hand flayed behind her in an effort to get Ruth's attention away from the dog. She could see the man was holding something at his side. Fear dug its claws into her brain. She stopped breathing as he pulled up his hand and slowly tapped a baton on his palm.

CHAPTER TWO

THE WAKING DAY HUNKERED DOWN on Tiger Morrison as he stepped out of his cabin and into his world. Still dark, a bird hollered out a call from deep within the woods, and the fragrant scents of mountain blossoms mingled with the smell of bacon wafting out from the mess hall.

He strode up the path of gold cast by the light pouring from the kitchen across the dewy hillside, then sprinted up the steps to the porch and opened the door to the lodge, taking care not to let the screen door slam; the campers would be up soon enough with reveille only an hour away.

He made his way through the lodge and across the dining hall to the kitchen. Katie barely responded to his greeting as she flipped over a spatula full of bacon. He resisted an urge to pat her on the butt he'd watched broaden a tad over the ten years she'd been cooking at the camp, and went over and poured a cup of coffee. How did that get into his head? He missed his chance with her almost twenty years ago when he didn't take her up on her proposal the last summer she worked as a counselor. He wasn't over Susan enough then to love her the way she deserved. A practical mountain girl, she just moved on and found someone else.

She was all business, and he knew enough not to interrupt the urgency of getting breakfast ready for one hundred and fifty kids. A battery of headlights bobbed in the distance. The ladies from the valley who helped in the kitchen were pouring in. He took his cup and walked through the dark mess hall onto the porch. This would be the only time he'd have to himself until his head hit the pillow that night.

The nickname he earned as a kid still fit Jack "Tiger" Morrison. Of medium stature and stalwart build, his manner bore a clear resemblance to the Scots-Irish, German, and Welsh mountain men who settled North Carolina's Green River Valley, following in the footsteps of the Revolutionary War veterans who came to claim their hard-earned land grants.

He leaned against the porch railing cradling the coffee in his hands and watched the forest slowly emerge all around him. Wisps of vapor snaked up from the lake. Times like this he allowed the kinds of thoughts too foolish to share with anyone else to roll around in his head. He was convinced something was going to happen this summer that would change his world. Not a premonition or fear. A fact.

He closed his eyes and imagined himself blind. He could handle that. He could tell the seasons of the year by the sun on his back and the wind on his face and the scents seeping from the woods; and he'd know the time of day by the sound of the birds.

He shook his head. What was he thinking? His sight was fine. It was just that he'd had this same damn feeling the summer he lost Susan. Ice cream of all things! Just like a woman, she had to make sure they'd have enough for after the talent show. He could still see her wave at him as she ran toward the parking lot, her white shorts crisp against her deep tan. Samantha had toddled after her, and she swept her up in her arms, buckled her into her car seat and took off.

They were in the middle of a talent show performance with the kids rollicking and laughing when he spotted the two troopers at the end of the mess hall, one holding a dazed Sammy. He couldn't remember the officer's exact words, just the solemn tremor in his voice as he said a drunk driver swiped the side of the jeep; then after he took a deep breath, asked if there was some other relative that could identify the body.

The lights went on in the dining hall. Tiger turned and saw Euva

Freeman setting out pitchers of milk and orange juice. He went inside, and she said good morning with a smile and kept at her chore as if it were for her own children. He smiled inwardly. A lot of the camps had signed on with contract workers to dish out their meals, but he hired as many people from the valley as he could get. Quite a few had been with him since he started and, over the years, just like him, watched a lot of the campers grow up. Euva had run the kitchen for years before retiring, and now came back every summer to help Katie.

It was one of the things he couldn't explain to people. How from the time he was a kid and his father bought the property, these folks who had lived in the valley for generations taught him reverence for the land by weaving its lore in a cloth of stories. He wasn't but five when their neighbor Charles Cox, while rocking on his porch in the evening, told him the story of Joe Capps who walked five miles to the Poe Cotton Mill in Greenville for five years earning five dollars a week so he could buy a bigger spread.

That's how lore comes about, Tiger figured. Stories that capture man's respect and awe are told over and over on porches and hearths until they exist in the collective memory of a people.

Spotting something under one of the chairs, Tiger bent down and picked up a cap one of the kids must have left behind. He slapped it against his leg and stuffed it in his back pocket while he thought. His indecisiveness must have caused that grim mood to wash over him this morning. He had to make a decision about the camp. The way things stood right now, the only way Sammy could pay her inheritance tax if anything happened to him would be to sell off a chunk of the camp's property. Judging from what the Ledges had offered him in the spring, she'd have to come up with nearly nine million. Hell, he'd never even seen that much money in his whole life. He couldn't dump that in her lap.

The land. That was what the place was all about. The camp, the program, the naturalists, counselors, mentors, kids, him—the whole shebang was there to appreciate and preserve the land and the creatures that roamed its three thousand acres. His father dreamt of it. He knew it. Sammy was raised on it. Why, the main reason he built Camp Green River in the first place was to have somewhere to pour his love for the valley and respect for its beauty, and let it overflow into the lives of every kid who ever came near it.

The wake-up bell rang and he looked up to see the assistant director, Charlie Morgan, walk into the lodge and throw him a wave before heading straight to the coffee urn in the dining hall. After last night's final campfire he had to be exhausted. Tiger finished answering a few questions from the camp nurse and joined him.

Charlie patted his shirt pocket. "I've got a few announcements."

"Who's doing the morning reading?" asked Tiger.

"Since this is the last one of the session, I thought I'd let Johnny Baird and Judy Wilson say something about the Woodcraft Laws and then ask all the kids to recite them."

Tiger smiled and nodded. This was his favorite way to close a session. By now, there wasn't a kid in the camp who hadn't memorized the laws written by the famed naturalist, Ernest Seaton, one of the founders of the Boy Scouts of America. Of Scottish ancestry and Canadian by birth, Seaton started the Woodcraft movement in the early nineteen hundreds. Tiger felt empathy for Seaton's early support of the rights of the First People and, after studying his writings, adopted the Woodcraft Laws of personal responsibility, respect for ecology and respect for others as a cornerstone of Camp Green River.

Win-de-ah-ho, win-de-ah-ho, win-de-ah, win-de-ah .....

The ancient Cherokee morning song, welcoming the sun and giving thanks for another day, echoed over the lake and drew Sammy from her desk. She strolled out onto the porch perched on a knoll next to the lodge and listened to the pulsating rhythm. The kids were pouring their hearts into it. She fed on the emotion and wished she were there; but the parents would start arriving at nine and she had to make sure she had all the paperwork set for checkout.

She went back inside and stacked up all the group pictures, then stopped and shuffled through them for one last look. Jimmy Larsen grinned at her from the second row of the one on top. Sammy laughed as she pictured him feverishly scribbling out an escape plan no less than an hour after his parents dropped him off. The little rascal wrote home saying he was going to sneak out on Monday after lunch when everyone was resting and walk the four miles to the main road. His mother was to pick him up at two. In the time it had taken for the letter to arrive, he had settled in and had no intention of leaving.

Sammy glanced at her watch. The counselor who was going to answer the phones during checkout wouldn't be there for another fifteen minutes, so she decided to take the time to plan a hike. Everyone was getting tomorrow off, but she needed to stay and answer the phones the day before the new session started, and would go hiking this afternoon instead.

She opened a desk drawer and slipped out her three guide books. Each trail she'd hiked had the date and the time it took penned in. Carefully written notes ran along the margins, especially of flowers and plants she'd identified and also noted in a collection of botanical books. She fanned through a dog-eared paperback the camp's botanist had given her when she was eight and smiled at the large uneven printing from her earliest entries.

She practically grew up learning to look for and recognize anything that grew on or crawled around the forest floor. Over the past twenty-four years she'd hiked every trail on their three thousand acres a hundred times and bushwhacked deep into the woods and along the ridges, once discovering a waterfall they hadn't known existed. The fantastic views from their lookouts had ignited a flame to walk every trail and climb every mountain in the southern Appalachians, if it took her the rest of her life.

Sammy smoothed her hair behind her ears and flicked through the guide book, finally settling on the Craggy Pinnacle Trail off the Blue Ridge Parkway. She didn't have that many parkway trails left to do in North Carolina and was anxious to get going on the Smokies. The trail was only a mile and a half, but it was going to be hot, and the first session of the season had tired her out; she'd knock it off after lunch and be back at camp early enough to have dinner before the session wrap-up meeting at seven.

CAMPERS WERE BURSTING WITH EXCITEMENT over the anticipated arrival of their parents and clamoring for attention. They crowded around Tiger and the staff assembled on the deck of the lodge. Through the jumble, Tiger got a glimpse of Sammy unpacking her paperwork. She was taller than he or Susan with a nicely curved lanky build she'd inherited from her mother's side of the family. A picture of her Aunt Betty floated across his mind like a dark shadow. She'd done her level best to turn Sammy into a girly girl, but as much as Sammy loved her, it hadn't stuck. He smiled to himself; score one for the Morrison side.

He kind of wished she'd let her blond hair grow long, but she wore it bobbed with bangs brushed to the side across her forehead. He knew enough not to say anything or he'd just be inviting her to tease the devil out of him, especially about getting married. He suspected that's why she got an apartment, figuring if he got lonely enough he'd finally talk Liz into marrying him.

Sammy noticed him gazing at her and gave him her old "aren't I a good girl" grin she threw out every time she caught him looking at her with too much pride, making him laugh.

ONCE THEY GOT THROUGH THE COMMOTION of greeting parents and seeing all the kids off, a huddle of grown men and women ate lunch while discussing the challenge of getting the camp ready for the new session by the day's end. Conversation ricocheted around the tables.

Katie came out of the kitchen wearing an apron and holding a heaped plate. She slipped onto a chair at the end of a table next to Bob Davies, the archery instructor who also played the part of the camp's hilarious mascot, Ortman. His wiry build vibrated with energy.

Bob stopped recounting a tale and gave Katie one of his trademark expressive looks, hamming it up as if he'd been rudely interrupted. He slowly made eye contact with the faces in the room as he spoke. "Well, look what we've got here." He tossed his head in Katie's direction. "Now that she sees none of us has keeled over from her cookin', she's decided to take a chance on some of it herself."

Amidst the laughter, Tiger waved a hand in the air. "Wait a minute, folks. I want you to know that we've got the best darn camp cook around. In fact, we're famous for it."

Bob put an arm around Katie and gave the crowd a big wink. "Well, now that you're so famous, instead of teaching this winter, why don't you go get yourself one of them cookin' shows."

Katie pushed some food around on her plate with her fork. "I'll

23

admit I've had to put on quite a few performances to keep my students interested in algebra, but I'm not quite ready for prime time."

"I can see it now," said Bob. "Katie the Camp Cook...*we dish it out.*"

Everyone could tell Katie liked the teasing by the way she flipped her thick chestnut braid back over her shoulder and looked around at the smiling faces, a halo of wispy curls framing her face. Deep dimples appeared as she tossed a hand into the air. "I'm no Paula Dean. Heck, I don't have the jewelry."

Tiger enjoyed the good-natured banter. Katie, who had just hit forty, was a Green River Valley gal who taught math at Hendersonville High, the main reason she had given him for wanting to stay in the kitchen every summer: she didn't want to get burned out.

Their maintenance supervisor butted in. "Why, Katie, you'd put that Paula Dean to shame. She may have all those long drawn out *y'alls* to slather around, but honey, you've got the *might coulds*, *tidy bits* and *ye-alls* to work with. And as for that thirty-minute meal gal, just show them our tin can casserole. Heck, between slinging all the barbeque and pullin' together a poke salad or hog jowl and beans, you'd be spellbinding."

Bob stole the attention of the crowd in a way that came natural to him. "And be sure to tell your fans that chicken feet ain't half bad if you know how to fix 'em."

Amidst all the shouts and boos, Tiger came up behind Bob and made it look as if he were about to strong-arm him. "Okay, people. If y'all want Katie the Camp Cook to dish it out for dinner, we had better leave her be and get to work."

The crowd disbursed rather quickly after putting away their trays and grabbing bottles of water and snacks set aside for them on the counter. Before taking off to look at some work that needed to be done in the infirmary, Tiger signaled to Sammy who was coming out of the kitchen stuffing a sandwich in her backpack. They could take a minute to talk while the maintenance director gathered his tools.

"Are you taking Skippy with you?"

"No, Dad. I'm hiking a steep climb on the Blue Ridge today and it's going to get too hot for him."

"Will you be back in time for the session wrap-up?"

She gave him a quick kiss and ran out the door. "Don't worry. I'll be back by four. Maybe five."

Seeing Sammy disappear down the road all alone made Tiger wonder, as he had been doing a lot lately, about Randy. Whatever happened last May to make her cancel the wedding had to have been serious. Just getting that sister of Susan's to put the brakes on what was building up to be the social event of her life was as hard as attempting to stop a runaway truck on a steep mountain road. For a moment back then, he was afraid Betty was going to offer to marry Randy herself just so she could go ahead with her plans. What he knew about Randy he learned mostly from the staff at Falling Creek, a boy's camp a few miles up the road. A former camper, he was working on his MBA at UNC in Chapel Hill where he met Sammy at a party while she was visiting a friend.

Tiger never quite warmed up to the guy, but it sure did his heart good to see Sammy bloom as the boy courted her. It picked up the whole office over the winter. Her mother's jaunty step appeared, and then the trickling laughter. It usually pained him to think about Susan, but this time, maybe because she almost seemed alive again in Sammy, it had made him happy and feeling young again. Since the big blowout with Betty, as if they had made an unspoken pact, Sammy never mentioned Randy or the wedding to him again.

Despite the whole thing tearing Sammy up, he was ashamed to admit to himself that he was glad it worked out the way it did. He knew it wasn't in his nature to feel this way about anyone. He always looked for the best in people, and he needed to come to terms with why he didn't like the guy.

Maybe it was because he'd always expected Sammy to end up with someone from one of the local camp families. That's the way things went around there. Operating a youth camp was a way of life. A mind set. A twelve-month-out-of-the-year job that turned into twenty-four/seven when the kids showed up. Almost every couple he knew either met at camp, worked together at camp, or got together through some camp connection, because that was who they knew. Camp was the world they lived in. He never dared push it because he knew all too well that picking the right partner was the most important decision Sammy would ever make, and he didn't want to tamper with the delicate balance between desire and reason.

Maybe he was rationalizing now that the two broke up, but Randy had seemed too good looking, too sure of himself. How could a guy, who half the time had a big grin on his face as if it were a permanent fixture, run the camp with Sammy? He couldn't imagine Randy having the fire in his belly for the place the way he'd need to.

Tiger suddenly felt pressured. He wasn't going to live forever, and sooner or later Sammy would take over. Something had to be done to make sure she could hold on to the camp. He would make that call to the guy at the conservancy and see if he could get together with him tomorrow for a few minutes before the next session started, even if it was just on the phone. It was rushing it a bit, especially after putting him off for the past two years, but once the new group of kids arrived, he'd be swallowed up in the mission of making their two weeks at Camp Green River a lifetime experience. He spotted the maintenance supervisor and grabbed one of the tool boxes and laughed to himself as they headed to the infirmary. Who, he wondered, was more excited about the upcoming session, him or the kids?

CHAPTER THREE

"LAURA, HOW MANY TIMES do I have to tell you, Alvin's going to be perfectly all right?" His voice was soft and his words spoken not so much to get a response, but more to drown out the sound of the sniffling he'd listened to for the past three days.

She said nothing and kept stacking the carefully pressed clothes into the trunk on the bed, their neatness an expression of her love. Every once in a while she stopped long enough to blow her nose and put a checkmark on the list attached to a clipboard lying next to the trunk.

Al Magee, his gray suit jacket hanging limply on the back of a chair, stood gazing through the lace curtains with his thumbs hooked onto his suspenders. He spotted his son, Alvin, putting something in the car in the driveway, then he shifted his weight from one foot to another a couple of times, waiting for the next flare up. Laura stopped, took a tissue from her apron pocket and blew her nose. No matter what she said, he wasn't going to be dissuaded. He only had to hold out for a couple more hours, then he'd have Alvin at a place where the kid could breathe.

From the reflection in the window he saw she had stopped packing and stood staring at his back. The sight of the woman he loved, wringing her hands in torment, broke his heart. He went over, put his arms around her and gently patted her graying brown hair as she sobbed softly against his chest.

This whole mess was his fault. Why didn't he listen to all her pleading about her biological clock? They burned up too much time getting their doctorates and landing assistant professorships. Once they tossed out all the birth control paraphernalia, he was stunned to find out how difficult it actually could be to conceive. If only his students knew through those seven agonizing years, the reason their balding economics professor kept ending classes early to rush home was because a dipstick had told his wife she was ovulating. By the time baby Alvin finally showed his darling wrinkled little face, they'd hit forty and were too worn out for another go-around.

He rubbed his cheek across her hair. "You need to wrap this up, baby. We've got to leave in an hour."

She moved away from him a bit and straightened his tie, then ran her hands down his chest.

Here we go again. She's going to give it one more try. He held her head firmly in his hands and looked straight into her red swollen eyes. "Honey, he's going." He studied every muscle in her face until the wrinkled brow slowly relaxed and the quivering lower lip melted into a look of submission.

She nodded, then compliantly went to the dresser and pulled out a cardboard box, took off the lid and pulled a bright orange piece of cloth from the tissues.

"What's that?" he asked.

"A shirt." She pulled out a matching pair of shorts and placed them behind the shirt on the bed. "I thought the tie-dyed effect would make him look a little more... filled out."

"You're not sending that outfit to camp with him, are you?"

"Yes. He can wear it when we come to visit." She stood motionless and stared blankly ahead, trying to adjust to the fact that Alvin was actually going to camp. "I might as well go downstairs and get some snacks for the cabin."

She was gone a few moments when Alvin walked in the room. He was on the skinny side with glasses, and looked a lot like his father. He sauntered over to the bed and picked up the shirt, a trace of disbelief on his face. "What's this?"

"Your mother bought it for you."

His mouth twisted as if he were biting hard on the inside of his cheek while he mulled the outfit over. It took a moment, but he finally muttered a pathetic attempt at appreciation. "I... like it."

His father put an arm around his shoulder and pulled him close and laughed. "Alvin, you're such a good sport. We don't deserve you."

THE TRIP TO FLAT ROCK took a painful four hours. Both the campuses at Harvard and Durham were flat, and since Alvin had never been in the mountains, he was possessed with the general idea that it would be like a jungle. He looked a little tense in the back seat reading all the words between the lines his parents spoke. They'd always treated him like another adult so he wasn't used to them talking so guardedly. Based on what he could decipher, he half expected that the car could turn around and head back home at any moment.

Alvin could tell his mother was about to cry again. Her voice got pinched and she began to snivel. He searched his brain for something to distract her. "Mom, are you sure you remember how to feed Molly?"

His mother pulled herself together and repeated the detailed instructions he'd given her for his Guinea pig. That was one of Alvin's favorite things about her. She was a stickler for getting everything exact, just like him.

He made eye contact with his father in the rearview mirror. Even though his dad was now the assistant dean of the School of Economics and he didn't see him as much as before, they could still read each other's thoughts, and the main one on his father's mind right now was that he go to camp.

Alvin had sensed things were going to change ever since his dad stuck up for him when his mother wouldn't let him play soccer in the spring again. His father usually kept still every time he begged to join in some team sport while his mother came up with some convoluted reason why he shouldn't, ending with, "Now, you can if you really want to, Alvin." And when he said he did, she would expand her reasoning to where it could go on for hours.

The massive Blue Ridge Mountains rose on the horizon, and his father turned off Route 26 onto 25 before Hendersonville. They made a right a few miles up and drove through a lush valley for a while, then turned onto a gravel road and stopped abruptly.

His father tapped his fingers on the steering wheel like he was reluctant to say something he knew he should. "Honey, your face is puffy. Maybe you should put on some powder before we drive up to the camp."

She stared out the window. "It's not necessary. I'm not getting out of the car."

His father pounded the steering wheel. "Laura, we're here and I want you to buck up for Pete's sake."

"Al, I would have been all right with this if you had let me get a job at the camp. I would have been willing to wash dishes."

"That idea is ridiculous and you know it!"

"Not as ridiculous as you insisting that we wait so long to have a baby. First it was our masters, then the damn doctorates, then the damn assistant professorships. That boy in the back seat is all I've got, and I'll never forgive you if anything happens to him!"

The sound of splattering gravel exploded as his father threw the car into reverse, swung back on the main road and slammed on the brakes. Everyone's heads smacked against the back of their seats as his father floored the gas and sped back towards Route 25.

"Stop, Dad! Stop!" The car screeched to a halt laying a coat of rubber on the road. Except for the sound of heavy breathing, all was still. Alvin unsnapped his seatbelt and slid an arm around his mother. His voice resonated with love. "Mom, you don't have to put on any powder. You're beautiful the way you are. But… I want to go to camp." He put a hand on his father's shoulder. "Go on back, Dad."

His father glanced up at the rearview mirror and shook his head. After twenty-five years of marriage, this was the first time he had heard Laura swear. For the past two months they had discussed, analyzed and debated this camp deal, and in all the hundreds of thousands of words, she never once mentioned his insistence that they wait to have children. He couldn't help thinking she really had to be hurting to throw it in his face in front of the boy like this.

As the car bounced along the mountainous four-mile climb to the camp, his mother donned a pair of sunglasses. Alvin squeezed her shoulder. "That's it, Mom. Now you look like Angelina Jolie."

30

"Who in the heck is that? I don't know if I should feel complimented or insulted."

Alvin laughed to himself. That was another thing he loved about his mother. Her bio-molecular research demanded she read so much that she rarely looked at the papers or turned on the TV, to say nothing of taking an interest in movie stars. But when they would browse through the stamp collection his grandfather left him, she knew the names and biographies of all the people on the stamps, as well as fascinating stories of the countries issuing them. Not everyone could make history come alive from a little square of paper.

The car crawled up the narrow gravel road that twisted its way through an old-growth forest, passing running streams and rock-faced mountains, until it came to a drive with a sign pointing to Camp Green River. They drove a short way and rolled onto the front field packed with cars and people unloading. His father pulled instructions from his breast pocket and read them aloud. They were to meet up with his counselor there, and then check in at the main lodge and go through the health screening. The parents could tour the cabin and grounds before they left, then all the kids were to assemble back on the front field for a Respect Ceremony.

When his father read that parents had to leave by eleven, Alvin glanced at the clock on the dash and, seeing it was already ten-thirty, wondered if his father had planned this late arrival so they wouldn't have enough time to take a tour. Anything and everything his mother saw would be grist for her imagination.

His father got out and went to the other side of the car, opened the door and helped his wife out. He put his arm around her waist and whispered in her ear. "Are you going to be okay, baby?"

She straightened the skirt of her light blue suit and adjusted her sunglasses. "I'll concentrate on looking like a movie star."

Kids were in all stages of settling in, and the air pulsated with a sense of adventure. They found Alvin's counselor on the front field, put his trunk on a wildly colored cart and headed for the cabin. Alvin skipped up the steps ahead of his parents and found one of the mothers closing a trunk and slipping it under a bed. Dressed in hiking shorts and a tee shirt, she stood up and put a hand on Alvin's shoulder. "You're the boy my son's waiting to meet. Tucker's going to be attending two sessions, too. Everyone's already checked in and they're touring the camp."

Laura had gone directly to the bathroom separating the two sections of the structure to check it out, while Al helped get the trunk off a cart that had just pulled up. Alvin and the woman went out on the porch and held the door open for him.

The woman could see a matronly lady she presumed was someone's grandmother in thick heels giving the shower a careful inspection, and turned her attention back to Alvin. "I'd really like to meet your mother before I catch up with my husband, and we have to leave." She glanced at her watch as Laura emerged from the bathroom. "When is she coming?"

Alvin went over to Laura and put an arm around her. "This is my mother."

The woman's eyes barely flickered as she got her bearings. "Of course. How stupid of me." Seeing that Laura was inappropriately dressed to hike around the hilly campus, the woman said, "We've got to be out of here in fifteen minutes, and I know you want to get your boy settled in, so I'll let you get on with it and go find my husband."

Laura barely had time to make Alvin's bed before the bell rang, and they had to rush to the car. Alvin waved them off and made his way to a circle forming on the front field. He found his counselor among those who had to be his cabin mates. The smallest kid in the bunch made room for him and pointed excitedly to the open space.

Tiger, in a well-worn pair of shorts and a tee shirt, burst into the circle. A playful kind of energy emanated from his warm smile as he welcomed everyone and introduced the staff. He explained that they were assembled to pledge three things: to respect themselves, to respect others and to respect the world around them.

As kids raised their hands and told what the three respects meant to them, a strange feeling came over Alvin, like nothing he'd ever felt before. There was something about taking an oath that, for the first time in his life, made him feel like he was responsible for himself and his actions. He was suddenly connected to something beyond family and school, and he felt empowered as he promised to play an active part in this unfamiliar world with honor.

After repeating the pledge and listening to it echo around the circle, he looked up at the vastness of the space, listened to the absence of sounds except those of nature and inhaled the smells of the forest. This wasn't home with all the love and frustration it stood for. This was exciting.

CHAPTER FOUR

"OKAY BOYS, THAT'S ENOUGH froggin' around." Patrick Kenney, Hemlock Hut Two's counselor, stood at the switch. "I'm turning down the lights."

A squeaky, high-pitched voice moaned out, "Don't turn 'em down. I'm afraid of the dark."

Everyone snickered.

"All right, Ricky. That's enough clownin' around. We're gonna play *Rose, Thorn, Bud.*" Patrick turned down the lights and lay down. "Okay Ricky, what was your thorn for the day?"

The room became silent as everyone listened. "Can I say my rose instead?"

"Sure. Go ahead."

"I dove off the diving board head first. It was the first time I ever did that."

"Not bad, Ricky. Who wants to go next with a thorn?" They were silent. "Tucker, how about you?"

"I wasn't able to hang on to the test bar to the count of eight, so I couldn't ride the pulley across the lake."

"How far did you get?"

Someone hollered out "two."

"Quiet down, guys. Go on, Tucker."

"Five. But this was my first try. Tomorrow I'll do better."

There was a low murmur as a few of the kids asked who had passed the count.

"That's good, Tucker. That's a thorn… and a bud."

Patrick tucked an arm under his head and listened to the kids assess their day's accomplishments and disappointments and chart some goals. This was one of the best ways to wind them down for the night. After they all had a chance to share, Patrick told them to get to sleep. A couple of kids were talking to each other, and someone shouted out, "Shut up everybody, I'm tired." Patrick laughed to himself. In another ten minutes it would take a cannon to wake the little buggers up.

By habit, he reviewed the day in his mind and got a fix on the following day while he waited for everyone to settle down and doze off. He ran through the seven kids one at a time, matching them with the information he'd culled from their folders.

Thankfully, Alvin Magee seemed eager to fit in. At the wrap-up from the previous session, Tiger took him aside and told him he had personally selected him as the boy's counselor because he wanted someone who could empathize with him. That statement made him take a hard swallow before studying the kid's folder.

Tiger had said that after interviewing the parents on his recruitment tour, he was all set to cross the kid off as a candidate. He'd seen nervous mothers before, but this one gave him genuine pause. But then the father phoned. He was obviously an intellectual, yet spoke in the simple heartfelt words of a concerned father and husband. The man said he needed the four weeks to start weaning his wife from her obsession with the boy, and planned for both of them to see a counselor.

Tiger had told Patrick that the man's candor and determination earned his respect. At least he had a plan. But it wasn't until he had a conversation with the teacher who recommended the boy that he agreed to enroll Alvin Magee for back-to-back sessions.

Patrick gazed out the window at a star peeking from between the dark heavy foliage and recalled the way Alvin smiled all through evening song. It was good Tiger gave the kid a break. So what if he had to give him a little special attention.

The room had grown still. He crept out of bed, went over to the bunks and made sure everyone was tucked in. When he got to Alvin, he shook his head. The kid was lying on his back in a prone position, uncovered and out cold. Patrick had kept an eye on him all during the vigorous camp-wide game that night, and his heart went out to him when he started to drag pretty badly near the end. But he would call up enough energy to keep on going, as if he had promised himself he wasn't going to drop out, even if it killed him.

Patrick managed to wrestle him under the blanket without waking him up, and went back to his bunk thinking about the boy. He was way too thin and seemed uncoordinated, but his calm nature and mental alertness gave him a likable kind of maturity. Yep, Green River's non-competitive, yet challenging curriculum might be all the kid needed to get up to speed.

Patrick laughed to himself recalling the way Alvin started to get into bed, then spontaneously turned around, ran over and gave him a big hug. With the way a couple of kids stared at him when he went back to bed, he didn't think Alvin would do it again; but the gesture sure did seal their commitment to each other.

THE NEXT MORNING, EUVA FREEMAN sat with Katie at a small table in the kitchen. It was covered with a red checkered tablecloth; a plastic tray jammed with the usual condiments sat in the center. This was the first chance the women had to take a breather since breakfast.

Euva Freeman put the *Times-News* down and took a sip of coffee. A halo of white hair framed her finely crackled face. She was thin to the point of looking frail, but her shriveled frame could still split a log with one slam of an ax.

"Says here a couple of elderly ladies have gone missin.'"

Katie had her own problems with a missing carton of olive oil and kept studying the delivery slips from the shipment that had just come in.

"They think the two women went out hiking together," added Euva.

Katie's ears perked up with the mention of hiking, and she looked up. Katie, who was an avid hiker who went out regularly with her son,

Jason, noticed that after Sammy called off her wedding, she'd been going out alone with Skippy, and she didn't think it was a good idea.

Euva continued. "The one woman's daughter was a little worried because she hadn't heard from her mother for two weeks. And when a neighbor called and said the mail and newspapers were piling up, and her cat had been seen roaming around the neighborhood, she flew down from Connecticut and broke into the house."

Katie put down her list. "You mean she didn't do anything for two weeks?"

"It says here that the daughter didn't think it was unusual for her mother to go on bus tours with her church group, and figured that's where she was. She found everything in the house like it should be. Only things missing are her mother's hiking boots and backpack; and her car, of course. One of the neighbors mentioned it to someone at church who said her neighbor's mail was piling up, too. Turns out they're friends and go hiking together every week."

Sammy came into the kitchen holding a tray of dirty dishes she had brought over from the office. The ladies greeted each other, and Sammy got a cup, poured herself some coffee and slid onto a chair next to Euva. Katie went unnoticed as Euva showed Sam a picture of her newest grandchild. There was a strong bond between the two, mostly because Euva and her older daughters had a hand in raising Sammy after her mother was killed. Sammy was pretty much part of the family and invited to all their doings.

The newspaper lay on the table. Katie picked it up and skimmed over the article about the two missing women. "Sam, did you hear about the ladies they think got lost hiking?"

Sammy nodded. "Uh-huh. I got a call from a friend of mine who runs the rescue training program at the Pisgah National Forest. Evidently, the neighbors contacted the daughter of one of the women, and when she flew in from out of town she noticed her mother's computer was still on. She jiggled the mouse, and the nature trail in Lake Lure appeared on the screen. She guessed that was the last thing her mother looked up, so she went up there and found her car sitting in the parking lot. The sheriff has called for a search. Becky's group is joining them this morning."

Sammy brushed her bangs to the side. "They're pretty sure the lady went out with a friend who wasn't very athletic, and think they might have been looking for a shortcut and got lost. It's also possible one of them might have had a medical problem and they couldn't get out."

Sammy reached for the paper and studied the pictures of the two women. Her brow wrinkled. "They look like two nice grammas." She put the paper down and focused on Katie. "Rescue squads from two counties are out there today with everything they've got. All-terrain vehicles, search-and-rescue dogs, helicopters, searchers on foot." She shrugged her shoulders. "That whole park area is only around two hundred acres. Face it; it's been over two weeks since they were last seen. If they were alive, they would have made it out of there by now. My friend said they haven't given up hope for a rescue, but chances for a good outcome look pretty slim."

Sammy glanced at her watch, then jumped up and started for the back door. "I better get over to the lake. My swimming session's starting in ten minutes."

The swinging door to the dining hall rocked on its hinges, causing the two women to look up. Tiger threw them a wave, but before they could ask him what he wanted, he was out the door again. Katie's shrug asked what that was all about.

Euva got a piece of chocolate cake left from Sunday's lunch, peeled off the plastic wrap and ate it leaning against the sink. "He doesn't much like the news about old Jeb Ryan selling out. Looks like it's got him kind of preoccupied."

"You mean that mountain farm across the road?" asked Katie.

"Yep. That's it. My Jim was over to Jeb's place yesterday to talk about getting out some timber, and he told him he didn't want to make any arrangements since he was talkin' to someone about buying the place. They want to put in a golf course and a bunch of houses. You know. One of them gated communities." She rinsed her plate and fork and set it on a rack next to the dishwasher. "I told Tiger about it this morning on my way in."

Katie nodded. "That's probably why he didn't come in for breakfast."

"Jim knows every inch of Jeb's property. He's been hunting in there since his teens. Said from the ridge you can see right down on the camp."

As Euva sprang up from her chair and started unpacking the cartons, Katie hoped she'd be that agile at seventy. She got up and spread out the twenty-five large bowls they needed for serving the vegetables at lunch.

"Yep," said Euva as she set about chopping some lettuce for the salad bar. "I hate to see him so distracted. This place means a lot to him."

Katie went into the cooler and brought out a bushel basket of fresh picked green beans. Shouts from kids on the nearby path drifted in. She looked up and smiled at Euva. The kindly look the woman returned made her angry with herself for being so bothered by the affectionate touch Sammy gave her before she left for the lake.

Euva continued her usual chatter. "Katie, you've done a lot yourself for this camp. I couldn't handle runnin' this kitchen any more, yet I couldn't be done with it either. It took a heap of doin' for you to swallow your pride and ask Tiger for the job… after all the gossip and such."

Not again, thought Katie. If she lived to be a hundred, she wasn't going to live down the story of her last year as a counselor.

"The whole thing was your ma's fault. She's kin and I love her, but what she did to you is a cryin' shame. Once she got everyone talkin' about Tiger not askin' to marry you, it was no surprise you just upped and left for Wilmington."

Katie wished she would stop.

"It sure is a shame that husband of yourn didn't amount to nothin.'"

The remark stung. Mostly because her kids had probably heard it, too.

Katie bit her tongue and kept snapping the beans. She could still feel the pressure of everyone knowing how it was between her and Tiger back then, especially the valley folk. Hurt pride made her give him the ultimatum before she left for the teaching job in Wilmington. She had gone over that decision in her mind a thousand times since.

TIGER DIDN'T HAVE FAR to drive. Just a long climb up the winding road across from the entrance to the camp. It had been a while since he took this trip. Too long, in fact. He hadn't visited Jeb since after the old man's wife, Sara, died, and that had to be three or four years back. He made the tight turns on the narrow rutted road with his emotions bouncing between guilt for failing to look in on the man who taught him all he knew about hunting and tracking, and shame for only coming to see him when he needed a favor.

He rounded the final curve, and a log cabin with a rusting tin roof came into view. The raised chicken coops with their narrow ramps stood vacant, and the clutch of banty hens that usually ran helter-skelter all over the place had disappeared, giving the place an eerie atmosphere. Fence posts barely stuck up from the weeds occupying the space where the garden used to be.

Tiger expected ole Blue to come bounding out from his dog house and rouse everyone up, and when he didn't, he wondered if he should beep his horn. No water or food had been set out next to the dog house. Not a good sign. He got out and knocked on the door. After a wait, the door creaked open and Jeb appeared in overalls and a long-sleeved undershirt. Blue stood at his side, wobbling some and looking awfully gray around the muzzle.

Tiger shook Jeb's hand, then crouched down and petted the dog's head. "Hey, boy. Don't you run out and greet folks any more?"

"Oh, he's given up on that. Once them chickens were gone, he didn't have nothin' to chase when he took a fancy to doin' it, and the play went straight out of him."

Jeb shuffled aside and motioned for Tiger to enter. The musty smell of a damp fireplace permeated the air and brought back memories of the times he would tag along with his father when he came to visit. Sara would whip up some batter, pour it into an iron skillet, and in a matter of minutes have a spread of cornbread on the table. It had taken Tiger years to break himself of the habit of crumbling cornbread into his milk like Jeb did.

Tiger could almost feel the pain as the old man slowly made his way to a rocker in stiff arthritic movements. He rushed over and helped him lower himself onto the frayed cushion.

Jeb motioned toward a chair. "Sit down, son. I know why you're here. Doesn't take long for word to get around this valley, does it?"

Tiger pulled up a chair and sat with his shoulders hunched forward, bracing his forearms on his thighs. He wrung his hands not knowing where to start. "I hear you're talking to the Ledges?"

"Yep. They said they already talked to you some, but you turned them down."

"I wish you would have called me about it."

"I guess they just got me on the right day. My boy, Joey, kept tellin' me to see one of them estate planners and I kept tellin' him I hain't got no estate. He finally brought one of them fellas up here, and they got me so fuzzed up with all their inheritance tax talk I could hardly think. It's the darnedest thing. Our clan got this here land for service in the Continental Army, and we done owned it free and clear for over two hundred years. When I pass, how can the dadburn government make my boys pay a tax to keep what we already own? After they left, I was so mad I found the card them Ledges people left and told 'em I was ready to do business."

"Have you signed any papers?"

"No. They're drawin' 'em up now. But I shook on it."

Tiger knew, to Jeb, this was as good as a cast iron contract. He also knew if he told him how a Ledges development would ruin the land, he wouldn't be telling him anything he didn't already know. There had to be a compelling underlying reason he was doing this. It had to be the money; and if it were, it wouldn't be for himself. "If I can come up with the funds to meet their offer, would you sell your two hundred acres to me instead?"

Jeb stopped rocking and rubbed his chin. "Son, I've never gone back on my word."

Tiger rose and went to the window. He stared out onto the abandoned garden and spotted a sunflower poking its head above the weeds, and the ramifications of the sale rolled over him like a tidal wave. His eyes welled up. He couldn't deny the Ledges access to their land, and they'd probably use the four-mile graveled drive to the camp to bring in all the heavy equipment they'd need to build roads all over their property. The noise would be unending. With the land stripped, silt-laden rain runoff could spill onto the western edge of the camp property and disturb the headwaters of the Green River, legendary for its trout fishing.

This meant war. If the environmental watchdogs so much as blinked, the Ledges or one of their subcontractors might jump on any shortcut they could find and cause the kind of environmental damage that would take years to heal. He knew they wouldn't give a damn if they were fined. They'd just chalk it up to the cost of doing business.

"Tiger, did you hear me?"

Tiger wiped his eyes in a way he hoped Jeb wouldn't notice, then turned and faced him.

"Son, I said I'll give you four weeks."

Tiger's emotions see-sawed. He pulled up his chair again, this time close enough for their knees to touch. "Now, for the sixty-four-thousand-dollar question. How much?"

"Four million." Jeb scratched behind an ear. "I know that's a heap of money to raise in four weeks, but that's about as long as I've got the strength to hold everybody off fer."

Tiger fell back in his chair and ran his fingers through his hair. "Whew… that's twenty-thousand an acre."

Jeb rocked and seemed to be talking to himself. "The boys don't want this place no more. Can you imagine, after eight generations. The minute they left for college, they set their sights for places other than this here. When I pass, they're gonna sell out, but not 'fore they have one big fraction 'tween 'em. The family's already torn apart too much for my likin'. Greed's what's done it. Sara would turn in her grave."

He leaned toward Tiger as if he were sharing a secret. "Joey's lady, Pat, is running the show at their house. What with his coaching the football team and doin' all that volunteerin' over in Raleigh, he's lettin' her do what she wants. And she wants one of them big houses at the beach. Can't really be faultin' her with them six kids of theirs; heck, I lost track of all the grandkids."

He rocked, shaking his head. "Every time she pulls in here with some of her cookin', she's only got one thing on her mind. She used to sidle up to me with sweet talk, but she's way past that now. She's at the outright demand stage." He laughed somewhat bitterly. "I imagine I must be gettin' pretty lonely; I actually look forward to her visitin'." He looked straight at Tiger and winked. "Her cookin's pretty good…'cept I've got to eat it hearin' all about how expensive it is for her kids to put their kids through college, and all else she comes up with."

He scratched behind his ear. "I think that's why Joey brought them estate planners round. He's probably sick and tired of hearin' her go on 'bout this place."

Tiger folded his arms. "How about Jody?"

"He's the one sicced the Ledges on me. His big real estate plans in California can't hardly wait for me to die." He shook his head wearily. "Had about as much of this as I can rightly stand. My sister Mary is alone now in Fletcher and kinda hurtin' for company, so I reckon I'll go live with her."

Tiger rose and put his hand on Jeb's shoulder. "Don't get up. I'll let myself out. Jeb, I really appreciate the four weeks. I'll get back to you as soon as I can." As Tiger opened the door to leave, Blue barely lifted his head off the worn braided rug.

Tiger got into his truck and took a long look around. His eyes landed on the vacant dog house and realized why this man, famous throughout the region in his day for his hunting and trapping skills, finally decided to sell. He didn't want to be the only one left behind once the last of the family's long line of bluetick coonhounds was gone.

On the drive back, Tiger's mind raced through ways to get the money. Last year, together with a neighbor, he borrowed four-hundred-thousand to buy the farm on the camp's Northern border. The main reason they did it was the parcel connected both their properties, which in total constituted a "bear run" of more than twelve miles for wild animals. If a developer had gotten his hands on that land, it would have been a big jolt to the wildlife pattern and dealt a blow to the possible value of hunting rights to both their parcels.

It took at least six months for his neighbor to put that deal together. He'd worked with the Carolina Mountain Land Conservancy to get matching money from the state's Clean Water Management Trust Fund. Without it, they never could have pulled it off. Four weeks wasn't enough time. Looming in his head, almost like a sinister drumbeat, was the realization that he might have to go to his sister-in-law, Betty, for help.

He pulled into camp and checked the time. Six-fifteen. Sammy should be in the house getting ready to go to dinner. He walked swiftly across the lawn and met her coming out. Earlier that afternoon, he had told her what Euva had said, and the walk to the lodge was an opportunity to bring her up to date on his conversation with Jeb.

"How are you going to raise the money?" she asked.

"Honey, we're going to need a grant to make this happen, and I'm hoping the conservancy can put it together."

"Dad, you know how these things work; it's going to take months for that to happen, not four weeks."

"That's why I want you to get your aunt up here. If she can just give me a temporary loan, one way or another, I'll find a way to pay her back. Right now I need to get time on my side."

Sammy's cheeks ballooned as she slowly blew her breath from her pursed lips. "Dad, she'll never go for it."

Tiger waved at a group streaming from the woods on their way to the lodge, and he and Sammy fell in behind them. Tiger continued. "I've racked my brain. Betty's all I can come up with right now. If I can only get her to understand how much this place meant to your mother, I think she might consider it. After all, she's leaving everything to you anyway."

"That's true. She gave me a copy of her will." Sammy took another deep breath and slowly exhaled. "Okay, Dad. I'm willing to try anything. I'll call her after dinner and get her to come up."

"Have her stay right here at the camp. That way, we can work on her together."

They climbed the stairs and melted into the crowd pouring into the lodge. Sammy tugged on her father's arm. "Dad, I think you better read the will tonight after evening song." She put an arm around his shoulder. "But I'm afraid you're not going to like what it says."

CHAPTER FIVE

Liz's spacious screened-in porch brought a smile to Tiger's face. How many hours and how much money had it taken to create the impression of a simple homey place to hang out? Flowered chintz pillows on wicker chairs and elegant pots of pink geraniums sprinkled about gave a vibrant first impression, but it was the ubiquitous cast iron boot scrapers, framed prints depicting country life and subtly colored antiques scattered around that made him want to pour himself a cool drink, pull up a chair and let the afternoon drift by. He laughed. His day was barely beginning and was going to end with him sitting on the ground in front of a campfire.

A catalog lay open face down on the table next to Liz's favorite chair. He picked it up and saw her reflection on the faces of the stylish women... all younger, but not more beautiful. He glanced at the prices. Two hundred and seventy dollars for a blouse? He laughed and shook his head. He'd never understand women. Careful not to lose her place, he put it back just as he had found it.

He picked up the *Times-News* lying on a chair. The headline, *Search for Missing Women Called Off*, blazed across three columns. Anxious to learn any new developments, he began to read. "The unsuccessful two-day search that included over sixty law enforcement personnel and search and rescue teams has been called off." Tiger studied the pictures of two smiling women and shook his head. Probably got lost and won't be found until the winter.

Suddenly Liz's cat appeared on the porch railing. Tiger went over and picked it up. Noticing snarls on the Maine coon's fur, he unlocked the door and went to the laundry room beyond the kitchen, opened a drawer and pulled out a brush. He put the cat on the dryer and listened to it purr like a distant outboard as he brushed its long white and orange fur smooth. He glanced over at the two bowls in the corner. "I bet you're hungry, too."

After putting out some water and cat food, he strolled through the house feeling a little neglected himself. He looked at his watch. Liz was already a half-hour late. He'd called her that morning to see if he could stop by before his four o'clock appointment with the land protection director at the conservancy. She'd lingered in his mind ever since she said for him to come two hours earlier.

They'd agreed to disagree about the camp years ago, but he felt he would burst if he didn't share the demons swimming around in his brain with someone. A disturbing feeling came over him. One of the demons was his relationship with Liz. The intense desire they'd shared when they met ten years ago had mellowed into a true friendship, but something was missing and he knew how important that was because he had shared it with Susan.

It boiled down to the fact that his life revolved around three-thousand acres nestled in the Green River Valley and the camp he'd created to inspire children with the wonders of that incredible world... and Liz wanting nothing to do with it. The golf course at the country club was her idea of the great outdoors, and she refused to marry him until he turned the camp over to Sammy.

Not being able to share with her the euphoria he felt for all the wonderment and camaraderie he'd experienced every summer with eager, happy children always seemed to leave the joy of savoring an accomplishment flat. A couple of times in past summers he had decided to break it off, but then camp closed and he moved back to his house in Flat Rock, and everything returned to the way it was—comfortable and easy, with him commuting to camp every day and spending most of his evenings with Liz.

A car pulled into the driveway. Moments later, Liz sailed through the door. She tossed her purse on the couch and threw her arms around his neck. "You handsome dog, you. Oh, how I wish I had you here full time so I could show you off." She kicked off her heels, curled a finger and motioned for him to follow, then swung around and padded through the house to her bedroom, sing-songing, "Wait 'til you see what I've got."

Amused, Tiger folded his arms and leaned against the bedroom doorway as she opened her closet and pulled out a silk-covered hanger holding a lacy teddy. She held it up in the air and jiggled it until the feathery fringe along the hem danced. An eyebrow raised seductively. "Why don't you pour yourself a drink and give me a few minutes."

Just as he was ready to take her up on it, he noticed the digital clock on the dresser. For Liz, a few minutes could easily turn into a half-hour, and he needed to be fresh and alert for the meeting at the conservancy. He went over and took her in his arms, then gently ran his lips along her neck, thinking how good she smelled. "Honey, believe me, there's nothing I'd rather do, but I've got to leave for downtown in forty-five minutes. Keep that little number ready until after the meeting. Charlie Morgan's in charge of the camp tonight." He pulled away enough to look her in the eye. "But I'll take you up on that drink."

She frowned and put the teddy back. "Damn. I recognized that edgy 'I need to talk' look on your face the minute I walked in." She slid her feet into a pair of slippers. "Go sit down. I'll get us some wine."

Tiger was pacing on the porch when Liz came out and handed him some merlot. She sank into a chair and watched him empty his glass. "Okay. Let's have it," she said in a tone as dry as the wine.

The emotions swirling around in Tiger's head momentarily tongue-tied him.

"Nothing's happened at the camp, has it?"

"No. No. Everything is great as far as the kids go." He sat on the edge of the railing, careful not to press against the screen, and crossed his ankles. "It's the land across the road from the entrance. Yesterday I found out that old Jeb Ryan agreed to sell it to the Ledges. I went up to see him and he's given me thirty days to match their offer."

Liz ran a finger along the rim of her glass. "And... how much *is* their offer?"

"Four million."

Liz threw her head back. "Good Lord. Didn't you buy a lot of land from a neighbor *last summer?*"

"Yes. But a developer's involved in this deal."

"Tiger, this whole thing's starting to get ridiculous. You can only buy so much land."

He paced, waving a hand in the air. "We're talkin' roads, houses looking directly down on the camp, spill off in the river... you name it."

"What's a little spill off. We see it here every time it rains."

Tiger winced and ran a hand through his hair. "Do you have any idea what sediment does to trout? Clogs their gills... kills their young... they can't see their prey to eat..."

"I don't want to hear another word about those stinky trout!" They looked at each other in silence until Liz said, "I'm sorry. I didn't mean to sound so uncaring; but let's be real. How in the world are you going to dig up four million in a month?"

Coming here this afternoon was beginning to look like a big mistake to Tiger. He'd never seen her show so much resentment toward the camp and it worried him. "It's possible I can borrow it from my sister-in-law and work out a deal with the conservancy to pay her back."

"I've always gotten the impression your sister-in-law doesn't like you."

Tiger let out a cynical laugh and tossed his head. "Maybe if I make my case to her face-to-face."

"How about the bank?"

"I called all morning. Nobody's willing to come up with that kind of money in this short of a time. Hell, we can't get it surveyed and appraised in the time we've got left."

Tiger listened to the street noises as Liz sat staring into space mulling everything over. She snapped out of it and looked him in the eye. "Why don't you examine this thing a little more positively. Find out how many houses will actually be looking down on the camp and buy those lots yourself. It'll certainly be cheaper."

"Liz, you don't understand. It's... it's the impact on the whole ecosystem." The wine hit Tiger and he sat down across from her. "Let's not talk about it anymore. This is my problem, and I'll just have to solve it. Hopefully, the conservancy will come through with something."

She stared deep into his eyes and ran a hand down his face as if she wanted him to read her thoughts, then squeezed his hand. "Tiger, please forget about that farm. It can get you in so deep you'll never be able to get out." She let go of his hand and sank back in her chair. "That camp has always been a wedge between us. I've got plenty of friends to go to the playhouse and parties with, but it's not the same, Tiger. I get lonely."

They'd had enough arguments about the camp for Tiger to know where this conversation was heading. Why in heaven's name did he think he could talk this over with her?

She stood up, folded her arms and strolled over to the railing, glancing out on her garden. "I'm going to be fifty in a couple of months, and I can't help wondering how many more years I can stand living like this."

Tiger sat with his elbow on the arm of the chair, resting his head on his fist. He wanted to kick himself. He should have known better than to come over while camp was in session.

Still gazing out at her garden, Liz said, "Tiger, I hate to inform you of this, but you're not getting any younger either. Instead of buying land, you should be trying to sell it to the Ledges yourself."

He said, almost off-handedly, "I'll never sell, no matter how much they raise their offer."

She spun around with a horrified look on her face. "You mean, what my cleaning lady told me is true!? I… I… never thought to talk to you about it. It was too fantastic! Just another nutty rumor from one of those gossipy ol' valley people." Her forehead wrinkled. "Is it true they offered you sixty million?"

Tiger stared up at her. He had to keep his mind clear and his emotions checked for the sake of the one hundred and fifty kids entrusted to him. "Liz. I'm not going to get into this with you. If you want to fight about it, you're going to have to wait until the season's over."

Incredulity morphed into contempt. "Tiger, I've got to be out of my mind sitting here every summer waiting for you to be done with that place."

Tiger rubbed his forehead. Her mood was rapidly disintegrating, and he was getting a headache.

She paced around the room, then came over and sat down next to him. He could see her demeanor had softened. She took one of his hands. "Tiger, you know how I feel about you. And I know I'm never going to find anyone else like you, but I'm tired of all this. I don't want to wait until you turn that place over to Sammy. There's a big world beyond these mountains. We can travel and meet exciting people while we're still young enough to enjoy it. Promise me you won't buy that land... and that you're going to talk to the Ledges about your place."

The remark stymied him. She didn't get it. Not one ounce of it. He stared at the beautiful face. She was good and kind, and he would always care about what happened to her, but she didn't understand that he belonged to his land. It was his job, who he was. If he traveled the world over with her a million times, he'd never find a place as wondrous.

She got up, disappeared into the house and came back holding a lit cigarette. Her ring-laden fingers trembled as she took a puff and blew it out. "Well? Are you or aren't you?"

He stood up, took the cigarette and put it out in an empty candy dish. "Liz, let's not do this."

Her eyes were steely, the muscles in her face taut. "You're crazy. That's what it is. You're crazy." Every shred of charm evaporated. "This is the last straw. I've always hated the Green River Valley and I always will, and I'm sick of waiting for you to grow up. We're finished!" She folded her arms. Tightly, like she was afraid she was going to fly apart. "My looks aren't going to last forever, but they're still good enough to find someone who knows how to live... and Tiger, I intend to do just that. While you were playing Tarzan, Larry Elders made me an offer I'm going to accept."

The room grew silent, like someone suddenly turned the sound off. Tiger rose, walked to the screen door and started to push it open. He stopped and looked back at her. "I love you, Liz. I'm sorry."

CHAPTER SIX

Patrick awoke before daybreak. He lay there knowing the minute his feet hit the cold floor the chilly mountain air would pierce every pore. He glanced at the navy blue travel clock on the bench next to him that his stepsister had given him at graduation. Just enough time to shower and trim his beard before the seven o'clock bell.

Finished in the bathroom, he slipped into shorts and a tee shirt, then made his bed as he heard the first wake-up bell. "Okay everyone. Up and at 'em," he yelled over his shoulder as he fluffed up his pillow. Getting everyone rustled up and dressed was the biggest challenge of the day. "Anyone wanting to shower better do it now." He went over and helped a groggy kid down from an upper bunk, then went around ruffling the heads of those still tightly curled up under warm blankets.

Noticing that Alvin, barefoot and shivering, was having trouble with his trunk, he went over, gave it a rap and got it open. The fastidiously ironed and folded clothes inside grabbed his attention until a pair of socks flying across the room hit him on the back of the head.

The next half hour had all the order of rounding up a bunch of cats.

The 7:30 bell sounded. "Okay guys, we've got to start for the

51

lodge." He managed to hustle five of the boys out the door, leaving Alvin pawing through Tucker Watson's trunk. Tucker stood bare from the waist up. Patrick snapped his fingers a few times. "Come on, guys. You're holding us up."

"Is this it?" yelled Alvin as he yanked out a shirt with a whale on it.

A big grin spread across Tucker's face. He put it on, and the two ran out of the cabin.

The sun had risen over the mountain and shafts of light streamed through the thick forest, sporadically warming Patrick's group as they made their way in the crispness of the morning along the path to the lodge. Sunday night's camp-wide game had coalesced the group just like intended, and Patrick could see the kids had already formed friendships.

This natural tendency was the reason the field trip groups were composed of boys and girls from different cabins, allowing everyone to get to know other kids in the camp. Likewise, counselors were assigned groups that didn't include anyone from their cabin in order to expose the campers to a variety of role models. Patrick wished this wasn't the case today. He remembered how Alvin had buried his head in his chest as he hugged him that first night at camp, and he felt an uncomfortable need to be on his morning nature hike. The trip up Gold Creek Falls was the camp's most strenuous trek.

ALVIN TRAMPED ALONG THE TRAIL next to Tucker on their way to breakfast feeling a little light-headed. His body responded to everything around him, apart from his will. The smell of the hemlocks and sweetbush drifting in and out of the air made him feel raw and alert. Dark, rich scents oozed from the loamy moss-covered earth under his footsteps and mixed with the sweet perfume escaping from mysterious shrubs hidden in the woods.

His ears tingled as he listened to the wind in concert with the rustling trees. Other than during a storm, he couldn't remember ever hearing it before. The trill from a bird pierced the air, making him wonder if a song from off in the distance was an answer to its call.

Alvin's spirits soared. He'd been released into a world endlessly larger and more thrilling than the one his parents had created for him. He wanted to run and shout and give everyone high fives, but he smiled at Tucker instead. Just being happy would be okay for now.

Excitement rose as everyone assembled on the deck of the lodge for the morning reading. After a girl recited a poem she wrote, the Cherokee morning song echoed from the hills. Alvin glanced around at the joyful throng, then at Tucker, who had to be a head shorter than him. By the way he pouted about not finding his whale shirt, it was obvious he was used to having things done for him, but they were friends, and he'd go along with helping him out.

"Hey, String Bean, over here!" someone shouted as Alvin and Tucker streamed into the dining hall.

It was Ricky, waving him over to their table. They made their way through the crowd and sat down. The look on Ricky's face told Alvin that Mike Bailey, the mentor who was assigned to their cabin and ate with them at every meal, had said something to him about shouting out String Bean. Alvin looked up at Mike and said matter-of-factly, "That's okay. I'm used to it." He turned to Ricky and added, "But my friends call me String."

Everyone laughed, and Mike leaned toward him to read the name tag on a thin wooden disk hanging from a string around his neck, patted him on the back, and said, "You're a good sport, Alvin."

Alvin's eyes shot over to Patrick who gave him a wink.

Everyone passed the food and dug in. Alvin felt he ate pretty good, at least more than he was used to, until Patrick leaned across the table with a plate of sausages.

"Do you think you might want another one? You're group is hiking to Gold Creek Falls this morning and you might need some extra energy." His coaxing tone turned apologetic. "Now, I don't want you to take it if you feel you can't eat it." He reached a little farther, extended the platter even closer and jiggled it a bit.

Recognizing the same unstoppable approach his mother took to encourage him to eat, Alvin helped himself to a link.

After breakfast, one by one the mentors announced what hiking group they were taking where and what bus they were supposed to get on after cabin cleanup. They reminded the campers to empty and sort their scraps after they ate, separating the compostable food from the meat and dairy, then the paper items—recycling being a major lesson taught at the camp.

Once back at the cabin, Patrick announced that no one could leave for the morning hike until the cabin was shipshape. Alvin got busy arranging his backpack and making his bed while listening to Patrick answer a barrage of questions about everyone's trail assignments.

Noticing Tucker yanking a pile of tee shirts from his trunk, Alvin crouched down and picked up a handful, all with some sort of whale decal on them. He looked up at Tucker with a quizzical expression on his face. "Why did you pull these out?"

"I'm taking them with me."

"Aren't you going to Ruby Falls? I thought you had to wear a bathing suit."

"Yeah, but I'll need to put something on afterwards."

"Just put on the same thing you were wearing over your trunks before you got there."

"I'll want a new shirt."

Patrick's voice boomed from the bathroom. "Everyone get in here and brush your teeth."

Alvin decided one shirt was enough, so he quickly unzipped Tucker's backpack and stuffed one in, then pawed through the messy trunk until he found a towel. He zipped up the bag, tossed the rest of the shirts back in the trunk and slammed it shut, avoiding Tucker's glance. Maybe if he ignored all his faces, his friend would stop making them.

"All right, guys. Now, everybody get your beds made."

Ricky ran out of the bathroom and onto the porch separating their half of the cabin from one that had 12-14 year olds. He popped his head in the door. "Hey, everyone, you want to see something cool! There's a bunch of ants eating a moth in the bathroom!"

"Hey. Hey. *Hey!*" yelled Patrick at a kid who ran out the door and down the porch steps. "Get back in here and make your bed."

The kid picked up a shoe lying at the bottom of the staircase and slapped it against the railing to shake out the sand. "You evil man!"

Someone ran out of Hemlock One, opened the door to Patrick's side and yelled, "Does anyone in here happen to have a clean pair of socks?"

Patrick got a broom from the bathroom and handed it to Tucker. "Get busy. It's your turn to sweep."

The sound of a couple of kids singing *Welcome to the Hotel California* drifted out of Hemlock One. The screen door slammed and someone ran down the steps, quickly perused the clothesline strung around four trees and sagging with haphazardly bunched up towels, clothes and swimsuits, grabbed some trunks and ran back in.

Ricky hobbled around the cabin. "I can't find my shoe."

"Well, if you can't find your shoe, I can't find your shoe," said Patrick. "And if you don't find it in less than a minute, I'm going to beat you with a wet noodle."

The bell rang for everyone to assemble on the back field for their morning hikes. Kids streamed out from both sides of the cabin. Patrick stood on the porch and waved at Tucker and Alvin as they headed for the buses, yelling after them somewhat dramatically, "Goodbye, guys. I'll miss you until we meet again... in three hours."

Ricky came out of the cabin. "Patrick, I really can't find my shoe."

"Do you have another pair?"

"But I already have this shoe and sock on."

"Well take them off and put on something else."

With both sides of the cabin finally empty, Patrick and the other counselor made their way down the woodland path toward the buses with Ricky to the sound of a counselor on another path nearby hollering out, "Pick it up, girls. We're late."

The excitement level rose as kids eyed the seven camp buses lined up like a string of wildly colored beads screaming out fun and adventure.

Tucker ran to the one covered with wizards that had to be the Magic School Bus. Alvin recognized Dr. Seuss's bossy, mustached Lorax depicted jumping up and down on another bus as vividly colored wooly trees were being chopped to the ground. Alvin took a deep breath and got on. This was his fourth time out with his field trip group, but he still hadn't latched on to a buddy like at the cabin. No one seemed to pay much attention to him, except maybe Amy Whitmore from Winston-Salem. Good. The seat behind her was empty.

Amy talked to someone and didn't notice him slip into the seat. Everyone... with the exception of a girl sitting behind him who kept insisting she had to have a window seat or she would vomit...

bounced in excitement.

Alvin's cabin mentor hopped on. "Hi, everyone. My name is Mike Bailey and I conduct the Gold Creek Falls trek." He moved aside enough to let two counselors and another mentor crowd in next to him, and continued. "I teach rock climbing in the afternoon. And when I'm not at camp, do biological research at Cornell University in New York." He motioned toward the girl on his right. "Judy Somers is a naturalist with the North Carolina Wildlife Resources Commission and she'll be handling the cave hike."

He quickly glanced at some papers in his hand. "Okay. To get started, it might be a good idea if Unit Two finds seats on the right and Four on the left, so we can check to make sure we've got everybody."

A roar of confusion arose. Mike bent down and let one of the counselors talk in his ear. He stood upright and raised his arms. "Okay… sorry everybody. Unit Two has been renamed by you guys as The Slug Lickers and Four, Soggy Bottoms."

After a lot of seat swapping, Alvin looked over his shoulder and could see that the girl who wanted the window seat had a satisfied grin on her face as she sat in the recently vacated spot. Good. He didn't have to worry about vomit any more.

Once everyone settled down, Mike ran through all the safety rules again, then introduced the two counselors. He jumped in the driver's seat, and the minute the bus took off, someone yelled out, "I've got a repeat-after-me song." A big cheer rose. *The little worm…* The bus filled with the voices of kids repeating the round. Alvin studied some writings penned on the ceiling with markers. *Love all, trust few, do wrong to no one. —Shakespeare.* He read one running along a strip over the window. *How do people blowing each other up solve any of the world's problems?*

Suddenly the bus groaned to a stop. Mike hollered out, "All right, Slug Lickers. This is where you get out."

The scent of sweaty, heated bodies filled the bus as the kids jounced along the aisle on their way to the door. The bus continued climbing through the mountains, splashing through streams and rivulets as it made its way to the farthest end of the camp, an almost five-mile stretch of deep woods. Sunlight kept breaking through gaps in the forest canopy, striking the bus like lightning.

Amy bobbed her head as she talked to the kid sitting next to her, making her long, thick blond hair tied back with a rubber band swish around like a horse's tail. The boy sitting next to Alvin nudged him, before reaching over and pulling it just hard enough to make her turn and give Alvin a dirty look.

Embarrassed, Alvin instantly piped up, "Hi, Amy." He expected another dirty look, but she smiled instead.

The bus stopped and everyone got out and started to walk up an old logging road. The isolation of the place made Alvin feel small, especially when he looked skyward at the ancient oaks and poplars, some towering a hundred feet overhead. The woods were much quieter during the day, and he imagined all the night creatures were asleep, but he kept a wary eye out just the same, recalling some of Tucker's stories about kids being dragged away by bears and mountain lions. They came upon a cluster of deer in a clearing. The animals froze and studied the intruders for a moment, then turned and loped into the woods. The troop crossed the field and veered off onto a trail that seemed to get steeper by the foot, finally forcing them to proceed in single-file. A few times, when Alvin had to climb up on a boulder but couldn't find the strength to heave himself up, a couple of kids gave him a boost by pushing on his rump until he was able to wedge a knee into a crevice and move on. He kept grabbing onto laurel bushes or overhead limbs to pull himself up, but the space between him and the kids in front kept lengthening. When the line came to a wider stretch, everyone ran ahead, leaving him last with the counselor bringing up the rear.

"Don't worry, buddy, you're doing fine," the counselor kept reassuring him. Every once in a while, he stopped and pointed out a plant or shrub that could be eaten or had some medicinal benefit, giving Alvin a rest. The counselor found a sassafras tree, took off a leaf and crushed it. "Notice that citrus scent? They used to make root beer out of the bark." The counselor looked around for a sourwood tree and asked him to taste a leaf, but not to swallow. Sure enough, it *was* sour.

It had been a while since they had seen anyone from the rest of the group. They climbed over a large promontory next to a stream tumbling down from the mountain and came upon Mike crouched on the edge of a small pool with everyone gathered around. He lifted a rock, revealing a brown salamander with black spots.

As Mike explained the life cycle of the creature he called a Mountain Dusky, Alvin peered over the shoulder of a boy who had found a crayfish. The kid offered it to him, and he picked it up and raised it high enough to look underneath. It wasn't cute like furry-faced Molly, but the fact that it was a living thing made an impression on him. It kept snapping its two pincher claws and moving its eight legs in a valiant effort to get away from something that was a thousand times larger, making Alvin want to protect it. He filled with admiration and curiosity, but mostly, with respect for this creature that wanted to live as much as he did.

Mike reminded them to be careful not to hurt or move any of the creatures they found in the woods since they might have eggs or offspring nearby. Alvin studied the crayfish and thought about his mother and the tender way she cared for him, then the oath he had made at the respect circle. In that remarkable pivotal instant, he knew from that moment forward, not only would he respect, but he would protect and nurture the earth and its creatures for as long as he lived.

They continued climbing alongside the stream, refreshed by cool droplets bouncing off rocks. Voices and shouts of glee rose at the sound of a waterfall pounding on granite in the distance. The line had tightened up by now, and Alvin, after a few slips, started to get his footing. The counselor had told him to pick up his feet and keep his eyes on the rocks ahead of him, and it worked.

The reward for the rugged climb was an endless ribbon of water cascading from granite outcrop to granite outcrop until it reached a clear cool pool twenty feet below. Everyone stripped down to their bathing suits and jumped in.

They frolicked in the water and under the falls with Mike pointing out antennae and eyes on the movable stalks of the crawdads they discovered in cracks and under rocks. He kept pointing out aquatic insects like mayflies, caddisflies and stoneflies. After forty-five minutes, a counselor handed out snacks, and once all the wrappers were carefully collected, they dressed and changed from their water shoes to dry socks and hiking shoes, before setting out again.

The path down the mountain wasn't as steep, but a lot longer. Just before meeting up with the logging road again, they came upon a huge oak lying on the forest floor. Everyone climbed on, but Alvin didn't think he could make it. Standing alone on the path, the kids shouted for him to come over and then yanked him up. Alvin managed to stand on the broad old mammoth, but as he began to leap off, lost his footing and tumbled to the ground.

Everything was a blur until someone handed him his glasses. Mike examined him and proclaimed he just had a few cuts and bruises, and they continued. On the bus trip to base camp, Mike put on cream and Band Aids with Amy watching intently as she knelt on the seat in front of him.

The bus stopped to load on the Slug Lickers, and kids clustered around, curious about his fall. Amy answered all their questions as if she were the official spokesperson. Mike, noticing the way she had taken charge, eyed Alvin with a slightly raised eyebrow. When Mike returned to the front of the bus, Amy assumed authority and shooed everyone away.

The bus bounced along. Every once in a while an overhanging branch scraped along its side. Voices in song flowed from the open windows. *Calamine, Calamine, Calamine lotion…* A counselor stood up and at a precise moment pointed to Alvin's side of the bus, and they enthusiastically joined in the next round of the verse.

The bus wound through a deeply shaded stretch, and the air whooshing through the windows suddenly turned cool. After a few songs, Alvin sat listening to the kids chattering and laughing, and thought. Everyone helping him out the way they had made him feel like he belonged, and he was pretty sure he could count Amy as a friend. As much of a friend as a girl could be, anyway. His mind landed on the incredible hike, and he swelled with pride. He had just climbed a mountain. It was true, he had to be boosted, yanked and pulled, but he had done it just the same.

CHAPTER SEVEN

BETTY TALBERT USUALLY CAME UP from Greenville for a couple days at the end of every summer to visit her niece. The tradition started years back when she felt it her duty to outfit Sammy for the first grade, and eventually evolved into an annual outing after the camp closed so she wouldn't be bothered with all the comings and goings of a bunch of kids.

She'd had enough of that growing up. At fourteen, she took over the care of her baby sister when her mother died shortly after childbirth. And that was on top of helping her father and older brother with the farm chores and doing most of the cooking. She swore she'd never wash another diaper, so when Arthur asked her to marry him, she only accepted after he agreed they wouldn't have children. He never complained about that, but kept reminding her that he never agreed for her not to cook. Her brother had passed on; Arthur too. So Sammy was all she had left.

She stopped at a light in Hendersonville and examined her Cadillac STS with a fair amount of pride. She didn't know how to operate three-quarters of the gadgets... Lord, what in the world did she want with a Bluetooth... but the Cadillac brand had always represented the ultimate in luxury, and she deserved it.

Who would ever believe that someone would come along and

pay six million dollars for Arthur's rundown old farm? All it had been good for in the past twenty years was as a graveyard for her husband's junked construction equipment.

She laughed in the realtor's face when he suggested the listing price. *It's the last major parcel left on this highway,* he insisted.

Other than the car, she hadn't done much with the windfall. She had worked as an office manager up until the time she was almost seventy and had everything she ever wanted, that is except her sister, Susan. Dusting her bedroom yesterday, she knew she shouldn't do it, but she opened the bureau drawer where she kept her most cherished treasures. The gold on her mother's locket was rubbed clean away, and the picture her parents had taken on their honeymoon in one of those tiny photo booths at Myrtle Beach's Pavilion was faded to an almost ghost image.

Her hands shook as she reached for the heart-shaped frame. The cheap kind they sold at the old five and dime when she was a teen. Her hair was in pigtails and she had on her Sunday best, which wasn't saying much. She was holding Susan in her arms. The trusting way the baby cuddled against her with the playful smile on her face brought back a flood of memories. Afterward, she remembered glancing at the clock, then putting everything back in the drawer and scolding herself after realizing she'd stood there with tears in her eyes for more than an hour.

The Waverly Inn came into view up ahead. When Sammy called and asked her to come and stay with them in the main house, she told her straight out that it was bad enough she had to come see her at that godforsaken camp, she certainly wasn't going to put up with all the weird noises in the night coming from out of that wilderness of theirs. Instead, she had called up the bed and breakfast she stayed at every time she came to visit. They knew how to treat a civilized person.

The possibility that the wedding might be on again was the only reason she agreed to come up and meet Sammy at the camp. That place was responsible for killing her Susan, and God knows, if it weren't for a drunk doing her in, that man she married would have worked her to death.

She checked into the Waverly and was pleased they gave her the room on the first floor across from the Victorian parlor where she could visit with other guests before settling in for the night.

The next morning, she ate breakfast wearing a sensible cotton wrap dress, then went back to the room and took it off. A plastic garment bag was carefully unzipped, and the yellow suit inside spread out on the bed. A pair of yellow high heels was taken from a tote. Standing there in a slip, she caught her reflection in the full length mirror. Her figure hadn't changed much since she was twenty. In fact, she felt she had held up rather well; all the plastic surgery certainly helped. She gently touched her flawlessly coiffed short silver hair with both hands to make sure she'd put on enough spray to keep it in place at the camp.

She stepped out of the sandals she'd worn to breakfast and slipped her feet into the heels, then put on the skirt, careful not to muss her hair. After putting on the jacket, she reached in her overnight case for a bag of jewelry. First a pearl necklace and matching earrings, then a ring with a large amber stone. Satisfied with the overall effect, she got packed and checked out, with plans to head back home directly from the camp, hopefully to get right to work on Sammy's wedding. Why else would this little visit of theirs be so urgent?

SAMMY HAD BEEN EDGY ALL MORNING, and was now pacing the porch of the main house, keeping an eye out for Betty. Where was her father? No matter how important this was to him, she knew if a camper or staff member stopped him to ask a question, he would take whatever time necessary to give them an unrushed answer or explanation. But, by the same token, Betty's Southern manners would force her to take the time to settle in with a gracious greeting, commenting on how nice everything looked even though nothing could be up to her standards. She'd inquire about everyone's health down to the very last person she'd ever been introduced to. That ritual would take at least fifteen minutes. After that, she would want to get right down to the business of why she had been summoned.

A screen door slammed in the distance, and moments later her father came tripping down from the lodge. He walked with his usual spirited stride and sprinted onto the porch. "Hey, gal. Ready for the dragon lady?"

"Aw, Dad. She's really nice."

"Wait a minute, sweetie. Remember, I read that will of hers last night."

A big cream-colored Cadillac emerged from the woods and crept down the camp road like the driver wasn't sure they wanted to be there.

"Brace yourself Sammy; we're in for a bumpy ride."

She nudged him and grimaced. "Come on, let's go down and greet her."

Tiger opened the car door and helped Betty out. Sammy gave her a big hug and the two walked with their arms around other's waist down the stone path to the house. The second time Betty's heels got stuck between stones and had to be wrenched loose, Tiger tried to hold onto her arm, but she yanked it away.

"Good grief," she said in a high-pitched squeal. "Haven't you made enough money on this place in twenty-five years to afford a decent sidewalk?"

"Betty, if you promise you'll grace us with more of your visits, we'll put one in just for you."

She stopped and looked him in the eye, obviously biting her tongue. She agitatedly motioned toward the house. "Let's keep going."

Everyone concentrated so much on keeping Betty from taking a spill, they didn't see Skippy come out of the lake and race over. At the sight of the dripping wet dog, Betty's face twisted in terror and she threw both arms around Sammy's neck. Tiger lunged for the dog; but it was too late. He shook himself off and splattered water all over her suit.

Tiger held him by the collar until Betty was safely in the house, then entered to find her busy blotting her skirt and talking under her breath. As serious as their mission was, he had a time stifling his laughter, until he saw the genuine concern on Sammy's face. Betty was as near as his daughter had come to having a mother. And oddly, the same was true for Susan. In fact, he knew enough when talking to Betty not to refer to his wife as her sister, because they both knew darn well that wasn't the way Betty thought of her.

Sammy got everyone a glass of lemonade while Betty proceeded with small talk. Tiger marveled at how composed she was under the circumstances. Seventy years of practicing the genteel manners of the South… he was sure she had started at the age of one… gave her the aplomb to smile and cheerfully chatter away as if nothing had happened.

When Sammy sat down on the couch next to her, Betty put an arm around her and beamed. "Well darlin', do you have good news for your auntie?"

Sammy's forehead wrinkled and her eyes shot over to her father, who responded by clearing his throat. It suddenly dawned on the both of them that Betty had come expecting that the wedding to Randy was back on. Just like the woman, he thought. She can't let go. He suddenly feared the resentment she held for him might be too big an obstacle to get around. He braced himself and looked at her through squinted lids. "Betty, we wanted to ask you for help."

"Help? What kind of help?" Her voice had raised another octave and she appeared both surprised and oddly fragile.

As Tiger explained what dire events would transpire if the development across the road went through, Betty began to relax, sinking back on the couch and resting an arm on the back. Her lips curled upward a bit as if the prospect thrilled her.

"Betty, Jeb Ryan gave me a month to get together the four million. I know I can raise it one way or another in six months to a year, I just can't swing it in four weeks."

"Did you try the bank? Isn't that what they're for?"

"They can't act that fast. They'd need an appraisal, a survey." He shook his head. "Plus I'd have to come up with twenty percent down. And, no matter how good the terms, there's no way I can pay the interest on a four-million-dollar mortgage. The only way I can afford that land is if I can get some grant money by giving up easement rights to a conservancy. I've got an appointment with them on Monday, and they're pretty sure it's doable… but not in this short of a time."

Betty raised an eyebrow and tilted her head back to one side, the quiver of a smile on her lips broadening. "I suppose you want me to lend it to you."

Tiger eyed her keenly and nodded.

Betty crossed her legs and tapped her manicured nails on the end table. "And when the next neighbor to your precious camp wants to sell out… what are you going to do then?"

"There's no parcel that can cause as much damage as this one if it's overdeveloped."

"What makes you call it overdevelopment? There are a lot of people out there who want to enjoy the mountains as much as you do. And let's not forget all the jobs they'll create."

"I'm not saying there's anything wrong with a gated community or anyone building a house, it's just that these things need to be planned. There are just so many uncluttered vistas left. This mountain land here is in one of the most beautiful undisturbed valleys left in the Southern Blue Ridge. Hell, we've got the headwaters of the Green River right outside that door." He rose and pointed to a wood fish hanging on the wall, traced from an actual catch. "You can still haul in the biggest, best trout in North Carolina. Once those roads are under construction, and you get four or five days of solid rain, you'll see the surface of that mountain dissolve into a sea of mud and slide right down into that river. There are deer, bear, beaver… you name it… that have run out there for centuries. We're part of twenty miles or more of forest that are uninterrupted by paved roads. This place is special. Worth preserving."

"As far as I'm concerned, Samantha's the one who's worth saving. When you married Susan, you were all set with that big job in Raleigh. Then, when you inherited this land, you could have sold enough to set you and Susan up in luxury for the rest of your lives. But, oh no! You dragged my poor darlin' into this wilderness and made her work like a dog building your dream. She'd be here right now if it weren't for this blasted camp."

"Betty, this wasn't just my dream, Susan wanted it as much as I did."

"Not only won't I lend you the money, I want you to know I made sure Sammy won't ever be able to do it either. She's not getting a dime from my estate until ten years after you're gone. Hopefully, by then, the camp will be in someone else's hands. Nothing would make me happier than for Samantha to marry a man who will take her away from all this." She stood up and wobbled a bit on a loose heel. "I don't care one whit about the money for myself. If I didn't have Samantha, I'd leave every penny to the church." She reached for her purse. "Tiger, you threw your life into this place. You threw Susan's life into this place; and Sammy's already paid too big a price for it. But, my dear brother-in-law, you're not going to throw me in, too."

She took a step to leave, and the heel on her shoe gave way. Sammy jumped up and offered to get her some slippers as Betty steadied herself on the arm of the chair. Suddenly Betty stood erect and stepped out of her shoes, then bent down and picked them up. "Don't bother, darlin'; I can just as easily go in my bare feet." She glared at Tiger. "After all, I didn't own a pair of shoes 'til I was four."

As Betty hobbled toward the car, Sammy ran down the walk and retrieved some shoes from her aunt's suitcase. She glanced up at the house and saw her father at the door holding onto Skippy, the joyful grin that naturally appeared the minute he spotted anyone wiped clean away. Heat radiated from her cheeks as she kissed her aunt goodbye and waved her off.

By the time she got back to the house, her father was pacing around the living room, rubbing the back of his neck. She wanted to say something, but the whole situation seemed overwhelming. Not knowing where to start, she collected the glasses and took them to the sink. She didn't turn to face him when he said he had to teach a fly fishing class. What would be worse, her seeing the defeated expression on his face or him seeing hers?

When she finished straightening up, she rushed back to the office. Linda Turner, the office manager, gave her a message and a curious look, but she just dove into her paperwork, hoping she could catch up before the free swim. She took a minute to read a memo mentioning the search for the two missing women, then returned the call to her friend from the Carolina Mountain Club.

"I thought they called that search off?"

"They did, but when they checked the activity on the one lady's bank account... Annie Winslow... they found a $300 withdrawal at an ATM in Tennessee two days after she was last seen. The bank's surveillance cameras showed a guy taking out the money, but his face was obscured by the hood of his jacket."

Sammy made a face. "That doesn't sound very good."

"They tracked her cell phone records today and found Winslow tried to call 911 on the day they think she went missing, but the call was dropped by the tower because of a weak signal and never reached the emergency call center. They used search dogs trained to pick up scents the first time. Now they're handling it as a recovery mission and going out tomorrow with cadaver dogs. Can you come?"

Sammy told her she would try, and when she hung up, Linda, without being asked, gave her a sympathetic smile and said she could handle the office.

Sammy heard the bell for the free period, but before she left for the lake she wanted to email a few pictures she took yesterday to Alvin Magee's mother. They rarely did that sort of thing, but her dad had told her about Alvin's predicament and asked her to give his mother special attention, and they had developed a cordial email relationship.

The close-up Sammy took of Alvin lying next to the words *I love you* that he had scribbled in the sand was priceless. His matted down wet hair and red water goggles over his glasses made him look like something from outer space. She gave the shot a tight crop so his ribs weren't in the picture, then quickly attached the photos and sent them off before heading out.

The sound of screaming kids rose from the lake as Sammy walked down the path that led from the main lodge to a narrow earthen bridge between two bodies of water. On the left was a small trout pond, and on the right, a two-acre lake with two docks. The dock for boats and equipment was next to the earthen bridge, and the other for diving and swim lessons was at the far end. A cable was strung between the two, and kids were already climbing the stairs to the deck where they could grab on to a bar hanging from a pulley that would carry them across the lake. Kids in life jackets jumped into the water as they reached the midpoint, and a rope retrieved the pulley for the next daredevil. Dozens of campers in life jackets bobbed all over the lake—floating, hollering, swimming, diving off Styrofoam floats, or just lying spread eagle on the surface staring up at the sky.

Four of the staff were already at the far end watching the kids in the shallow water. Sammy could see she wasn't needed, so she went back to the office to help Linda with a mailing. She walked back across the sports field where a group was playing soccer, and laughed to herself when she heard someone shout out, "Play fair," and then quote from the Woodcraft Laws. "Foul play is treachery!"

Sammy walked into the office, rolled her chair up to Linda's desk and joined in folding and stapling the camp newsletter. "Are you going to be okay by yourself tomorrow?" she asked Linda.

"Sure. If we get these done, it'll be fine."

They settled into folding and stapling. Linda, somewhere in her mid-fifties, was dressed in a Camp Green River tee and jeans; but with her trim figure, neatly coiffed short hair and ready smile, she still managed to project a breezy professionalism in sync with the overall character of the camp.

"I like to see you get out," said Linda. "Just wished it wasn't for what has to be a pretty sad search for the two missing women. I know you're frustrated having to work in the office all day. It's not exactly what you want, is it?"

"I thought once I got my degree in biology, my dad would let me mentor... for a couple years anyway."

"You can't blame him. He knows you're going to take over some day, and it makes sense for you to act as the liaison with the parents. And, besides, you do get to sub as a mentor from time to time." She got up and grabbed more sheets from the copier. "And let's not forget the swimming lessons."

Sammy looked up and gazed thoughtfully out the window for a moment. "I wonder what my life would be like if it wasn't just me. You know. A brother, sister, whatever. It's got to worry my dad that there's just the two of us to make sure this place stays the same. I keep telling him he's got to see the conservancy and set something up."

"Well, you're not always going to be alone. You'll be getting married some day."

Sammy giggled. "For the past two months, Dad's been trying to throw me into the arms of Barry Sullivan... or one of his four brothers."

Linda laughed. "The last time he sent you over to Camp Mountainview to borrow some copier ink, I told him he should be ashamed of himself. We had a whole carton in the storeroom, and he knew it."

"Of all the families to pick!" Sammy laughed. "That Sullivan bunch needs a camp just for that brood of theirs. Euva said the old-est brother and his wife… you know, Mary Plover who used to teach swimming at Glen Arden… just had their second set of twins."

It was close to five-thirty by the time they finished and Linda left for home. As Sammy finished up some paperwork, Patrick drift-ed into her thoughts. She had caught him staring at her when he brought a group down for their swim lesson yesterday. In fact, lately, she'd noticed him looking at her a lot. The last time their eyes met, she hated herself for blushing.

Sammy rose and meandered over to the corner office, leaned against the jamb and glanced around. She vaguely remembered how the room was fixed up for her to play in during the winters before she was old enough to attend school. There was a doll house and a cot. She recalled drifting off at nap time to the muted office sounds com-ing through the closed door and wondering what it would be like to have a mother. She would pat the pillow and nestle her face into it the way she'd seen children snuggle against their mother's breasts.

She remembered how her father would pop open the door and toss her jacket at her, yelling, "Saddle up kid, we're goin' for a ride." They'd bounce all over the valley in the jeep. He took her along with him on so many business runs into Hendersonville and Asheville, she grew up as familiar with lumber yards and supply houses as some kids were with McDonald's playland. Maybe that's why she and her dad were so close and at ease with each other.

It was like that until she had to start school, and her father bought the house in Flat Rock and found a housekeeper who could live in. It was either that or Aunt Betty was going to take matters into her own hands and bring her home with her to Greenville.

She went back to her desk and put the instructions on how to get to the search the next morning in her pocket and headed out to the lodge. It was already starting to fill up. She spotted her father intently listening to one of the campers, and it made her marvel. His ability to compartmentalize everything that happened insulated all his responsibilities from being affected by each other, a characteristic she'd noticed from the time she was a kid. She'd tried to emulate it, but got too swept up in things. Her dad insisted that was her strong point, but she knew better.

After the kid went off to his table, Sammy pulled her father to the side. "Dad, I got a call from the Carolina Mountain Club. Is it all right if I help with the search for those two ladies tomorrow? Linda said she can handle the office, and I'm sure I can get someone to trade with me for the swim sessions."

"I thought they called off that search."

She told him about the dropped cell phone call to 911 and the ATM withdrawal.

Their eyes met.

"They're asking all their trained rescuers to participate in a grid search starting at 7:30 in the morning."

Tiger nodded. "Sure honey. Go on out, we'll cover for you here. Just be careful."

CHAPTER EIGHT

Iᴛ ᴡᴀs sᴛᴀʀᴛɪɴɢ ᴛᴏ ᴄʟᴇᴀʀ as Katie turned into her driveway. Good. They could have the cookout after all. Jason's bike was leaning against the garage under the eave, but her daughter's car was gone. Must be working late at the store. There was a split second of relief when she realized Hal's car wasn't in the driveway either, and she felt ashamed for feeling that way.

She pulled into the garage and saw her son, Jason, working on the lawnmower on the bench in the corner. She blew a kiss into the air as he ran over and took a couple of bags she'd taken out of the back seat.

"Jeez, Mom. You should have let me get these for you."

Their dog, Lucky, who always showed interest when groceries arrived, followed them into the house. The kitchen was neat with nothing left out except a stack of mail that Jason must have brought in, proof that Hal hadn't been in the house.

Jason started emptying the grocery bags. He dangled a bag of chips in one hand and cheese dip in the other. "Can I have some?"

"Sure, baby. I'm not going to start dinner 'til your sister gets home."

He straddled a stool at the counter and dug into the treat as Katie put things away. He dipped in a chip and thrust it in the air toward her. Clutching an armful of cans, she opened her mouth wide enough for him to pop it in. Everything out of the way, Katie pulled up a stool and fell into her habit of running a hand along her long braid as she perused the mail.

She threw her stock investment statement aside, then thought for a moment. Lately the news was filled with the rise in the market, so she decided to see if the kids' college fund had gone up any. Maybe she wouldn't need that loan when Jason graduated from high school. She worried about putting two kids through college at the same time—for a couple of years, it would be a real struggle.

She pulled out a chip and gave it to Lucky, then got out another one and scooped up enough dip to practically break it. "You ready for camp next Sunday, honey?"

Jason nodded. "I can't wait. That's the best part of my summer. All except for the cookin.'"

Katie laughed. She loved the way he always found some way to kid her. "How about Lisa?"

"You know her. She won't start packing until the night before."

"Have you seen your father at all today?" she asked, trying not to sound concerned. The look he gave her showed that he was worried too. She scooped up another chip full of dip and thought about Hal, something the pace of running a kitchen for a hundred and fifty kids helped her escape. All the signs of another gambling binge stared her in the face, and she wondered what it would cost to bail him out of trouble this time.

Lucky jumped up and ran to the kitchen door wagging his tail. Had to be Lisa or he would have barked. Hal walked in and said hello, sheepishly. He needed a shave by at least three days and his clothes looked like they'd been slept in.

Jason tried to make everyone feel comfortable by asking his father about the lawnmower as if nothing were wrong. Hal's eyes darted over to the mail on the counter and landed on the envelope with the Edward Jones logo. He studied Katie's face as if he were gauging her mood, then went over and started to pick it up.

There was something about his cagey grin that made Katie grab it out of his hand. The sudden fear in his eyes sent a streak of terror through her brain. She quickly slipped off the stool and backed away from him to the far end of the room until she bumped into the fridge, all the while fumbling to get the envelope open.

She stopped breathing as her eyes fixed on the underlined figure next to *Total Value of Your Account*. She could see half of it was gone, but it didn't register until she looked up at Hal and saw the pathetic look of guilt. Her brain was suddenly pelted by every fear, every suspicion, every ugly memory their nineteen years of marriage had wrought, and she wanted to puke.

Jason's forehead turned into a mass of wrinkles. "What is it, Mom?"

Just then, Lisa walked in.

Katie managed to pull herself together in spite of having trouble breathing. "Jason and Lisa, I want… both of you to go up to your rooms. Your father and I… have to talk."

Lisa smirked and said, "Here we go again." She gave her father a quick kiss and shuffled out of the kitchen. Jason stood firm.

Katie knew if she looked at him she'd fall apart, so she stared at the floor and said, "Please, Jason. Go to your room." Once she heard the sound of his footsteps on the stairs, she looked pleadingly at Hal. "It's not *all* gone, is it?"

A sickening silence followed.

The enormity of the deed began to sink in. "How!" she screamed. "How in God's name could you have done this to your kids!?"

He put a finger to his mouth and rushed toward her. "Hush! Do you want all the neighbors to hear?"

"You mean Jeannie next door? Ha! She's been telling me to leave you for the past seventeen years. And if I hadn't gotten pregnant with Jason, I would have."

"Oh come on, baby. Let's not make a Federal case out of this. I'm just on a losing streak. Once my luck changes, you know I'll put it all back." He took a glass out of the cupboard. "What you need right now is a drink."

As he poured, his hands shook so much the bottle kept hitting the side of the glass, spilling vodka on the counter. He handed it to her, but she pushed it aside, then collapsed on a stool and dropped her head in her hands. He quickly guzzled down the drink and looked at her steadily, trying to size up the situation.

She looked up at him. "How in the hell did you do it?" The eva-sive look on his face told her he was thinking fast. "You got my code from my desk. Didn't you?" She pounded her fists on her forehead. "How could I have been so stupid to leave the sheet with all my pass-words in my desk!" Her face twisted in incredulity. "But they only would have issued a check in my name."

It didn't take her long to figure out he had ordered a withdrawal on line, waited for the check to come in the mail, forged her signa-ture and then put the money in his account. When it dawned on her that all the dire warnings she'd gotten from family and friends over the years had suddenly materialized, her face froze in disgust. "If my own mother told me you'd do such a thing, I wouldn't have believed her."

She pounded a fist on the counter. "Hal, I can't believe you did this after all I've done to help you." She kept pounding with every statement. "Did I ever throw it in your face that you haven't sup-ported this family the whole time we've been married, that you've lost every decent job you ever had because you either were gambling at Cherokee or in some poker game?" Her voice rose to a shout. "Tell me! Have I?!"

Not expecting an answer, she got up and paced erratically. "I could have fixed everything in this house with the money I've thrown away on your counseling." She slammed a fist on the counter next to him. "Goddamn it! This time I thought it was going to work!" Whip-lashed by emotions, her voice started to crack. "I've stayed with you all these years so my kids would have a father. It wasn't their fault I married you." She swung around and looked him square in the eyes. "I still can't believe it. After all your promises, all your begging for forgiveness, all the new starts... you had the nerve to gamble away what's taken me years to scrape together so our kids can get a decent start in life."

She was quiet for a few moments, then swiftly brushed away a few tears as if they were a nuisance, went over to the counter and carefully folded the top of the potato chip bag. She pulled open a drawer and took out a clip and snapped it on, then put the bag in the cupboard. The door was slammed shut, deliberately, as if she meant it to be the period at the end of a sentence. "I'm done, Hal. I'm get-ting a divorce. You managed to ruin my life, but I'm not going to let you do the same to these kids." She turned and leaned back against the counter. "I want you out of this house, and I don't want you to ever show your face here again. Anyone who could do what you did is out-and-out dangerous."

His stunned look turned into a hideous mask of defiance, erasing all traces of any attractive feature he still had left. "You can't do that. This house is just as much mine as yours."

"Have you forgotten? This house belongs to my mother." She turned her back to him and popped the lid onto the cheese dip. She threw a glance over her shoulder. "Besides, you don't live here. The last time we saw you was almost a week ago." She shoved the container into the fridge, knocking over a few jars; but instead of righting them, swung the door closed as if they were the least of her problems. "I'll have all your things at the end of the driveway tomorrow at five. Just pick them up and don't ever step foot in this house again, or I swear I'll kill you." She turned and looked into his eyes. "In fact, right now if I had a gun in my hand, I'd pull the trigger."

She stared at him with a resolute expression on her face as he studied her. He raised a hand slightly and started toward her as if he wanted to hold her, then a shadow of defeat fell across his face, and he turned and left.

She must have sat there for almost an hour with the walls vibrating with the heavy metal music coming from Lisa's room. Jason came in and climbed on a stool. Katie sat slouched forward with her cheek collapsed on a fist, distorting the line of her mouth. Without stirring, she managed to lift her lids enough to look up at him.

"We heard everything," he said.

She reached over and patted his arm in a way to say she was sorry.

"Lisa's locked herself in her room." He hesitated for a moment as if he were afraid he might say something he might be sorry for. "Is there enough left for her to start UNC in September?"

"We'll be all right for a couple of years. But I don't know what we're going to do when you start."

"Don't worry about me, Mom. If my grades stay the same, I'm pretty sure I'll get a scholarship."

She squeezed his hand. "I know, baby. I've talked to your placement counselor. I just don't want to put a lot of pressure on you. Anything can happen." She rose, took a deep breath and slid open a drawer. "You want to get the fire started while I make the salad?"

He gave her a hug. "I love you, Mom. You take a lickin', but you keep on tickin.'"

Katie finished the salad, and Jason came in and said the fire was going good.

"Do you want me to set the table?" he asked.

"No. That's your sister's job. Just call her down." She changed her mind. "No, better go up and get her. You'll break both our eardrums if you have to shout loud enough for her to hear."

"Dinner's not going to be much fun."

"You mean your sister?"

"You know how she likes Dad."

The remark summed up Jason's relationship with his father and made Katie feel bad. Hal hadn't spent any time with the boy, any time with anyone really; but Lisa being the first, he'd held more affection for her and always managed to make her feel special.

Jason took some plates from the cupboard. "Mom, I think we should go easy on Lisa for a couple of days. I'll set the table."

The music stopped and the room grew quiet as the two went about their chores. Katie got out some bleu cheese to spread on the London broil. "Honey, you want to put the meat on the grill for me?"

He came over and took the platter and watched as she made a vinaigrette dressing. She looked up at him. He was short and brawny like all the men in her family, and his dark curls, still wet from a shower, glistened. "You okay?"

"Yes, Mom. I just wanted to tell you that I'm glad you did it. Dad hasn't belonged to this family for a long time. It's not fair that all you do is work and take care of us. I want to see you have some kind of a life like all my friends' parents. Gettin' all dressed up... goin' out to dinner... that kind of thing. You're still young, Mom. And you're pretty, too. There's got to be somebody out there who will treat you real nice."

That night after everyone had gone to bed, Katie made her way up the stairs with a basket of folded clothes still warm from the dryer. Dinner hadn't been what she had hoped for, and she had ended up taking Lisa's plate to her room. Lisa hadn't looked up from her Game Boy when Katie laid the tray on her desk, but later, after watching TV in the family room, she said goodnight before going up to bed. Katie figured it was due to some nudging by Jason, but it still felt good.

Katie stood under the shower until the hot water ran out, put on a terry robe and made her way down the wide hall to her bedroom. The house was an old Victorian, expensive to heat and always needing some kind of repair. She loved it mostly because it was filled with the memories of her two children growing up.

Her parents bought it for her after Jason was born. They wanted her to live near them in Tuxedo, but she felt it was better to be close to the school where she taught. Her father held the deed and made her mother promise that after he died she wouldn't turn it over to her as long as she was married to Hal—something Hal never forgave him for.

She put on some hand cream, and feeling her wedding rings, eased them off her finger, went over to her jewelry case and dropped them in. She slipped out of the robe and looked at herself in the long oval dresser mirror that must have been brought into the house by its original owners. In spite of all the hard work and scrimping, she still had her figure.

She studied the curves of her body and wondered what it would be like to have a man run his hands over them again… and what it would be like to be filled with desire for it. She pulled off the band holding her braid and unraveled it so her dark chestnut hair hung down over her shoulder. She took her two firm breasts in her hands and squeezed them together, trying to remember what it felt like to have them caressed in passion.

She couldn't keep Tiger from drifting into her thoughts. If only he had committed to her. But then she wouldn't have had Jason and Lisa. She'd seen him with Liz once. At a silent auction to benefit the high school sports program where she worked as a volunteer. The woman was beautiful. She wore a dress that must have equaled the value of her entire wardrobe, but she was very gracious when Tiger brought her over and introduced them. One of Euva's daughters cleaned her house and said Tiger practically lived there. She remembered thinking for weeks what a shame it was that he couldn't commit to her either.

She put on one of the oversized tee shirts she slept in, slipped into bed and stared at the ornate ceiling, dimly lit by a street lamp. It had been years since she had thought about Tiger this way. Years of mostly trying to survive. Every time she had gotten ahead a little, Hal had racked up just enough gambling debts to clean her out. All except for the kid's college fund. Until now, that had been sacred.

The math teacher in her made her calculate. Nineteen years of covering up and trying to make a go of it—all going up in smoke within an hour. Everyone had been right all along. All those years she was just enabling Hal. She was guilty of gambling too—betting if she tried hard enough she'd make him all right.

CHAPTER NINE

"**I** MISS MY NINTENDO," moaned Tucker.

Alvin, who was sitting next to him in the dining hall, nudged him a little with his elbow. "Oh, come on. Give the place a chance."

"I am giving it a chance. I promised my mom I would… and I will." His eyes darted to a kid who just walked in. "That's number ninety-seven."

"Why in the heck are you counting everyone?"

"My dad said that they have a three-to-one camper-to-staff ratio and I'm checking it out."

Alvin didn't know what to say, so he just nodded like he didn't think it was a nutty thing to do. Alvin put a big heap of mashed potatoes on his plate and pushed the bowl to Tucker.

"Now, take this group for instance," Tucker said as he helped himself. "There are seven kids and two staff. That's a three-and-a-half-to-one ratio."

Alvin adjusted his glasses and said, "You got to take into account the folks in the kitchen and the infirmary and everything."

Tucker's eyebrow raised a tad and he looked at Alvin from the corner of his eye. "I'm workin' on that."

By the time the meal finished, Ricky was firmly established as the cabin clown, and it seemed to Alvin that things were going to be just fine… once Tucker got everyone counted, that is. Charlie Morgan stood up and raised his hands until the din calmed down before making some announcements.

Expectations rose as everyone started clearing their places and sorting what the camp called "Ort," which stood for organic recyclable trash. There were three buckets—one for compostable food like lettuce and veggies, one for paper, and the last for what they called "Sad Ort:" meat and dairy. The reason it was considered "sad" was because everyone was expected to eat what they put on their plates.

Once everyone got reseated, the table banging began. The sound of one hundred and fifty kids simultaneously pounding on the tables to the same rhythm, along with intermittent claps and stomps, reverberated throughout the hall.

Suddenly a whistle blared and Bob Davies, dressed in a ridiculous homemade caped superhero outfit and cycling helmet, ran out from the kitchen, then up and down the hall to the delight of screaming kids. He was followed by his befuddled sidekick, Scrappy. The kid's already knew he was from the planet Compost and would give them the Ort Report after inspecting the trash.

He raised his Ort detector—nothing more than a flashlight dangling from a strip of duct tape—into the air. That alone made everyone laugh. He proceeded to examine the compost bucket for any paper, meat or dairy. "Ah, ha!" He pulled out a paper cup, shined the flashlight on it, and announced that his detector would lead him to the culprit. Kids screamed and cringed as he skulked around the tables holding up the detector, every once in a while stopping and checking someone over. He crept along, abruptly stopping at Patrick.

Scrappy jumped around screaming "It's him! It's him!" generating a raucous response from the kids, which quickly evolved into a chant of *Throw him in, Throw him in.* The delighted mob led him out of the lodge and all the way to the far end of the lake. Patrick and Ortman climbed up the high-dive platform with the kids cheering and waving on shore.

Ortman raised his arms for silence, took out his cell phone and shouted, "Put me through to the governor of the planet Compost." He raised his arms again to quiet the sudden uproar. "Hello, governor! I want to ask you to commute Patrick's sentence."

Throw him in! Throw him in! the kids demanded.

Ortman raised his arms for silence again and shouted into his phone. "What? You won't commute the sentence?" The kids worked themselves into a frenzy, wherein he and Scrappy grabbed Patrick and tossed him in the lake.

The dunking ended with Ortman shouting, "Fight the Ort wars forevermore!" He led the whole rollicking assembly in the camp mantra, "Waste not, want not!"

Everyone frolicked on the green for a while, giving Patrick a chance to run back and change before they proceeded to the back field for the start of the camp's famous *Predator or Prey* game. The cabins were divided into species teams ranging from insects as the lowest, to hawks at the top of the food chain, with everyone trying to survive.

THE GAME KICKED OFF with Alvin's cabin being designated as insects. There was something about being chased by a hundred frogs, snakes and hawks that quickly made Alvin forget his sore knees and shift into survival mode. What he lacked in stamina he made up for in brains, and by the time Hemlock Hut Two had risen to hawk status, he was being looked to as the point man on the team.

At the campfire afterward, a few kids shoved a little so they could sit next to him, and it made him feel good, but he still made room for Tucker.

That night, Alvin curled up in bed with the events of his first week at camp rumbling around in his head. Keeping up had been tough, but at least he was still alive to talk about it. He'd earned some status in the cabin by using his head and a lot of animal cunning at *Predator or Prey*, but he had to do a lot better with his hiking group tomorrow.

He rolled over, and the pull of the blanket across his knees smarted in spite of all the new Band Aids and salve Patrick had put on. He kept thinking back to the morning he went on the field trip to Gold Creek Falls. When Mike jokingly said he fell off the log because he was growing so fast, he had looked around at the kids' faces and could see they didn't swallow that even though it was true he was the tallest.

They'd all treated him pretty good, though, especially the way they pitched in to find his glasses after he fell; but he didn't want this to keep happening. It was like everyone was making special allowances for him, and he was sure they'd be sick of it after a while. Tomorrow he absolutely had to keep up the pace on the hike. At least with the girls. And as soon as he could, with the boys.

Amy had a bossy way about her, yet he liked how she moved over so he could stand next to her when Mike showed them the salamander, and the way she gathered up his backpack when he fell. Her blond ponytail bobbing around when she talked was kind of cute, too.

At free swim, she seemed impressed with his crawl. Thank God, Mom let me get those swimming lessons at the college. It's the one thing I don't look like a complete doofus doing. Suddenly he felt torn. He had only thought about his mother once all day, and he should have written her a letter at rest period instead of passing out again. He had to be sure to do it tomorrow.

As he started to doze off, Alvin wondered about Tucker's idiosyncrasies, especially his fascination with all the gory stories he'd read on the internet about people being bitten, gored and dragged from the mountains by everything from coyotes to mountain lions. There was his odd fixation with numbers, too. Tucker had told him his father was a renowned mathematician and that's all they talked about together.

Alvin giggled to himself remembering the last thing Tucker had said before getting into bed. After telling him about a Boy Scout who was dragged into the woods by a bear and had to be taken home in several bags, he said, "Don't worry, buddy. We only have twenty-three more days, 552 hours, 33,120 minutes and 1,987,200 seconds to go."

PATRICK ROSE FROM HIS BUNK at the sound of the screen door opening. Mike had come to relieve him until midnight. On the stroll to the staff rec room, Patrick scrolled through his day. Alvin seemed to be making it through the field trips in high spirits, but little Tucker Watson didn't appear to be enjoying himself as much. Alvin had to have noticed it too, since he looked after him a lot. Tomorrow he had to give Tucker some one-on-one attention to see if he could get him more engaged.

Patrick became aware of utter quiet, an interlude that wouldn't last long. All the creatures in the night were just taking a breather. Suddenly, the whole symphony of peeps and croaks rose up again. He wished he had put on a sweater as he walked through the misty woods, wet from a sporadic shower that had just let up. With the valley being one of the wettest places in the continental United States, the air was soft and the scent of hemlock pervasive. Passing by the lake, he remembered how great Sammy looked on the dock that afternoon. With those legs, no wonder she was a champion swimmer.

Two of the girls' counselors were at the computer in the rec room. He said hello and read the paper while he waited for them to finish. He finally got on the internet and booted up his email. Three messages from his stepsister. He smiled as he remembered barging in on her pajama party when he came home from school at spring break. All the girls ran around screaming in the family room like they'd seen a rock star. He couldn't get up the stairs and behind a locked door fast enough.

He sent his father a short message, even though he knew his stepmother was the only one who was going to read it. The door slammed and he looked over his shoulder to see Bob Davies walk in. Finished, Patrick went over and flopped down on the couch across from him.

Bob looked up. "You want to go into town and get a beer?"

Patrick flicked a clump of dry mud off the side of his sandal. "No. Let's just hang out here."

Earlier that day, Patrick had been talking to Bob about being a mentor the following summer since this was Bob's fourteenth year at the camp.

"Have you talked to Tiger yet?" asked Bob.

"Yeah. It's all set."

Bob reached over for a ukulele lying on a bench and started strumming it. "Well now that that's done. What are you going to do about Sammy?"

"What do you mean?"

"Come on, buddy. Everybody knows you've been crazy about her ever since she started looking different in a bathing suit."

"I don't know. I'm pretty stuck in the 'pal' position." Patrick couldn't help thinking that didn't stop the bottom from falling out of his world when he heard she was marrying Randy. All the bunk about them being a beautiful couple made him sick. If looks were what she was after, that dude certainly had them.

"Patrick, you've got to make your move. Just do it without making a complete ass out of yourself."

"That's going to be the tricky part."

Bob strummed and grinned. "I remember the first time I laid eyes on you. What were you then? Ten? Brother, was that a trip. When you stepped out of that limo in a three-piece suit straight from Paris, I said, 'he ain't gonna last a week.'" He looked up at him. "And, now look at you."

Patrick pressed his lids tight and tried to erase the image of an overly sophisticated ten-year-old raised by his divorced mother in hotels on two continents. He could order dinner in three languages and tell you where every painting was in the Louvre and the Metropolitan Museum, but the only contact he'd had with nature before coming to Camp Green River was the opulent bouquets scattered around expensive hotel suites.

"My father got the same impression when he came to get me when my mother died." Patrick picked off some debris stuck on his sandals. "My mom always referred to my stepmother as Doris Day in a sort of condescending tone, so before my father came to get me, I went to this run-down theater on the Champs Elysees to see *Pillow Talk* so I'd know what I was in for. My mother's friend, Monique, asked me where I had gone after the funeral, and when I told her 'the movies' she screamed *mon Dieu!*"

Bob laughed, and considered the situation. "Okay, Patrick, we all know you're crazy about Sammy... and buddy, if you don't go for it now, someone else is going to get her, and you'll kick yourself for the rest of your life." He put the ukulele down and hunched forward. "Listen. Sammy and I both have Thursday night off. I'll trade with you, and tomorrow ask her... casual like... if she wants to grab something to eat and catch a movie. Nothing fancy. Maybe take her to West First, that hip pizzeria with a brick oven on First Street downtown."

Patrick listened, but said nothing. The two played chess for a while, then had a few laughs with two counselors who dropped in. On the way back to the cabin, Patrick mulled over what Bob had said. I'll have to see what movies are playing. Definitely not an action or chick flick. A comedy's the safest bet. He thought for a moment. They'd be sitting close to each other in the dark. Boy, what a cheesy plan. The movie bit was as old as the hills. But then again, if there was a part where he could put an arm around the back of her chair, natural like, her next move would tell him if he was in the game... or not.

CHAPTER TEN

Sᴀᴍᴍʏ ꜱᴛᴜᴅɪᴇᴅ ᴛʜᴇ ɪɴꜱᴛʀᴜᴄᴛɪᴏɴꜱ she'd jotted down last night. She was supposed to turn right onto Route Nine a couple miles beyond Lake Lure and meet up with the search party in the Ingles parking lot across from the Tate Nature Park trailhead. There were so many cars, sheriff's vehicles and rescue trucks that she had to park halfway across the lot.

She got out of the Jeep. The thumping of a helicopter swooping over the trail and the solemn faces of the usually jovial members of the Carolina Mountain Club set a grim tone as they quietly unpacked and strapped on their gear. The oppressive heat and humidity so early meant a grueling day ahead, especially in jeans, boots and a long-sleeved shirt. She'd done enough bushwhacking to know she needed a good pair of gloves and well worn-in heavyweight boots to support her ankles over rough terrain.

The crowd drifted toward what had to be the main staging area. Joe Wilson, the Rutherford County Sheriff, stood on the back of a pick-up with a megaphone.

"Taking into account the age of these women and their hiking experience, we've narrowed down the area of greatest probability to a five-hundred-foot-wide section and will begin a grid search starting from the parking lot. You'll be put in position ten feet apart by Ted

Sutton from the Lake Lure Rescue Squad. Everyone should have food and water to last all day, as well as a first aid kit. We expect each of you to be a self-contained unit. North Carolina Search and Rescue will be in the lead with their cadaver dogs. Please keep your radio on and check your compass regularly. We don't want the line drifting off the 250 degree bearing."

Someone neared the open tailgate and motioned to him. He bent down so they could whisper in his ear, then he stood up and said, "I'm going to turn this over to Ralph Juston, the county coordinator for the North Carolina Division of Emergency Management."

The coordinator hopped up on the truck with a fistful of papers, and the Sheriff handed him the megaphone before rushing off. "As you all know, we've already been over all the trails and done a search of the park. As Sheriff Wilson said, due to the age of these women, we've picked the area between the lot and the Mountain Vista Trail as the area of highest probability. A helicopter went out yesterday with a thermal camera and didn't spot anything, but they're trying again today. Once we get off the trail, the foliage gets thick and you won't be able to see more than ten to fifteen feet ahead in some places. Remember, we consider every search area a crime scene. Our support team will be right behind you. If you come across anything that looks like evidence, radio us so we can process it and get a GPS coordinate."

Except for a few stragglers, everyone assembled at the park across the road in a matter of minutes. Sammy got between two men she knew from the hiking club. They both had machetes but she preferred to crawl under and over rather than chop her way through. That was the only way to get by a batch of mountain rhododendrons anyway.

The going was easy at first, then the line started to descend through thick brush. Her clothes were already getting soaked with sweat. It helped a little when she stuffed her hair under her baseball cap. She stepped on a long bramble, but as she started to go forward, it slipped from under her foot, sprang up and slashed across her cheek. Without stopping, she reached in her pocket and pulled out some antiseptic cream she kept handy.

"Halt progress until further notice," boomed from her radio. Sammy glanced over at the guy on her right. They hadn't gone but a hundred feet. He shrugged his shoulders in a silent response. She plunked down on a log and took a bottle of water out of her back pack. She gulped it down, then took out a bandana and wiped her face and neck, wincing at the feel of the abrasive grit. She could see the guy to her right doing the same, but the one on her left was hidden behind a boulder.

After another ten minutes, the guy next to her said, "They must have found something pretty important, or they wouldn't be holding us up this long."

Just as she was about to agree with him, a voice came over the radio. "Folks, we found a body. It was buried under brush and accounts for our missing it the first time. Everyone, the probability factor that we're going to find another one just got greater. The recovery team's here processing the site. Take five more minutes, before we get moving again."

SAMMY SLID OUT OF HER JEEP, and leaned against the door, sucking a deep breath of the pure Green River Valley air into her lungs. The chorus of "She'll be Comin' Round the Mountain" echoed through the woods from the back field. She closed her eyes and let the joyful energy erase the grim mood that had enveloped her all day.

The singing stopped. The campfire had to be over, with everyone on their way to their cabins by now. She took a couple of steps toward the house, but when her numb feet couldn't feel the impact of hitting the ground, she wanted to sink down and curl up on the lawn.

Skippy, his black coat glistening in the moonlight, ran from out of the dark and licked her hand. Knowing her dad couldn't be too far behind, she trudged the thirty yards to the door so she could peel off her clothes and get into the shower before he saw what she looked like. They had stopped the line for a half hour at five, giving her a chance to change her shirt and socks, but no one would guess it.

Sammy came out of the upstairs bathroom in her pajamas with a towel wrapped around her hair, and the weather report droning from the TV in the living room. She went downstairs and found her father asleep in his favorite easy chair with papers that must have fallen from his hands lying on the floor.

He stirred. "Hi, honey. I was thinking about you all evening. Heard about them finding a body."

"They kept us looking for the second one until dark. We covered the woods almost to Island Creek Road that borders the area." She fluffed her hair with the towel. "Dad, can I put the eleven o'clock news on?"

"Sure. I want to hear it myself."

The reporter rattled off the events of the day as if she were talking about a Sunday school picnic. "The investigation is being treated as a homicide, but only as normal protocol. Rutherford County Sheriff Joseph Wilson said there is no evidence of foul play, and the search will continue throughout the weekend."

Joe Wilson appeared on the screen. "The body was taken to the county coroner's office and will be sent to the State Medical Examiner in Chapel Hill tomorrow to determine identification and cause of death. It could be as late as Tuesday before we have a positive identification."

The sheriff continued. "We have stepped up the search after locating the one body. We're not going to take anything for granted. You only have one chance to investigate the scene. If we just chalk it up to some lost hikers, two months down the road we could find out it was more than that and have lost every opportunity to process the scene or gather evidence correctly. It is always better to treat every death suspiciously until the facts of the case tell you in what direction to go."

Sammy figured the news clip had been shot mid-afternoon. When the guy next to her on the line came back after the half-hour dinner break, he told her someone on the Chimney Rock rescue team had heard the body had too many injuries for where it was lying, and it was definitely a woman.

TIGER DROVE TO HENDERSONVILLE in a somber mood and pulled into the lot between the library and the office strip where the conservancy rented space. With nothing but a sea of asphalt and cement, the sterile unearthliness of the place added to his angst.

No one sat at the reception desk, and Tiger assumed it was because the conservancy didn't want to spend money on a task they could juggle themselves. He picked a newspaper off the table and read. *Two days after searchers found a body in the mountains of North*

Carolina, the search for Annie Winslow and Ruth Rodham, missing for more than three weeks, has been permanently suspended. The active search concluded over the weekend after authorities involved in the search met and officially suspended it. The identity of the body found in the Tate Nature Park in Lake Lure on Friday could be known as early as today, Rutherford Sheriff Joe Wilson said yesterday.

He put the paper down. The camp was secure with counselors sleeping in every cabin... he always slept with one eye and one ear open... but he didn't want Sammy to go out hiking until they knew what happened at that park.

A young woman in jeans poked her head in, and finding he was there to see Tom Gibbons, led him through a maze of hallways and offices jammed with desks and file cabinets. The crowded, yet orderly, look of the place gave the impression that the business that transpired here was too demanding for anyone to waste time on amenities. In spite of the total absence of décor, plants in cheap plastic pots and makeshift containers were stuck in every available niche, as if to remind them why they were there.

Seeing Tiger at the door, Tom Gibbons grabbed a notepad and shepherded him into a conference room at the end of the hall. Charts, maps and marked up aerial views of mountains and farms plastered on every inch of wall space gave it a war room quality.

Tom turned to Tiger. "I've asked our development guy, Ben Beckham, to join us." Ben appeared in the doorway, shook Tiger's hand, and they all sat down.

Tiger guessed the two men were younger than him by a little more than ten years. In fact, everyone he'd seen in the building ranged in age between twenty and forty. This was a healthy sign. Thirty years ago when he was twenty, a vibrant conservation organization of this size would hardly exist in a small town like Hendersonville. Hardly exist in any sized town for that matter.

Tom took down an aerial view that was pinned up on a wall, and spread it out on the table. Tiger's comfort level jumped up a notch seeing the camp and Jeb's property outlined with all kinds of notes tacked on, as well as comments scrawled in the borders. They had evidently spent some time studying his situation. The way the man put aside all the lawyer-speak and framed the facts in a straightforward conversational tone put Tiger even more at ease.

"We knew the Ryan property was a key element in keeping the headwaters of the Green River intact, and we've had it on our radar screen; but, frankly, we've got so many parcels at risk, we figured you were probably all over it like a rug and put our efforts elsewhere."

"I hear you," said Tiger.

Tom glanced at his notes. "We don't have much time, but it's not hopeless. I suggest that we all get to work on every available avenue open to us. Ben's already been beating the bushes for "angels" and might be able to come up with someone."

Tiger turned his attention to Ben. This former wide receiver for the Giants, who'd played in two Super Bowls, made quite a stir when he hit town, giving members of the conservancy's board considerable bragging rights. Tiger had heard a lot of favorable comments about him at cocktail parties over the winter, and now understood why. The toned athlete, in a navy blazer and white open-collared shirt, projected an easy confidence without a trace of arrogance.

Ben was leaning back in his chair fingering a paperclip he'd picked up off the table. "I've been talking to The Nature Conservancy. It's possible they have a line on someone who's looking to buy the sort of land Ryan has, and put it in a conservation trust for the tax write-off. Also, I'm having lunch tomorrow with someone who's in a position to consider a loan until you come up with the financing..." His eyes shot over to Tom, then back to Tiger. "... but the timeframe here is pretty tight."

The talk about finding an "angel" that would kick in four million dollars to save a chunk of land from development excited Tiger. This environmental movement sure had gained traction.

Tom stood up and strolled around the room. He was tall, lean and tanned like someone who tramped around outdoors a lot. He didn't have Ben's casual confidence; this guy was driven. "For the moment, let's assume that we get some kind of temporary loan to secure the property. If you want to absorb the land into the camp, our best bet for a long-term solution is to get a matching grant from the Clean Water Management Trust Fund. That would take the nut down to around two million... maybe lower."

Tiger swallowed hard. Hell, two million was better than four.

Tom sat on the edge of the table and pointed to stream beds they had outlined on Jeb's property. "This State agency was set up to help finance projects that specifically address water pollution problems, and they've got money to help conservation non-profits like us acquire easements to protect stream and river buffers. You'd have to give them rights to fifty feet on one or possibly both sides of all the streams, and you wouldn't be able to disturb that land... build cabins... anything like that. If you're willing to bump that up to three hundred feet instead of fifty, they'll actually pay you for the easement."

Tiger was quickly getting the impression that these guys knew all the options.

Tom folded his arms. "A problem we see here is that they're not going to consider any new projects until next February and won't release the money until August, which means you're going to have to borrow the money for at least a year. Another issue is that it's not a sure thing. They don't grant every project." He looked thoughtful. "Though, with the streams on Jeb's place part of the Green River's headwaters, I can't see them turning it down."

He looked directly at Tiger. "However, right now, the least we need to shoot for, in case we can't raise the money and the property does go to the Ledges, is to get Jeb to give us an easement on the east slope facing the camp before he signs. Runoff from there would do the worse damage. I think we should start Jeb thinking about it as soon as possible, and my plan is to go over and give that a shot tomorrow."

The "angel" idea was quickly starting to look like the only way out to Tiger. "Won't an easement affect the way the Ledges look at this deal?" he asked.

"If he gives us one, they're certainly going to try to leverage that fact, but if I can get Jeb's confidence enough for him to let me help in the negotiations, we might be able to work it out. And... you better be prepared to pay Jeb the difference if they want the price reduced. We won't know until we get into it."

Tiger liked what he was hearing. The conservancy was committing time, talent and valuable relationships to help him out. Yet, with only twenty-one days left to go, everything seemed too iffy.

Tom strolled around the room, tapping a pen on his palm and

thinking out loud. "You said Jeb hasn't signed the contract yet. What we need now more than anything is time." He turned to Tiger. "Do you think we can get him to give us another couple of months?"

Tiger shook his head. "His going back on his word to the Ledges was something I never thought he'd do. It had to be his relationship with my dad... and me, too. But I think that's all we're going to get out of him. Mentally, he's walked away from that place. Knowing his land is passing out of the family's hands is killing him, and he wants it over with."

"Hey, girl, you look pretty darn good in them new jeans of yours. It's about time you stopped hiding that figure of yours 'neath them bib overalls," said Euva as Katie got up to get more ice tea from the fridge.

That was the second compliment Katie had gotten on the jeans. She hadn't worn them in years, but since she was going to see her brother this afternoon, and he always complained about her dressing like an old lady, she dug them out of her closet last night and put them on. Jason had come in her room to ask her something, and whistled as she inspected herself in the mirror.

Euva's remark made Katie self-conscious, and she found it hard to look her in the eye. She was used to Euva doing all the talking during their breaks. Mostly valley gossip. Between Euva's five daughters and six sisters, the Freemans knew just about anything that was happening anywhere, so she assumed she'd heard about her and Hal by now.

"Why are you leavin' early?"

Katie hated telling this strict Baptist who faithfully read her Bible every day that she was going to see a lawyer, but the facts would be coming out sooner or later. "Euva, I'm sure you know I've been struggling with Hal's problems for years, but it's gotten where I can't handle it. My brother, Matt, is working on a divorce."

Euva took her hand. "Katie, I haven't walked in your shoes, but I know you wouldn't be doing this unless you felt you had to. I'm here for you if you need to talk, and I'm going to pray for you and your family."

Euva's words ran through Katie's mind on the drive into Hendersonville. She'd drifted away from her religion since college, but the warmth Euva expressed brought it all back to her. She missed the comfort of a strong faith that had in her youth kept her from feeling afraid and all alone.

She pulled into a parking space behind a brick building that must have been there since the early 1800's. She'd never been to Matt's office before… at least not on business… and going to see him in a professional capacity gave her a strange feeling. The casual way he'd spoken over the phone, as if divorce was an incidental event, had somehow denigrated her years of trying to make a go of her marriage. *My own brother, instead of respecting me for going through hell to keep my family together, considers me a chump.* The divorce was acceptance of defeat, making her ashamed… especially when she thought of Hal. A feeling that she was cutting and running nagged at her.

The building was right off Main Street and the first floor housed one of a handful of antique shops Hendersonville was known for. She took the elevator to the second floor and entered the law offices of Keene, Puckett & Sheetz, Puckett being her brother.

He was on the phone when she was ushered into his office. He finished running through his weekend golf scores with one of his friends, hung up and laid back in his swivel chair as if to say, *How do I look, Sis? Do you think I've made it?* She smiled back at him as if to say, *Yes, big brother, you have.*

Katie proceeded to repeat everything she'd already told him over the phone.

"Sure we can go to Edward Jones, but it ain't gonna buy you nothin'. They'll only go after Hal… and we all know he doesn't have anything. Then, there's the scandal. Sis, consider the money gone. By the way, I hope you've changed all your passwords."

"Before he was out of the driveway."

He pulled out some papers. "It'll be pretty cut and dried. You don't really own anything jointly since Mom's holding the deed. Dad was no dummy." Noticing the unresponsive stare on Katie's face, he said, "No one can say that you didn't give this marriage a try, Sis, but it's time to move on." He held his breath for a moment. "We put adultery as the main complaint."

She looked up at him, puzzled.

"Sis, what do you expect with his lifestyle? We've all known about it for a while. He stays with her in Cherokee. Sally Freeman's sister-in-law works at the casino and told Mom what's been going on."

Katie slowly shook her head. Hal hadn't missed a betrayal.

Her brother handed her a pen and started to point to where she should sign and initial. He put the papers in a file folder, and said, "We'll serve him tomorrow. After that, I'm going to get his ass in here and squeeze like hell to get an uncontested divorce out of him. With what he pulled with the kids' college fund he's got plenty to be afraid of. I'm pretty sure he'll cave right in and you'll be rid of him in a couple of months."

A voice came over the speaker on his desk. "Your four o'clock's here."

Dazed from the revelation of Hal's affair, Katie rose.

Her brother watched her walk to the door. "Sis." She turned and looked at him. "I hated like hell to see you stuck with that guy all these years. I hope you can finally find someone nice." He looked her up and down. "By the way, have you lost weight?"

"No. Why do you ask?"

"I don't know. You look good. Maybe it's those jeans. In fact, do yourself a favor and throw out all that old junk of yours, and for heaven's sake get rid of that braid. Katie, you've got a long life ahead of you, and you're not going to latch on to some great guy if you're lookin' like an old granny. And, by the way, don't get too friendly with anyone until this is over."

EUVA WAVED AT SAMMY who was headed to the lake, then made her way down the shady path to her car. She was done for the day, and bone tired from the extra work with Katie being gone. She pulled out of the driveway and headed for home just over the mountain above the camp in what they called Mountain Valley. She passed Jeb's land and felt saddened. It was a shame neither of his boys wanted to carry on the Ryan legacy. It had to be killing Jeb to hand his land over to the Ledges. But she figured that's what happens when boys go off to college and marry outside the valley.

She was a Maybin before she married into the valley's Freeman family, and most of the Maybin clan still lived on or near the three square miles of land old Mathew Maybin was able to get his hands on, including the twelve hundred acres he received for his service in the Revolutionary War. The land had been split up amongst family over the generations, but all together they were still pretty much rooted in the Green River Valley.

Everyone in the family could mouth the story of Mathew Maybin coming by ship to Charleston from Ireland and working here and yonder until he discovered the valley. He had believed he had gotten hold of one of the most beautiful places on earth, and now, more than two hundred years later, the clan was still agreeing with him. Her brother, Theron, who lived between Mountain Valley and the Green River Preserve, with sixty-six years on him, was still farming forty acres on his bottomlands and shipping beans and squash from Florida to Maine.

She turned onto Cabin Creek Road and started the climb up, worrying about Katie. She'd known her since she was born. Her parents lived on the mill hill in Tuxedo when she was a kid, but once the mill closed, her dad became a master tool and die maker and earned a good living up until his passing. He put great store in education, and all four kids graduated from college.

Everyone always said those Pucketts were a smart bunch, recalled Euva. All except that mother of theirs. It was a shame how she whipped up that heap of trouble when little Katie started going with Tiger. She just couldn't keep her nose out of it. She pushed Katie into demanding an ultimatum from Tiger instead of letting the two of them work things out. After it was all said and done, poor Katie couldn't lift her head in church any more.

Now that her mother had a little bit of age on her, Euva was hoping she would stop causing trouble with her gossip. But Euva was afraid. With Katie getting a divorce and word leaking out that Tiger had broken up with his lady, she could start making the same kind of mess of things she did twenty years ago. Tomorrow she'd hurry up and let Tiger know about Katie's situation. It was about time he settled down with a good woman.

CHAPTER ELEVEN

Sᴴᴇʀɪꜰꜰ Wɪʟꜱᴏɴ ᴛᴏꜱꜱᴇᴅ ᴛʜᴇ ʀᴇᴘᴏʀᴛ on the table. The coroner from Chapel Hill had called him with a heads-up last night, and now the detailed autopsy report was fresh off the fax.

"Should I notify the press?" his administrative assistant asked.

He took off his glasses, dropped them on the desk and massaged his eyes. He was up for reelection in a couple of months and all the barbeques and potluck dinners had made him look like something they were fattening up for slaughter. In a couple of hours he'd have the pleasure of debuting his puffy new double chin in front of a bunch of TV cameras. He could hear them all now. *Gee, he's puttin' on weight.*

"Aren't they already sittin' out there in the hall?" he answered.

The woman rocked a little in her sensible low heels. "What do you expect? They all know you're releasing the coroner's report this morning."

"Get Lieutenant Williams in here. As head of homicide I want him at the news conference. Tell him to be prepared to release all the footage from the bank's security cameras. Also, get Mrs. Rodman's son on the phone, and then Annie Winslow's daughter. They should be the first to get the official word that this is now a murder investigation."

"They've both called Lt. Williams already and are standing by to hear from you." She handed him a piece of paper. "You can dial their numbers yourself."

He nodded, thinking to himself that he should have expected that. He looked at his watch. "Set up the conference for ten."

Just as she disappeared through the door, he shouted. "Did you make copies of their joint statement for us to hand out?"

She peeked in and said she had. He started to dial Ruth Rodman's son. They both knew the body was Ruth's, but had to wait for the coroner to confirm it from dental records. Now, with the autopsy done, at least the family could bring her home and start their closure. He was hoping the man wouldn't ask for a copy of the report. It wasn't going to bring his mother back, and it would haunt him for the rest of his life.

Jim was surprised how calm the son was, and it confirmed his belief in being available, open and candid with victims' families. He was also glad the man didn't ask to see the report. All he wanted was the death certificate so he could wrap up his mother's affairs.

The call to Annie Winslow's daughter was going to be harder. She was still desperately holding out hope that her mother was still alive, and had appeared on CNN and *America's Most Wanted* to stimulate possible leads.

He had to be careful not to disclose too many details of Ruth Rodman's autopsy report. Under the circumstances, the viciousness of the assault could send Marcie Winslow over the edge. He picked up the phone and dialed. She was pleased the bank footage was going to be released and felt it would give her another shot at national coverage. He ran through some of the ideas Lt. Williams and his team were working on even though he knew she was in daily contact with him. Every bit of reassurance was going to make this easier for her. At this point, there wasn't much else he could say, except that they would be handing out the joint statement from the families thanking everyone for their help.

The sheriff ended the call. He picked up the report and leafed through the sheets until he found the drawings showing all the injuries. He'd known from the minute he looked down on the body lying in the woods that it couldn't have sustained all the apparent injuries falling from such a gradual incline. But he had to follow strict protocol and keep speculation out of the press.

His detectives had jumped on the case right after they got their hands on Winslow's financial records and discovered the ATM withdrawal. They started by examining files of slaying victims and missing persons in Georgia, South Carolina and Florida. So far, forensics hadn't come up with anything, but at least now they had a positive identification that the body was that of Ruth Rodman and she was killed by blunt force trauma to the head.

He scanned the drawings. The guy who did this to a seventy-year-old woman had to be a real animal. Four blunt force injuries to the skull and a broken jaw. She must have put up quite a fight to break three fingers and both bones on her lower right arm.

This was the county's first murder this year, and it was just a matter of time before the second one showed up. Annie Winslow's body was out there somewhere and this press conference would only ratchet up the pressure on him and his department to find her and the monster who did it.

The only thing solid they had so far was the photo from the security camera at the ATM in Reedville, Tennessee. The perp was tall and thin, and wearing a black hooded sweatshirt, but they didn't have a clue about his age or if anyone else was involved. There were thousands of black hooded sweatshirts out there, but if the killer discarded it, and someone brought it in, they might get a lead.

Why Reedville? Did the guy have some connection to the place, or was he just on his way through town? The day they found out about the ATM withdrawal, Annie Winslow's daughter had gone over there and talked with the local law enforcement officials and even managed to get on TV in Johnson City to plead for anyone who might have seen anything to come forward.

What those old ladies must have gone through for a lousy three hundred dollars, he thought. Only a real sicko would have turned this two-bit robbery into a murder. Those two couldn't have posed a physical threat to anyone and would have just handed over their wallets. Lt. Williams' hunch was probably right. There had to be a reason the perp couldn't afford to be recognized. He had to have some kind of record. A frequent offender with his photo and prints on file.

An ugly picture formed in Sheriff Wilson's head. This guy evidently couldn't take any chances and would just as soon kill two defenseless women as risk having anyone start looking for him. The hiking trail was a major factor here. After the conference, he'd ask Williams to go back over those files from the surrounding states and see if any of the slayings or missing persons could have possibly been connected in any way to a park or mountain trail. And if they were, take a good look at all the people they pulled in for questioning. Someone in one of those files could be their man.

He flipped the page and read the list of items received with the body. *Tee shirt, pants, bra, underwear...* The autopsy report continued. *Accompanying the body within a paper bag labeled right hand was the decomposed and partially skeletonized disjointed right forearm, wrist and hand.* He read on. *Also accompanying the body around the neck was a rope cord attached to a pair of eyeglasses, and within the pants, a handkerchief.* He sank back into his chair and swiveled slowly around as he wondered what he'd be wearing when he dropped dead. Hopefully he'd be in a pair of pajamas in a nursing home looking forward to his ninetieth birthday.

THE CALL CAME INTO the Cherokee County sheriff's office at 10:04. Deputy Olsen was in his cruiser coming back from serving an eviction notice on some squatters in Maggie Valley when he heard the dispatcher's instructions on his radio.

"The man said the guy's been trespassing on his property for two days now and wants him off."

Olsen took down the address. It was on Reynolds Road, just off I-40 next to the Pisgah National Forest. Probably some cheapskate that didn't want to pay park fees. He swung around and headed out, stopping once at a gas station to use the john and pick up some gum. Ever since he promised his wife he'd quit smoking, he chewed so much of it he went to sleep every night with an aching jaw.

He pulled onto Reynolds Road and drove about a half-mile until he came to the dirt road the dispatcher said for him to search. Sure enough, he hadn't gone one hundred yards before he saw a beat up white van in a clearing with camping gear sprawled all over.

A tall, sunken-eyed man came from out of the woods zipping up his fly. Must have just taken a pee. Olsen radioed that he had arrived at the scene, gave them the Georgia license plate number on the van, and said he was going to turn on his video recorder and get out and talk to him. He described the man as somewhere in his sixties and pretty harmless looking. By the looks of things, probably a drifter. He had a dog tied up to a tree.

He slicked his hair back and put on his hat, grabbed his clipboard and got out of the car. He kept his ears open as he slowly approached, one hand holding the clipboard and the other resting on his gun. His eyes surveyed the scene, carefully, in case anyone else might appear. He didn't want *his* wife driving over a bridge named after him.

"Officer, is there a problem?" the man asked.

So far, so good, thought Olsen. The guy was too relaxed to be dangerous, but you could never be too careful. Some of these drifters were pretty slick con artists.

"I'd like to see your driver's license."

"Sure thing, buddy. It's in my van."

Olsen followed him to the back of the van, and before the man opened it, he said, "I want to warn you, I've got an expandable baton among my belongings. Don't let it get you nervous. I just never want to get out of my van without it, man. You never know what crazies are out there. That's why I've got my dog with me."

He retrieved his wallet hidden in a wheel well and handed over his license. Olsen glanced at the name on the Georgia license. "Stay right here, Mr. Skinner, I'll be right back." He went to the car and radioed the information.

"Okay," said the dispatcher. "We'll check him out and call you right back."

The deputy got out and positioned himself in front of the car so he'd be sure to get a good recording. "Step over here, please," he said.

Gary Skinner had an affable look on his face as he sauntered over.

"You know you're trespassing on private property."

"Officer, I got lost trying to find a shortcut to 441. I'm on my way to Tennessee."

"Then why don't you explain why you've been here for two days."

"After the first night, when I woke up I saw the place was beautiful. I served as an Army paratrooper in the 1960s, and camping just comes natural to me."

Skinner didn't appear as nervous as he did excited to have someone to talk to. "Typical training would be a 20-kilometer land navigation problem… carrying a heavy load, moving as rapidly as possible. We would run that stuff over and over. I got it in my blood. What I'm doing is I'm on perpetual field maneuvers."

By now, Olsen was wondering why it was taking so long for the dispatcher to get back to him.

"It relaxes me to be in the woods. I've had multiple sclerosis for years." He pulled something out of his wallet. "Here. I carry a doctor's written diagnosis right in with my license because sometimes it will make me stagger. It affects my posture and my gait. What I call this, is camping therapy. And I do it just like in the Army, subjecting myself to hardship."

Olsen heard the dispatcher's voice on the radio. "Stay here," he told him. "I'll be right back." He slid onto the front seat, closed the door and listened. "I'm with you. What do you have?"

"That guy you've got is a real charmer. He's chalked up quite a record of offenses in three states. This guy's been charged with petty theft, stealing a shopping cart, possession of marijuana. He's a career criminal with a record that goes back thirty years. He just served a couple of months in Buncombe County for assault and battery."

Olsen looked out the window at Skinner. This guy's got some balls, he said to himself. Look at him standing there with a shit-eating grin on his face when he knows damn well his rap sheet's being read to me.

The dispatcher continued. "We can't arrest him for trespassing if he agrees to leave, and since there's no outstanding arrest warrants for him, we're going to have to let him go. So just tell him to get the hell out of Cherokee County."

Olsen put the receiver back in its cradle, took a long look at the toothless grin and felt disgust. He got out of the patrol car and asked him to leave, hoping he would give him an argument.

"Right away, officer. I don't want to be a bother. You come back in… thirty minutes and you won't know I've been here."

As Olsen got back in his car, Skinner yelled out to him, "I love you, man!"

GARY SKINNER WAVED TO THE COP pulling out. He forced a big smile on his face and whispered, "You dumb ass," under his breath. He waited until the car was out of sight, but didn't fool himself into thinking it was going very far. He got in the van and backed it up next to the tent so it looked like he didn't want to lug his gear too far; but he really wanted to obscure the opening in the woods where he had hid his trunk.

He got out of the van, looked toward the highway for the squad car and casually entered the woods. The trunk was tucked under a clump of rhododendrons about twenty feet in. He hauled it to the clearing, put it in the back of the van and packed everything with lock-step speed.

When he opened the door for the dog to get in the front seat, he spotted the newspapers on the floor with the pictures of the two women on the front page. He grabbed them up and spied his black hooded sweatshirt sticking out from underneath the seat. God-damned! The paper had reported the man at the ATM was wearing a black hooded jacket. He was ten counties away from Lake Lure, but if that deputy had searched the front of the van, he might have put two and two together and gotten suspicious. He had to burn it before he left.

DEPUTY OLSEN PULLED INTO THE PARKING lot next to an old Ford tractor. A wagon filled with hay bales sat next to it. He un-wrapped a stick of gum and shoved it in his mouth, when he spied a man in overalls coming out of the barn. He got out, put on his hat and introduced himself.

"Yep. That feller's been there for two days now. I'm fed up with these folks thinkin' they can come on to my property anytime they want and stomp down my crops." He pointed toward the dirt road with a trace of blue smoke rising from the woods. "Look. I wouldn't be surprised if he sets the whole place on fire."

Olsen could see it was about as much smoke as you'd get from a small campfire. "He's probably just cleaning up after himself. He'll be gone in a few minutes."

They talked for a while, mostly Olsen listening to the man complain about everything from high taxes to imports from China. He kept an eye on the dirt road and chewed all the while. When he finally saw the van kicking up dust on its way to the highway, he waited for it to pass before touching his hat and saying goodbye.

He pulled out of the lot. Curiosity made him go back down the road to where the van had been parked. Neat as a pin, just like the guy had promised. Since he was there, he might as well get out and look around a little. He went over to where the campfire had been stomped out. Nothing out of the ordinary. He kicked the ashes around and something caught his eye. He bent down, picked up a nearby twig and poked around. A small piece of cord with a knot was looped through an eyelet set in what looked like black jersey material. He poked around some more. Nothing but remains of a newspaper. Just a corner was left. He bent down and read: *TIMES-NEWS*, then the date and page number.

Somehow, Skinner hadn't looked like the kind of guy who would pay fifty cents for a newspaper. He went back to the car, opened the trunk and put on a plastic glove, got out two evidence bags and collected the paper and the eyelet. He'd just store it in his locker at the barracks. You never know.

CHAPTER TWELVE

Sᴀᴍᴍʏ ᴛʀɪᴇᴅ ᴛᴏ sᴛʀᴀɪɢʜᴛᴇɴ the top of her desk, but it was hopeless. Ever since Bob stopped by and told Linda he was switching his evening off with Patrick she knew something was afoot. Especially the way he kept tossing his head in her direction. Then, when Patrick dropped in and casually mentioned that since they both had the night off why didn't they grab dinner and a movie in town, Linda couldn't wipe the grin off her face.

"Go on. Get ready. I can handle the office 'til five," said Linda. "And don't forget to take the dinner box you had Katie drop off."

Sammy sat biting the end of a pencil as she mulled over the prospect of the skinny kid who had shown up in camp at the age of ten wearing a three-piece suit now evidently planning on making a move on her tonight, and the whole camp knowing about it.

Sammy looked over at Linda and gave her an impish grin.

"Now don't you bedevil that boy. He's one of my favorites," said Linda, shaking a finger at her.

Sammy chomped on the pencil and then waved it in the air. "Oh, he's got it coming. By now, Bob's got the entire staff taking bets on how this is going to turn out." She squinted and thought. "I wonder what bathing suit I should wear."

"Bathing suit? Good Lord!"

"You can hardly bedevil someone in some ol' pair of shorts and a tee shirt," Sammy said as she sprang up and got the box lunches out of the fridge.

The phone rang and Linda waved goodbye as Sammy ran out the door. She half expected to see her father pulling into the parking lot on the way to the house. He'd been running back and forth to the conservancy in Hendersonville almost daily. She ran into the house and up the stairs, pulling her top over her head. She kicked off her shorts and panties and yanked open a drawer with the new outfits her aunt insisted on buying for her honeymoon.

A mood swept over her. She wedged a box from the drawer and opened it on the bed. A flowery floor-length gossamer tie-front beach dress was pulled out and put on. She stood in front of the mirror, and it took her breath away. It had to be the most beautiful thing she'd ever seen. She glanced back in the box at the matching bikini and an ugly image scraped across her brain, like a nail on glass.

She'd never forget the sounds coming from Randy's bedroom. He had wanted her to come visit him in Raleigh for the weekend, but she had promised to lead a hike for a Girl Scout Troop. With bad weather suddenly predicted late Friday, the hike was called off, so she put a message on Randy's answering machine that she was on her way and started the four-hour drive.

She sensed something was wrong when he wasn't on the staircase to greet her like usual. Music drifted out into the hallway as she unlocked the door. Clothes lay scattered on the floor and a bra was draped over a chair. *Turn around and go!* a voice screamed in her head. But a primitive predatory reflex made her follow the soft grunts into the bedroom. Candlelight reflected from the sweat on the bodies moving in rhythm. Long, silky blond hair spilled like glittering water across the pillow. She watched the hand clutch a large white breast tighter and tighter until the rhythm stopped and Randy sank onto his back, his face turning to stone as he looked up at her.

Sammy wiped her eyes and carefully put the dress back. She cut the price tag off a skimpy one-piece black thong bathing suit with a keyhole back and put it on, then slipped on a fresh pair of shorts and a tee. She felt good about going out with Patrick; it made her laugh. Yep, I'm getting more and more like my old man. Randy's in a different compartment, and I'm not going to let him spoil my day."

She grabbed the food as she ran out of the house to the parking lot, snapping her fingers for Skippy to follow. Patrick was leaning up against her Jeep, and just as she expected, dressed in casual cool. Thankfully, he wore a pair of solidly built sneakers. She was sure he picked out the white sports shirt to show off his deep tan. The fact that he had showered didn't get by her either, with the way a drop of water trickled from the lock of black hair that curled behind his ears. She opened the rear door and snapped for Skippy to jump in.

"I... don't think we should take the dog," said Patrick.

She showed him the bag holding the dinner. "We're going to Ruby Falls for a picnic." She was careful to study his expression, and smiled to herself when he grinned. Warily, like he didn't know if this was a good sign or a bad sign.

"I've got my suit on. Do you want to run back and get yours?"

"No, thanks. I'll just watch the champion demonstrate her world famous butterfly stroke."

"Sir, let's not exaggerate." She smiled. "... my *nationally famous* butterfly stroke."

She tossed him her keys and hopped in, happy she'd come out earlier to take down the top. She sank into her seat with her head nestled against the back so she could look up at the sky and watch the huge trees cantilevering overhead as the vehicle bounced along the gravel road.

Patrick glanced at her a couple of times, and she shouted "I love this place," loud enough for him to hear.

He nodded and shouted back, "Buckle up." She complied and laughed again. Five weeks at camp and he was solidly in his counselor mode.

Since he had to keep his eyes on the road, she didn't mind staring at him, even though he had to know she was doing it. Why not? She'd caught him staring at her on the dock plenty of times.

His arms were long like hers. Maybe that was part of the reason they were both such good swimmers. He'd come a long way from the pasty white kid who stepped out of the airport limousine fourteen years ago. He wasn't gorgeous like Randy, but the whole package definitely had merit. In fact, she had always thought of him in terms of his character.

He pulled off the road onto a trail and grabbed the food. Sammy got a blanket she kept in the back, and Skippy, knowing exactly where they were headed, jumped out and bounded ahead of them.

The two, intimately familiar with the terrain, fell into the same gait. Skippy kept on the path, sniffing but never disturbing the landscape or chasing the fauna, just like he'd been trained since he was a pup. A branch snapped in the distance. Two deer froze.

"Don't do it, Skippy. Stay, boy." Sammy's voice was steady but firm.

The dog grunted and turned toward the trail.

A couple of times Sammy felt Patrick's hands on her waist as she started to heave herself up and over a boulder. They both knew she didn't need any help. It was the language of touch, and she got the message.

The falls tumbling above from rocky ledge to rocky ledge splashed into the pool and gave off a cool mist. She spread the blanket on a massive smooth, flat boulder and pulled off her shirt, purposefully facing Patrick. Then she stepped out of her shorts. She smiled to herself as he put his hands on his hips and looked away.

The boulder was at the pool's deepest end, so she dove into the icy, clear water and swam around for a while, before floating on her back and watching the clouds crawl across the sky. She swam directly under the falls and let the water pound on her head and stream her hair over her face. She dogpaddled to within a few feet from the boulder next to Patrick who was looking down on her.

She slicked her wet hair tight behind her ears and asked playfully as she tread water, "Is it true what they say about Chrissy Hutchinson?"

Patrick's mouth fell open. He rolled his eyes and looked out in the distance. "It depends on what they're saying."

She swished some water around with a hand. "You know."

He looked at her. "No, I don't know. Why don't you tell me." His tone was stern.

"Well... Judy Billings' twin is also in Tri-Delt, but at Duke." Sammy glanced up at Patrick. He was rubbing his forehead like he had a headache. "...and she heard from a friend in the UNC chapter in Chapel Hill that you and Chrissy were getting married because you… *had* to." Sammy paddled with one hand and floated on her back in a small circle.

"Boy. Now I've heard it all. You Tri Delta girls have probably spread this tidbit to every corner of North Carolina."

"Oh, heck. It's reached California by now."

Patrick stood up and offered her a hand. "Okay. That's it. Come on out. I don't know why you're playing this little game of yours with what was a pretty serious matter to me, but you're going to listen to the straight story… *and then maybe we can talk about Randy.*"

He pulled her out and she skillfully swiped the water from her arms and legs like someone who did it all the time, then wrung out her hair with her hands, only furtively glancing at him from the corner of her eye. She sat down on the boulder and hugged her knees as water trickled off her body. She tugged on her lip with her teeth like she was ashamed.

Patrick hugged his legs loosely. "Okay, I knocked Chrissie up and was going to marry her. Only, we broke it off after she miscarried in the third month."

"You were going to marry someone you didn't love?"

"I loved her. Enough, anyway. She's a great girl."

"If she's so great, why did you break up?"

"First, you have to promise me you're not going to put it on the Tri Delta evening news."

She giggled.

"Well, after we decided to get married, we found out we didn't want the same things. For starters, she didn't want any part of this camp. Boy, that was a scary time. I planned my whole life around this place. That's the main reason I decided to be a teacher. I'd have summers off to come here as a mentor." He swatted at a gnat. "And that was only the beginning; so after she lost the baby, we decided it was better to just stay friends."

Sammy studied his face. His eyes were a deep blue and he had a fair Irish complexion with dark black hair. The planes of his face were placid and she imagined he'd never have deep creases since he wasn't given to facial expressions, except for an easy straightforward smile.

She brushed her bangs back. "I guess you want to hear about Randy now."

"Not if you don't want to."

After she told him the story, she sat looking off in space, nodding her head as if she was agreeing with her decision to end their relationship. She smirked and looked over at him. "My called-off wedding is definitely worse than yours. You're the first and only person I've been able to tell about it."

"Well, sweet thing, I beg to differ with you. Your drama wasn't dragged from here to Wilmington... excuse me... from here to California by a horde of Tri Delta gossip queens."

She sprang forward and thumped his shoulders. "Don't you be callin' us gossip queens."

He grabbed her and started to tickle her as if she were one of the boys, but she wasn't built the same. He held her for a moment before saying, "Why don't you put your clothes back on." She laughed and reached for her tee shirt. He shook his head. "That bathing suit has less material on it than one of my ties. I don't recommend you wear it out on the dock any time soon."

"Oh don't you worry about that. My dad would run up and cover me with a towel... that is if Linda or Charlie didn't get to me first."

They opened the box Katie had prepared and began to eat.

"Rumor has it that someone's thinking of building a housing complex across the road," said Patrick.

"Tiger's trying to get the property away from them." She referred to her father by name, something she started when she first worked in the office so she'd appear more professional.

"I wish him all the luck."

Sammy tucked her toes under and ran a finger along a vein in the granite. "You're really stuck on this place, aren't you?"

"Yep. I sure am."

"I never would have thought you'd turn out the way you did."

"Actually, I never would have if it wasn't for this camp." He glanced across the pond. "That's why I'm so intrigued with this kid in my cabin."

"Alvin?"

"Yeah. Alvin. It's good your dad let him come. If ever a kid needed a break, it's this one. Of all the good things this camp does, the one thing it does best, this little guy needs most." He laughed quietly, like he was embarrassed for going on about it, but he couldn't stop. "Kids today are never left to their own resources. Their moms drive them to school and then pick them up. If they want to play with a friend, they get taken over, or the friend gets brought over. I think of them as helicopter moms... always hovering overhead. And, I'll tell ya... Alvin's mother's got it in spades.

"They're hell bent on taking all the risks out of these kids' lives, so they never need to make a choice that lets them experience the consequences. Heck. When they come to camp, if they leave their shoes outside in the rain, they're gonna have to tramp around with wet feet for a couple of days. If they choose an activity and find out they don't like it, they've got to live with it. It was their choice. If they mess up their footlockers, everything goes to hell in a hand basket, and they can't find anything and end up wearing the same smelly clothes until they straighten everything out. These kids grow here in ways they can't at home."

"How's Alvin doing?" Sammy asked.

"It's funny. The kid's killing himself to keep up, but he's real happy. Like he's been tied up his whole life and has finally been freed. He's bright too... and sympathetic. He's actually helping out with little Tucker Watson. Boy, that kid's a trip. Talk about nature deficit disorder. He's not relating to anything at this camp. He's just counting the days 'til he gets his Game Boy back. And when I say *counting*, I mean it. He's got this weird thing for numbers. Yesterday at rest I found him lying on his bed memorizing the digits of Pi. He's been doing it every day since he got here. When we're walking to the lodge, I hear him repeating them to himself."

He crossed his legs and leaned toward her. "I got this idea about engaging him. You wanna hear?"

"Sure."

"Are you familiar with the Fibonacci ratios?"

"Uh-huh. I read about it in *The Da Vinci Code*. You add one and one and get two. You keep adding the last two numbers... two and one equals three. Three and two equals five."

"Yeah. Well Fibonacci discovered that this mathematical series is in the pattern of pinecones, pineapples, honeycombs... turtle shells. I'm going to get on the internet and bone up on it, so I can teach it to Tucker and try to draw him into connecting his number fetish to nature."

"My dad's got a book on it at the house. I'll bring it to the office tomorrow."

They were quiet for a while. At ease and thoughtful.

"You like kids, don't you?" asked Sammy.

"Uh-huh. That's the best part of being here. I love the joy that erupts out of them. All their emotions and senses get ratcheted up when they're suddenly part of a bigger, more challenging world. You can especially tell it's happening when you hear them sing. They're in another zone." He tossed his head. "I ought to know. It happened to me that first summer."

Sammy leaned back on her arms and looked up at him. "My theory on the way these kids break out in song at the drop of a hat is that it's a form of mass communication between them. A kind of medium they tap into to connect with each other... like holding hands, or hugging each other."

They sat quietly for a few moments. He looked at his watch. "We better start clearing out. We don't want to be caught up here in the dark. We can still make it to a movie if you want."

They were quiet on the walk back. Expectant. They reached the Jeep and Sammy put her blanket in the back. She turned to find Patrick standing in front of her, his burning glare asking her permission. Yes, she told him with her eyes.

He grabbed her up in his arms and kissed her with a fervor she would remember the rest of her life. He closed his eyes and murmured her name softly as he pressed her tight against him. She felt his hand follow the curve of her thigh.

She was ready to give herself to him, but not here and not now. She put her hands on his chest and pressed. He stopped, gripped her waist almost as if he needed to steady himself, and rested his hot, sweaty forehead against hers. She ran her hands along his chest and down his lean, muscular arms. "I think we better get going or *we're* going to end up on the Tri-Delt network."

He hugged her and laughed out loud, then picked her up and swung her around triumphantly like he knew right then and there she was going to be his.

When they got back to camp, they ran into a couple of counselors who had gone to Camp Green River since they were kids, too, and spent the rest of the evening talking and laughing about old times.

Later that night, Sammy was in her room when she heard her father come in and flick on the weather channel. She ran down to the landing in her pajamas to say hello.

"Well, how did your date with Patrick go?" he asked without looking up.

"You knew I went out with him?"

"Everyone in camp did."

"I'm going to marry him."

He took his eyes off the screen and looked up at her. "Well, I'll be darned. Never thought Patrick had it in him to win you over in just one date. Figured it would take him the whole summer." He snapped his fingers. "*Dang!* I bet Bob five dollars you were still too broken up over Randy to fall for him right away."

"*Oh, Dad!*"

He laughed and folded his arms as he strolled toward the stairs. "So Patrick asked you to marry him."

She turned and started back up. "No. But he will."

CHAPTER THIRTEEN

Tom Gibbons stood in the conservancy's reception room, which was nothing more than a couple of chairs and two old desks they used mostly for collating grant packets. His arms were folded and he looked appreciatively at the elderly couple standing in front of him. They were on their way out and seemed like they weren't so much having pangs about leaving, as they were about letting go. They had just signed the papers for a conservation easement on their one-hundred-acre farm, placing its protection in the hands of the Carolina Mountain Land Conservancy. They needed reassuring, and chatting with Tom helped them deal with the finality of signing the documents.

He had carefully crafted the transaction over the past year to include all their desires. The couple wanted whoever owned it after them to be able to farm the land like they did, or sell off lots no smaller than ten-acres each for a single home to be constructed; and they had asked him to include a provision about maintaining the woods. They were also getting a lower tax rate on their property, as well as Federal income and estate tax benefits.

Tom had put a lot of time into this easement, and the conservancy would have to spend a lot of labor in coming years to protect it, but their land was at the gateway to the Hickory Nut Gorge and their woodlands were habitat for the endangered plants and animals that roamed it.

Tom walked them to their car, an old clunker they could have replaced with anything they wanted if they had sold their land to a developer. He noticed Ben Beckham pull into the lot, and hoped he had some good news.

Tiger had been right about Jeb Ryan wanting out of there. He had struck out with him about extending the deadline. His two kids had all but spent the money, and the Ledges were all set to survey the property the minute the four weeks were up. When he asked Jeb if he would be willing to give them an easement on the east facing ridge, he just rocked and talked to himself, deaf to anything but moving on.

Tom waved goodbye to the couple and headed for the door that Ben was holding open for him.

"How did it go?" Tom asked.

"Not too good. My folks are looking for a bigger write-off than the Ryan property can give them, and decided to buy the one thousand acres the Foothills Conservancy has lined up."

"Anything else on the horizon?"

Ben stopped at the door to his office. "I've got one more possibility, but there are simply too many parcels on the auction block all at once. Too many people pulling the plug." He shook his head. "I'm going to keep on trying, but I think you better start talking with the Ledges."

THE KIDS HUDDLED AROUND the edge of the trout lake laughing and joking while they relived the highlights of the talent show the night before. This being the last day of the session, emotions were soaring and the camaraderie tangible, with a lot of kids hanging on to each other like they didn't want to let go. Most of them had chosen the fly fishing activity before and were there for the sheer pleasure of the sport.

Charlie Morgan strolled along the shore hollering out tips to the kids casting their lines. As the assistant director, he was in charge of several activities, including this one. Tiger, who had been taught the art by the best in the state, most of whom were right there in Henderson County, stood off to the side watching with his arms crossed, smiling and nodding.

With the best trout stream in the state on the property, Charlie was thankful fly fishing was one of his best skills. He knew it gave him a leg up when Tiger was looking for an assistant who would probably succeed him as director until Sammy was ready to take over.

Tiger watched for a while before spending some time with a kid who seemed to have a real knack for the sport. Charlie speculated that Tiger had come out to the lake to find some relief from thinking about the Ledges, and there was nothing like the concentration needed in fly fishing to do it.

Tiger had kept him in the loop, and it looked like hope for some kind of a deal was draining away. There were only two more weeks to go and as of yet they had nothing. At least tonight the upper council fire and closing ceremony should take Tiger's mind off Jeb's farm.

The bell rang, ending the session. Kids drifted out to the front field for games or to the lake for the free swim, leaving Tiger and Charlie to chat for a few moments.

TIGER WENT BACK TO THE OFFICE, threw a hello to Linda and Sammy who were finishing up the batch of final paperwork for the end of the session, then went into his office and closed the door. He drummed the eraser end of a pencil on his desk for a moment, as if he were trying to make up his mind. He picked up the phone, started to dial and put it back down again.

He looked up at the clock on the wall. An hour before dinner. He smiled to himself remembering the look on Sammy's face last night. He had felt like that once and wondered if he'd ever feel that way again. He sat sizing up his situation. They had made it more than half-way through the summer with no camper getting hurt other than the usual scrapes, sprains and sore throats; then there was Sammy and Patrick. Those two were as right as rain.

On the other hand, it was looking like he would lose Jeb's property to the Ledges. The call he'd gotten from Tom felt like a sock in the jaw. He knew the conservancy wouldn't be talking to the Ledges about rights to the property around the streams unless they were pretty sure their deal with Jeb was going to go through. By God, if he did lose out, he was going to ride shotgun on that project to make sure they were held to the letter of the law, even if he had to sleep up there!

He kept tapping the end of the pencil on his desk. Getting dumped at the age of fifty hadn't been fun. But if he thought his pride hurt now, wait until Becky Freeman, Liz's housekeeper, got wind of it. He expected that to leak out any day now. He'd tell Sammy tomorrow so she wouldn't get blindsided by the gossip.

He'd fought with Liz about the camp before, but not like the other day. Being called crazy for wanting to save one of the best watersheds in the state was one thing, but, boy, when she said the trout stank, she stepped over the line. He picked up the phone and started to dial again, then slowly placed it back in the cradle. Ever since Euva told him about Katie breaking up with her husband, he couldn't get her out of his head. He'd heard rumors off and on through the years and had hoped that things weren't as bad as they sounded. He remembered Katie coming and asking for Euva's job. He was just starting to date Liz back then. It hurt him the way she acted all formal and businesslike, handing him her resumé and all. Hell, all she would have had to do was call him up on the phone and the job was hers. The worse part was things had remained that way.

She was popular with the kids, and the staff adored her, but she kept her distance with him. He respected that she was a married woman, but he'd seen her joking around and flirting with the staff, all in good fun, plenty of times. Did she put up that wall between them because she harbored some kind of resentment? That doesn't make any sense. She was the one who broke it off. Dang! He'd beaten himself up a thousand times for not asking her to marry him before she left for that job in Wilmington.

He had wanted to go see her, but when the tornado hit, he worked himself into exhaustion cleaning up and fighting with the insurance company so he could rebuild. Sammy even had to stay with her aunt for a while. Just before Thanksgiving, when he had the place together enough to where he could shower and shave and walk around in clean clothes, he called her mother to find out when she was coming home and was told she was engaged. He could still remember the vindictive tone in her mother's voice, as if she were throwing it in his face.

He put his hand on the phone again, then paused. Maybe it *was* too early to give her a call. This could be a temporary situation, and he didn't want to barge into the middle of a misunderstanding between a husband and wife. But the way Euva talked, it was a pretty done deal. He felt resolute. If it wasn't, maybe it should be. If half the things people were saying were true, she should have left him long ago.

He put a hand through his hair and struggled with his emotions. What in the world am I thinking? She hasn't so much as smiled at me in ten years.

He checked his watch. Just enough time to get showered and changed for dinner. He shook his head. Those kids out there loved him, but he'd sure as heck struck out with most of the women in his life. Nope. I'm not going to call Katie. I've had about as much rejection for one week as I can take.

"OKAY, GUYS. COME ON OUT here and get your clothes," yelled Patrick as he pulled a towel off the sagging clothes line. The screen door slammed, and kids ran down the steps and started yanking things from the line. Someone snatched the towel from Patrick's hand and ran back up. Patrick pulled off a pair of green trunks dotted with dinosaurs, read the label and shouted, "Roger!"

"Here I am," piped up a kid on the porch. Patrick threw him the trunks, then bent down and picked up a pair of sneakers. "Okay, whose are these?" Someone scooped them up and raced up the steps. Patrick grabbed him by the shirt. "Clean them off a little first, buddy. You don't want to get all that dirt in your locker."

Patrick checked under the porch. Not finding anything else, he took the steps two at a time and entered the cabin. "Guys, listen up. Anyone who hasn't checked the laundry to see if any of your stuff's in there, better do so right now. And, if you've got anything missing, run over to the lodge and see if it's in the Black Hole. We've got to have your lockers on the carts tomorrow before breakfast."

Someone from Hemlock Hut One popped their head in. "Did you guys steal our broom?"

A pillow flew through the air and hit the screen door. "Heck, no! We don't sweep." Laughter rose. The kid disappeared and the door slammed shut. Patrick picked up the pillow. "Okay, guys. I know this is your last night, but let's settle down a little. Does everyone have their spirit stones ready to take to the council fire?"

Someone strummed a ukulele trying to find a tune, and shouts, hollers and the sound of slamming screen doors from throughout the boys' compound drifted in. A kid showed Patrick his stone with a bug-eyed frog painted on it. Ricky took a look. "Awesome! You're never going to have trouble recognizing that baby."

The bell sounded and after making sure everyone had put on insect spray and a warm shirt and had their spirit stones in hand, they tramped out toward the back field just beyond the cluster of cabins. A group of girls singing *This Land is Your Land* strolled down a path from the other side.

Kids trickled out of the woods and assembled quietly on the benches circling the back field fire pit. A counselor stood at the front, and seeing the benches fill up, started the cabin roll call. Satisfied everyone was there, she said, "At my signal, we'll all start singing *Earth, Air, Fire, Water*, and then file out one-by-one to the upper council. Stop singing when you enter the woods, and please be silent as you climb the mountain to the field of spirit stones. There'll be someone there with burning sage for whoever wants to smudge themselves. Native Americans felt this ceremony cleansed them of bad feelings and negative thoughts. Grasp some smoke with your left hand and throw it towards your body and turn around, then proceed to the council fire pit and be seated."

Suddenly the soulful sound of a flute drifted from the woods. Tucker nudged Alvin and whispered, "This is spookin' me out."

"Shush," Alvin whispered back.

The girl raised her arms, and voices started chanting, *The earth, the air, the fire, the water… return, return, return, return* as, one row at a time, the kids shuffled out and disappeared into the woods. Tucker kept bumping into Alvin as he peered around the darkened forest.

They reached the field of spirit stones eerily shadowed by the dancing flames of lit candles. Alvin waved his hand over the trail of smoke swirling from a platter a counselor held, and turned around. Tucker quickly passed his hand over the smudge pot, and kept on moving as everyone silently filed past hundreds of decorated stones left by generations of campers.

The flute's trailing Native American melody was the only thing heard except for the rustling of clothes and treading of feet as everyone found a piece of earth to sit on. Tiger stood solemnly behind the unlit council fire ring at the foot of the mountainside waiting for everyone to be seated.

"Let the council fire begin," echoed through the woods. Two girls came forward and spread sand in a circle around the kindling and lit the fire, sending sparks drifting upward and the smell of wood smoke floating on the cool air. One at a time, four campers came forward with a lit candle, placed it around the fire ring and recited one of the Woodcraft laws: Beauty, Truth, Fortitude, Love.

Once they finished, Tiger spoke. "I hope, more than anything else, your camp experience has taught all of you how all things are connected. I want to read a letter that Chief Seattle wrote to President Franklin Pierce in 1854 in response to the government's offer to buy two million acres of Native American land in the Pacific Northwest."

By firelight, Tiger proceeded to read from a sheet of paper he held in his hand. The prophetic words on behalf of the environment and the fate of the First People floated across the mountainside. "...How can you buy or sell the sky, the warmth of the land? The idea is strange to us. If we do not own the freshness of the air and the sparkle of the water, how can you buy them? Every part of this earth is sacred to my people. Every shining pine needle, every sandy shore, every mist in the dark woods, every clearing and every humming insect is holy in the memory and experience of my people. The sap which courses through the trees carries the memories of the red man. So, when the Great Chief in Washington sends word that he wishes to buy our land, he asks much of us. This we know: All things are connected. Whatever befalls the earth befalls the sons of the earth. Man did not weave the web of life; he is merely a strand in it. Whatever he does to the web, he does to himself..."

Patrick had heard the letter dozens of times, yet it still stirred his emotions. "When the last red man has vanished from the earth, and his memory is only the shadow of a cloud moving across the prairie, these shores and forests will still hold the spirits of my people. For they love this earth as a newborn loves its mother's heartbeat. So, if we sell our land, love it as we've loved it. Care for it as we've cared for it. Hold in your mind the memory of the land as it is when you take it. And preserve it for your children."

CHAPTER FOURTEEN

"GEEZE…YOU'RE NOT GOING to wear that are you?" Tucker asked Alvin.

Alvin finished buttoning up the short-sleeved shirt, then straightened the collar. It was bright orange with long swirling white streaks as if it had been tie-dyed. The shoulders hung way below where they were supposed to and the sleeves reached past his elbows. The matching shorts were equally oversized, hitting the middle of his calves.

Tucker reached in his locker and pulled out a tee with a smiling whale on it and *I'm Having a Happy Day* printed underneath. "Here put this on."

"That's okay. I want to wear this."

"I wouldn't if I were you. The kids are going to laugh."

"I know."

"Then why in the heck are you wearing it?"

"My mother bought it for me and she wants me to wear it when she comes."

Patrick, who was busy helping all the boys finish packing their footlockers, made his way over to Tucker's and helped him snap it shut. "We'll make sure this goes to whatever cabin you're going to be in."

"Aren't me and Alvin going to stay right here for the next session?"

"I don't know. When you come back on Monday, we'll find out. Okay?"

Patrick scooted over to Alvin's locker on his haunches and seeing him, said, "Where did you get that outfit?"

Tucker piped up, "He knows it looks awful but his mother bought it for him and he's going to wear it anyway."

Patrick stood up and gave Alvin a long, thoughtful look. "Okay. Let's do this." He bent down and twisted the waistband inside out to see if there were tabs to adjust it. Finding some, he made it as tight as he could, then folded the waistband over a few times until the shorts rose a couple of inches. He stood back and got another look. "Not bad, but we're going to have to do something about the sleeves."

He rolled the hems over twice, straightened the shirt over the pants and declared that Alvin looked terrific, when Ricky ran up and shouted out, "Hey, guys! Look at the orange popsicle!"

Patrick tapped him on the shoulder with a knuckle. "That's enough Ricky."

Three of the boys gathered round and stared. One even went so far as to inspect the outfit from the back as Alvin looked ahead with a stoic expression on his face. Patrick shooed everyone out of the cabin except Alvin. He crouched down next to him and grasped his shoulder. "Alvin, you don't have to wear this if you don't want to. There's still time to change."

"But I want to."

"I don't think your mother will mind."

"I know. But it's going to make her real happy if she sees me wearing it."

"Now, Alvin, sometimes kids say things that can hurt your feelings…"

The second bell rang.

Alvin put a hand on Patrick's arm so as to interrupt him. "Don't worry, Patrick. I can take it."

Patrick couldn't help himself. He gave Alvin a big hug. "I know you can, kid." He stood up and put his hand on his back and gently guided him out. "Let's go, buddy. It's show time."

LAURA AND AL MAGEE HAD CHECKED into the Lake Lure Inn the night before, even though it was an hour's drive from the camp, thinking it would be a great place to spend the two days with Alvin before he had to go back for the second session.

Laura had taken a pill to get to sleep and still hadn't awakened in spite of stirrings in the hall and the sound of traffic coming from the road. A string of motorcycles roared by. Her husband slipped out of bed, shaved and put on slacks and a golf shirt, then went over and sat back down on the bed next to her.

He tenderly fingered a curl framing her face, marveling at her determination to give this new path they were on her all. After they had dropped Alvin off two weeks ago, he'd gotten her to agree to put one day aside each week just for herself, and he still couldn't believe that the very next day she meandered into a beauty parlor for the first time in her life and asked for "the works."

That night, when she walked in the door, he barely recognized her. The thick eyebrows had vanished and the graying strands pulled taut against her head into a bun had turned into soft reddish brown curls tumbling almost to her shoulders.

She'd had a time mastering the curling iron... once when she dissolved in tears he even had to give it a try... but she finally got the hang of it, mostly thanks to all the tips she was getting from the girls at the lab. He suspected, just like him, everyone was willing to do their share to keep Mother Hubbard from rearing her head again.

He bent down, kissed her on the forehead and roamed her face with his lips. Her eyes slowly opened, and she put her arms around him and hugged.

"What time is it?" she asked dreamily.

"Eight-thirty."

She sat up. "My God! We're supposed to be there by nine!"

"Whoa, girl. We can pick him up as late as eleven."

She jumped out of bed and ran into the bathroom with him yelling after her that he had already put on the curling iron. She hollered out for him to bring her the outfit hanging on a chair. He opened the door to hand it to her and saw her brushing her teeth, wearing nothing but a bra. She grabbed the hanger with her one free hand,

and noticing him staring, garbled what sounded something like him being a naughty boy.

He had raised an eyebrow when she told him how much she spent in two days of shopping, but when she walked out of the bathroom dressed in a slimming pair of navy blue slacks and a stylish lacy white top, he wanted to sit right down and write a testimonial to the Durham Merchants Association. She'd never looked so smashing. The whole art of dressing and knowing what looked good on her had passed her by in the years of thinking about nothing but study, work and Alvin, and now it appeared as if she was catching on to the concept.

They hadn't had a chance to get a good look at the hotel last night. Over a quick cup of coffee in the dining room, they took in the homey elegance of the place before rushing off to the camp.

From the parking lot, Laura spotted her son on the deck and hurried toward the lodge. Alvin caught sight of her and ran down the steps waving to his dad, then flew into her arms. He grabbed his mother's hand and dragged her back up the stairs through clusters of kids saying goodbyes until he reached Patrick.

Laura clasped both of Patrick's hands and thanked him for taking such good care of her boy. Then, just as Al caught up with them, she almost got yanked out of her gold sandals as Alvin pulled her through the pandemonium to Tucker who was waiting for his parents to pay his camp store bill.

As Laura got caught up in a conversation with Tucker's parents, Ricky, spotting Tucker and Alvin, ran over and squeezed the two in headlocks. "You guys got my email address. Write to me and we can see each other again next summer. Everyone wants to be in the same cabin again."

Alvin's father barely got a few words in edgewise with Patrick who was fielding questions from all directions and getting rushed goodbyes. Al made his way over to Tiger amidst the energy exploding all around him and shook his hand. "I want to thank you for taking such good care of my boy. I've never seen him so happy."

"That's what we're here for," said Tiger. "By the way, how's your wife doing?"

"Thank Sammy for emailing all the pictures. It made all the difference. I really appreciate it."

Walking to the car, a couple of kids yelled, *Bye, String. See you next year.* One kid yelled out, *Great outfit, bud. Nobody's gonna forget it,* and gave him a high five.

Al shepherded Alvin into the car, listening to him chatter excitedly. Once behind the steering wheel, he turned to Alvin and said, "We've got a room at the Lake Lure Inn and thought we'd all enjoy the day in Chimney Rock."

Laura spent the whole drive facing Alvin in the back.

"Oh, Dad, you should have seen me sailing down the rock slide on the river on my butt! *It was awesome!*" His mother touched the scabs on his knees and wrinkled her forehead. "Awh, they're nothin', Mom. You should have been there. I climbed to the top of Ruby Falls and jumped into the pool! Mom! Dad! I stood under the falls long enough to say *Polar Bear* three times! It was freezing! Now I belong to the Camp Green River Polar Bear Club!"

His father reached over and patted Laura on the leg, then said, "I'm proud of you, son."

"Mom, how's Molly? Does she miss me?"

His father gave him a quick glance in the rearview mirror. *"Does she miss you?!* Heck, your mother feeds her carrots in her lap every night. Son, I don't think Molly's even gonna *remember you!*"

Alvin snapped his head back in mock indignation and looked at his mother through squinted lids.

"Well, you told me to keep an eye on her."

They all laughed—the "happy we're all back together again" kind.

Chimney Rock was packed with sightseers with cars bumper to bumper. Luckily someone pulled out of a spot in front of the Old Rock Café just ahead of them. Once inside, they ordered sandwiches, helped themselves to drinks and went out on the riverside deck and slowly began to decompress while watching the rapidly rolling Rocky Broad splash and twist its way downstream. Folks of all ages crawled and climbed over the masses of giant piled-up boulders that nature had haphazardly tossed off the granite walls of the gorge.

"How dangerous," Laura commented.

"Oh, that's nothing, Mom. You should have seen me crawl into Miner's Cave. Our mentor's shoulders barely… fit…"

Noticing his wife's blanched face, his father had quickly squeezed

Alvin's hand to interrupt him. "Laura, remember what Dr. Walters said. You've got to let go and trust people. These folks at Camp Green River are among the best in the business."

"Oh, don't worry, Mom. We got safety rules. They give us helmets, life vests… all kinds of stuff."

The next few minutes were a little uncomfortable with everyone mostly avoiding making eye contact, but then the food arrived and took their minds off Alvin's cave crawling.

"Are you going to eat your potato chips, Dad?"

"Why no, son. Take them." Al looked over at Laura and winked as Alvin tore open his second bag of chips. "You're looking pretty good, boy. I think you're putting on some weight."

Alvin pulled a chip out of the bag and said matter-of-factly, "They're still calling me String, though." His glasses slid forward on his sweaty nose, so he pushed them back and said, "But, don't worry. I'm eating good, and when I come back next summer…" He made a face meant to make him look tough, then raised a clenched fist and flexed a bicep. "…I'm gonna be a new man." They all laughed.

The afternoon was spent traversing all the stores along Chimney Rock's two-block-long shopping district streaming with people out for a day in the mountains. As they came out of Gale's, their eyes kept getting drawn up to the giant granite monolith towering four hundred feet over the town. Crowned by the Stars and Stripes proudly waving in the breezes wafting through the gorge, it beckoned them, and they decided to go up to the park the next day and climb the chimney themselves.

By the time they bundled the sling shot, Indian headdress, moccasins, tomahawk, coonskin hat and two bags of penny candy from Bubba O'Leary's into the car, it was almost five. They had dinner on the porch at LaStrada overlooking Lake Lure and the picturesque Rumbling Bald Mountain. Before settling in for the night, they took a stroll through the hotel lobby filled with antique upright disc music boxes popular in bars and saloons in the 19th century.

Alvin hopped into one of the double beds and his father turned off the lights and climbed in the other. A glimmer of light streamed into the room from the parking lot. Some people were saying goodnight in the hall outside, a door slammed shut, then all became quiet.

After a while, the light disappeared from underneath the bathroom door and Laura came out. She made her way to Alvin's bed and sat down. She ran her hand down his face. "I missed you."

"I missed you too, Mom." He reached up and touched her hair. "Do you like it?"

"Uh-huh… but you were real pretty the other way, too."

They were quiet for a moment, just enjoying being together.

"You're holding up pretty good, Mom. I mean about me being at the camp and all."

"Well, I've been talking with someone who's helping me out with that. She told me to keep busy so my mind's not always on you and the camp." She laughed and pressed down affectionately on the tip of his nose with a finger. "She and your dad have banished me to the malls one day a week and there's nothing to do there but shop."

"You looked terrific in those slacks."

She was quiet for a moment. "I don't know if that outfit I sent with you was as great."

"Aw… that's okay, Mom. You heard what Jerry Sutton said. "No one's gonna forget it."

It started with one of them snickering softly and grew to both of them giggling before laughing out loud. Laura hugged him, then ruffled his hair saying, "If we're going to hike around Chimney Rock Park tomorrow, we better get some sleep."

As she tucked him in, he said, "Mom, what exactly *is* molecular biology?"

"Why, honey, it's the study of biology except at the smallest level where you look at the tiny molecules. We try to discover how the systems of a cell interact so we get to know all about them."

"That's what Patrick said. He said it's helping all the plants and creatures in the world."

They were quiet and at ease with each other.

"Mom?"

"Yes, baby."

"I want to be a molecular biologist too when I grow up. I really care about all the things that want to live."

She grabbed him up in her arms and squeezed. "So do I, baby." She let him back down, gave him a kiss and tucked him in once more.

As she was getting into bed, Alvin said, "Mom?"

"Yes, darling."

"Thanks a lot for letting me go to camp. It's made me real happy."

She slid into her husband's open arms and snuggled up next to him. He kissed her and she tasted the salt in his tears.

CHAPTER FIFTEEN

No one seemed to care about the two wrestlers on the TV as the bartender picked up the empty beer bottle in front of an elderly man slumped on a stool, replacing it with another. A smallish dark-skinned girl scurried around in the rancid-smelling, smoke-filled bar clearing tables and dodging pinches from the grisly bunch of dead-enders sprinkled around the place.

Rosa Guadalupe was only nineteen, but she'd already seen enough of the grim side of life to fill up a year's worth of CSI episodes. People who rape and murder women in El Salvador are rarely brought to justice; and her year-long trek through the picking fields of Mexico and Arizona with her brother brought her more pain than she ever wanted to remember. They had arrived in Hendersonville in a stifling truck full of illegals last fall to pick apples, and were lucky enough to make friends with a family of Salvadorans who helped them find refuge in a Catholic parish in Asheville.

Finding work where they were paid under the table was easy. In fact, she cleaned motel rooms every day before coming to the bar. But she was afraid for her younger brother. They had a room on the west side where a lot of immigrants lived as well as members of the Mexican gang, Mara Salvetrucha. He'd been attacked a couple of times, so when he wasn't doing lawn work she made him stay inside as much as possible, but it was getting to be a struggle. Church members were searching for a farm where they could stay and work, but everyone was wary of getting caught by an enforcement agent from the Department of Homeland Security, and she feared Fernando was going to end up joining MS-13 for protection if they didn't get out of there soon.

She kept glancing up at the clock. A neon outline of a sudsy glass of beer blinked across it. She'd be home in a half hour and, between now and when she walked in the door, filled with anxiety about whether or not Fernando would be there. Better get as many of the glasses washed before closing as I can, she told herself. The sooner I get home the better.

By the time she finished at the sink, the bartender was coaxing everyone out. She quickly went about snatching up the last of the glasses and the few measly tips, before starting back into the kitchen.

"Wait up, Rosa. Let me pay you," said the bartender.

She put the tray on the bar and moved toward the cash register where he stood with his belly hanging over the open drawer.

"This is for the week, tootsie. I put something extra in there for you being so dependable."

She looked around the bar cautiously, but the only one left in the place was an old man slumped over a stool. He looked harmless enough. She reached under her apron into a deep pocket she had sewn into her skirt and pulled out a roll of cash, added the money and put it back.

GARY SKINNER DRAINED HIS BEER, picked up his change and left. He didn't know what door the girl would come from, but he'd already checked the alley and there was just one truck that he guessed belonged to the bartender. From the size of the wad the Latino pulled out of her skirt, she had to have had over two hundred dollars, even if they were all singles. She obviously had no bank account, and had to be an illegal or the bartender wouldn't have paid her in cash. A perfect robbery victim. The last thing she was ever going to do after he got her money, was run to the cops and get handed over to a U.S. Immigration official.

He stood in a dark recessed doorway of the store next door and lit a cigarette. The street darkened as the lights in the bar started to go out. A door opened. He dropped the cigarette. Careful not to be noticed, he could see her through the corner of the display window looking up and down the street. As she turned toward him and started to walk, he stepped deeper into the shadows until she passed, then stepped out and grabbed her from behind, deftly putting his gloved hand over her mouth.

Her strength shocked him. She reached back and tried to claw him with her fingernails as he carried her to the van. He threw her against the back door and she kneed him in the groin. Enraged, he grabbed her by the throat and squeezed until she slumped to the pavement.

He quickly regained his composure and looked around. No one. He opened the van door and threw her in, then got behind the wheel, but not before carefully scanning all the windows and doorways to make sure no one had seen him. The pickup that was parked behind the bar pulled out of the alley and cruised down the street.

Goddamned, now he had another body to get rid of. He drove down a few blocks and pulled into a dark parking lot behind a furniture store. He surveyed the scene. Nothing but huge empty cartons piled with used carpeting sitting in a corner. He lit up another cigarette and drummed his fingers on the steering wheel and thought. The bitch had put up such a fight she probably had his DNA all over her. If she had any family, he didn't think they'd go to the police with a missing person report. The bartender either.

Still, he had to stash her somewhere she wouldn't be found, otherwise there'd be an investigation. He'd worked as a day laborer for a trash removal firm for a couple of weeks and thought then that a dumpster would be the perfect place to get rid of someone. They'd haul everything to the dump and there'd be trucks lined up ready to dump on top of every load. Even if the cops were absolutely sure a body was in all that trash, they'd never find it. Remembering how the dumpsters outside of the grocery stores reeked, he decided to find one. But first, he had to get the money and shove the body into a sleeping bag.

He got out and climbed in the back of the van. After retrieving the wad of money and wrestling the girl into a sleeping bag, he remembered the carpeting. It wouldn't be a bad idea to roll the sleeping bag up in a rug to be extra safe in case he got stopped. He dragged a smaller piece off the pile, placed the body and roped it up. Back behind the wheel, he took out the money and thumbed through it. Had to be over ten twenties and a hundred or more singles. Not bad. This might be a sign that his luck was changing.

Skinner drove the van onto Route 240 and headed north. There was barely anyone on the road when he suddenly spotted a white squad car behind him. The first thing that entered his mind was that the cop was running his plate. He couldn't drive too fast or too slow; in fact, he kept at the same speed… four miles over the limit so as not to appear nervous. He must have stopped breathing, for he needed to catch his breath. His scalp tingled and he felt a little lightheaded, when suddenly the patrol car disappeared from the rearview mirror and he caught its red rear lights speed down an exit ramp.

Hopefully, something was coming off downtown and they were calling for all the cars. He pulled off onto Tunnel Road. A bunch of malls and shopping centers loomed ahead. He cruised until he spotted a plaza with a grocery store, then swung around to the back next to a dumpster.

The place, lit with a lone lamp, was desolate with the exception of a bunch of scrawny cats milling around. He quickly jumped out, looked around one more time, then unlocked the van's back door. The carpet made the bundle a lot heavier, but he was able to hoist it over a shoulder and pull it out, then stagger over to the dumpster. The way it was leveraged, he couldn't get it high enough to drop in. He'd have to get both arms underneath, then heave it up and over.

He dropped the bundle on the ground parallel to the container. As he bent down to get a hold of it again, he heard the crunch of tires on asphalt. A car had pulled in with the headlights off. Something a cop would do. He put a smile on his face and turned.

The officer zipped his window down. "What are you doing, old man?"

"You caught me officer. I'm just trying to get rid of some old carpeting." He hunched his shoulders and threw up his hands. "I'm a Vietnam vet kinda down on my luck, and I can't spend a lot of money on gas driving to the dump."

The officer got out of the car and walked over to the roll of carpet. He looked him over before studying the van. Gary's eyes surveyed the area, finding nothing he could hit the cop with. If he remembered right, his baton was right next to his wallet under the front seat.

The officer turned and came toward him. "Okay, old man. I'll give you a hand."

After they tossed in the bundle, Skinner thanked the cop profusely, humbling and ingratiating himself as much as he felt was called for. He got back in the van and drove off, now convinced that his luck had changed.

CHAPTER SIXTEEN

It was still dark, but the night had already passed for Tiger Morrison. It sounded as if all the birds had woken up at the same time, instead of sending forth intermittent waves of song that ascended throughout the early morning hours. He was keenly alert. He'd gotten through another session with everyone going home safe and sound, and now that he didn't have one hundred and fifty kids to worry about, Katie kept slipping into his thoughts. Ever since Euva told him about her leaving her husband, thousands of fragments of smothered memories had fused into an image he couldn't get out of his head. He had seen it once before, but he wasn't ready then.

He showered and dressed, careful not to wake Sammy asleep upstairs, then made his way toward the light from the kitchen striking across the dew-covered grass. Katie always arrived before the crack of dawn the day before a new session started, cranking out cookies, cornbreads and fresh fruit pies to have ready for their first meal. If anyone ever believed in making a good first impression, it was her. Once the parents left on Monday and the kids poured in for lunch, she was going to make darn sure, that even if they hated the place, they'd stay for the food.

Today, everyone had the day off so she wouldn't be starting up breakfast until the staff began drifting in around eight, and even then there wouldn't be that much to fix. Euva was coming later in the afternoon to prepare the annual staff barbeque with a couple of women who handled the evening supper shift.

He ran up the back stairs that led directly into the kitchen and spotted Katie at the mixer through the screen door. He went in, smiled and said hello. He wasn't certain she had said hello back as she continued pouring a quart of cream into the mixer. He poured himself a cup of coffee and strolled over to the stainless steel table where she was working.

Katie glanced up at him and then back at her work. He noticed something had changed. She was wearing shorts and a tee, and instead of a braid, her hair was tied back with a yellow silk scarf that trailed down her back. He hadn't seen her that way since the summer she left for Wilmington.

She switched on the mixer and looked up at him. He could see her eyes were still as big and brown as a fawn's. He stared into his coffee to keep from blushing, an affliction that had plagued him his entire life, making it impossible to ever lie to anyone or hide his deeper emotions.

The mixer stopped and she poured the batter into a baking pan. She kept her eyes on her work, and with a faint smile, said, "Are you here to steal my butterscotch cookie recipe?"

He took a sip of coffee. "No. I'm holding out for the secret ingredient for your cornbread."

She looked up at him and slowly raised an eyebrow. "Then I'd have to kill you." She took a spatula out of the drawer and concentrated on scraping the rest of the batter into the pan.

He smiled to himself. She even sounded like the old Katie.

"Are you coming to the barbeque tonight?" he asked.

She carefully ran the spatula around the bowl trying to get the last of the batter. "You know I never go to those things." She finished and took the bowl to the sink and ran the water.

"Katie?"

She turned with a shadow of exasperation on her face.

"I heard about you and Hal."

Katie wiped her forehead with the back of her hand, then turned to face the wall. Tiger went over and put his arm around her shoulder and drew her close. She pulled gently in the other direction and he held her even tighter.

"Katie, nobody can say you didn't give it your best shot. These things happen. Promise me you'll try to come tonight."

She nodded slightly and he felt awkward standing there with his arm around her, so he said he'd better fill up the coffee urns. As he went about getting out the creamers and juices, the smell of fresh baked brownies floated from the kitchen, and after a while the mixer started up again.

The dew-laden needles of the white pines on the edge of the lake sparkled in the early light of the dawn as he stood on the deck and watched the morning mist that resembled white cotton candy sweep across the ridge. He'd made a mistake all those years ago, and as he thought about it, figured he'd paid mightily for it. But his biggest regret was that Katie might have paid some for it, too.

A couple of the mentors going on a field trip came into the kitchen through the back door and Katie started fixing them lunches. He slipped out and went to his office and picked up his clipboard with all the weekend assignments. He skimmed over it and stopped at the barbeque. He folded his arms across his chest, hugged the board and thought. Something about the way Katie looked and the relaxed way she was with him gave him a hunch she might show up.

ALTHOUGH IT WAS SUNDAY, Tiger, Charlie and Josh Stepp, their maintenance supervisor, still had to see to some repairs before the kids arrived the next day. The infirmary roof had sprung another leak and a couple of the cabins were having trouble with slow shower drains. Josh had worked on it all Saturday afternoon, but in the end they had no choice but to call someone in to power snake the section of the sewer line running from the cabins. The rig was costing over a hundred dollars an hour and it took until mid-afternoon to get the job done. When the man handed Josh the bill, he looked at it and said, "Heck, I'd of been willing to come down and hose those kids off myself for this kind of money."

Sammy worked in the office all day answering phones and getting the packets ready for the next session. She was looking forward to taking the next Saturday off for a hike on the Richland Balsam

Trail with the Carolina Mountain Club. Bobbie Whitehall, a famous botanist, was going to be conducting it. She had studied his books in college and was anxious to hear him talk in the field.

Katie left just after two, and the camp became practically deserted until things started to pick up late in the afternoon. The big truck from the plumbing company finally pulled out, and Euva and some of the ladies who worked in the kitchen passed by the office on their way to the lodge. Sammy hadn't seen Patrick since noon when he left for Asheville with Bob. Patrick had acted sort of formal with her in front of him, but as they were walking out the door, Bob shoved him back in and said, "Go on... kiss her goodbye."

Sammy rolled a pencil back and forth between her finger and thumb as she thought. Should she, or shouldn't she call Betty and let her know an engagement was imminent? No. She'd ask too many questions, and when she found out Patrick was a counselor, she'd put two and two together and spazz out. The sole reason she was so crazy about Randy was that he had nothing to do with the camp.

It was best not to get her all riled up since there was still a slim chance her aunt might relent and lend her dad the money. She had an idea that might work, but didn't want to chance it unless they had no other alternative. Her plan could break Betty's heart, and that was the last thing she would ever want to do.

By the time she finished the last packet, it was five-thirty, and the aroma from the barbeque pit had already permeated the camp. Patrick had peeked in around four and she shooed him away lest she never get finished. The screen door opened. A slim, fine-boned woman in her late thirties with long brown hair timidly stepped in, followed by a boy around fifteen and a girl not much older. The children looked so much like the man behind them, he had to be their father.

The woman wore a white cotton dress sprinkled with delicate blue flowers. She stepped forward and offered her hand. "We're the Frasier Family Ole Timey Country Band. Mr. Morrison hired us to play tonight." She turned and introduced her husband, who she said played the guitar, her daughter who played the fiddle, and then her son who played the banjo. "I sing some and play the bass fiddle."

Sammy was a little taken aback. Her father had never hired a band for the barbeque before.

Just then, he came barging through the door rubbing his hands together. "Good! Good! You're here!" He shook everyone's hand. "Thanks for coming on such short notice." He introduced Sammy and told the Frasiers that they were the ole timey Morrison camp family and got a big laugh. He glanced at his watch and looked over at Sammy. His eyes sparkled and his movements were fused with energy. "Hey, girl, the party starts at six. I'll meet you at home in a few minutes." Then he shepherded the Frasiers out the door saying, "Let me show you where to set up."

Sammy knew her father was heartened over a call he had gotten from Tom Gibbons at the conservancy that morning, but she hoped he wasn't celebrating too soon. From what she understood, The Nature Conservancy was just talking to an "angel" and nothing was firm yet. She thought again. No, it was something else. She hadn't seen him quite like this before. Maybe he and Liz had patched things up, and she was coming to the barbeque.

She finished up and ran with Skippy to the house waving at a car rolling into the lot packed with staff returning from a romp in Asheville. After a quick shower she put on a new pair of white cropped pants and a navy and white striped tee, then reached into her closet and took out a pair of navy canvas skimmers, polka dotted with tiny white stars, and slipped them on. She quickly brushed her golden hair behind her ears and examined the outfit in the full length mirror. *Oh, Aunt Betty... do you know how to shop!*

She couldn't wait for Patrick to see her. The only time they'd been alone since their afternoon off was last night after the session wrap-up meeting. The staff had thrown together a campfire to celebrate, and by the way Patrick had let her know how he felt about her, it was easy to see how Chrissy Hutchinson had a hard time holding him off.

She winked at herself in the mirror. *Patrick darlin', I'm no Chrissy Hutchinson; if you want what I think you want, you're gonna have to put a little ring on my finger first.* Then she pictured his handsome Irish face and broad shoulders and felt her insides melt. She closed her eyes. *Oh, Patrick. You simply have to propose tonight or I'll die.* A giggle erupted. *Poor devil, he had no choice. The whole camp was betting on it.*

The bathroom pipes thumped. Her father had to be taking a shower. After straightening up the place a bit, she meandered downstairs to find him coming from his room. The vivid aqua polo shirt he wore made his eyes even bluer. His thick sandy brown hair framed the impish grin lighting up his face. She was awe struck. How Liz could have thrown him over, she'd never understand.

"Well, who do we have here?" he said as he circled her. "Aren't *you* the cat's meow."

She wanted to tell him Betty had bought her the outfit, but on second thought decided not to bring up that delicate subject. "You don't look so bad yourself, Dad. If I didn't know you better, I'd say you were steppin' out a little."

He clapped his hands and rubbed them together. "Let's go, kid!" He crouched down a bit and his voice took on a long playful drawl. "Watch out Henderson County. Here come the Morrisons!"

As they walked down the trail, the sound of fiddles and the voices of the Frasiers floated from the back field. *Yes, we'll gather at the river, the beautiful, the beautiful river. Gather with the saints at the river that flows by the throne of God.*

The delicate scent of the hemlocks, the promising waves of barbeque-laden smoke and the gospel song praising the river they loved, created a moment of sheer ecstasy for the two of them as they fell in with the crowd strolling to the field.

THE MINUTE KATIE WALKED in the door and spied the last of the Spartanburg peaches lying on the counter, she'd decided to use them to make the kids' favorite chicken recipe on their last night home before going off to camp.

Lisa walked in the kitchen. "Where are we eating tonight?"

"I thought the porch would be nice."

Lisa slapped a tray on the counter with more force than necessary, and loaded it with everything she'd need to set the table, as if she couldn't wait to get the chore over with. Katie, seeing her daughter making her way to the porch, rushed over and slid the glass door open.

As she prepared the salad, Katie mulled over the roller coaster ride her relations with Lisa had been on since Hal left and hoped

everything would run smoothly tonight. She didn't want anything
to spoil Lisa's last summer at camp. Without fail, for the past ten
years, every time she came home she had proclaimed her two weeks
at Camp Green River as the best in her life.

It always made Katie feel grateful. When Tiger hired her, he had
agreed to adjust the cost of her kids attending camp. She'd heard rumors that he usually cut it in half and put the money aside. Weeks
after their first session she still hadn't gotten a bill so she called Linda
and told her she had to know so she'd be sure to have it when it was
called for. She remembered Linda's blithe response. "You mean you
haven't figured it out yet? Tiger told me not to charge you anything."

Jason came in from mowing the lawn and interrupted her reverie.

"Hi, Mom." He kicked off his shoes covered with grass clippings
and said, "Gramma phoned a couple of times this morning and wants
you to call her. She seems kind of hyped up."

Katie barely rolled her eyes and kept at the salad. "I will after
dinner. Why don't you run up and take a quick shower? Dinner's
going to be ready in a few minutes." She worked in the kitchen for a
while, then took the salad along with some rolls and green beans out
to the porch. Lisa was lying on a lounge chair thumbing through a
magazine.

"You all packed, sweetheart?"

She didn't look up. "Uh-huh."

"I made a bunch of peach pies to serve tomorrow. Be sure to get
a piece."

Lisa turned a page, and Katie went back into the kitchen. Jason
came down and helped her bring the rest of the food to the table,
and they all sat down, held hands and bowed their heads. Katie
gave the usual blessing and added something about them all being
safe at camp.

So far, so good, thought Katie as the food was passed.

Lisa served herself some beans. "Are you going to the doins' at
the camp tonight?"

The question surprised Katie. "You know I never go to those
things, honey." She looked over at Jason and smiled at the way he was
digging into his chicken. Then she glanced over at Lisa, and seeing a
self-satisfied smirk on her face said, "What?"

Lisa stuck her fork into a green bean and twirled it in the air. "Nothing. It's just that now that Dad's not... huh... you know... not here anymore, Gramma said she thought you would go."

"Why would that make any difference?" The words hadn't escaped before she regretted uttering them. Lisa hadn't said two words to her in the past three days, and this sudden talkativeness had to be leading somewhere she didn't want to go.

"Gramma said now that Tiger Morrison has broken off with his girlfriend and you with Dad..."

Katie put her fork down. "*Sweet Jesus!* Where does this kind of gossip come from?"

"Becky Freeman cleans that woman's house and she told Gramma the lady threw him out."

Katie put an elbow on the table and dropped her chin on her fist. She took a deep breath, shook her head and picked up her fork again. "Tiger's personal affairs have absolutely nothing to do with me."

Lisa gave a bitter little laugh. "Oh, come on, Mom. We've heard all the gossip. How you two had a 'thing' before you married Dad. Everybody knows he dumped you."

Katie filled with humiliation. Unable to face either child, she jumped up. "I forgot the lemonade. I'll go get it." On her rush into the kitchen she caught sight of Jason making a face at Lisa. Just then, the phone on the counter rang. She was relieved at the distraction.

"Katie, it's your mother. I told Jason twice today to have you call me the minute you got in."

"I ran some errands and just got home a while ago. I was aiming to call you after I fed everyone."

"I certainly hope you're getting ready to go to the to-do at the camp tonight?"

Katie stared at the ceiling. "Mother, telling Lisa all those things really put me in a difficult position tonight. I wish you wouldn't do it. Especially any kind of speculation regarding Tiger. Remember where that got you the last time?"

"Well, are you getting ready!?"

"No, Mother. I'm not getting ready. I just want to have a nice evening at home with the kids before they leave for camp."

"Lordy me! You make it sound like you're never going to see

them again! Euva says that barbeque lasts until eleven. You've got plenty of time to get gussied up and over to that camp. The Frasiers are fiddlin' there tonight and nobody can clog like my Katie."

"Mother, I haven't clogged in years. I don't want to talk about this anymore. I'm going to hang up and take the kids their lemonade." She slowly put the receiver into the cradle and gazed off into space. She thought about Liz and felt sorry for her, and also a kind of kinship. The woman probably got tired of waiting around for Tiger to marry her. She thought back to the way he had put his arm around her at the sink that morning. Ha! It certainly wasn't taking him long to move on.

She hugged herself tightly. Darn! How can I be so hateful to a man who's been so good to my kids? His hugging me was no more than a good man showing some kindness to a fellow human being. She shook her head vigorously to chase away all the crazy thoughts, then focused on her mother. She had already caused havoc in her life. Tomorrow after work, she had to go over and settle her right down before she got everyone in the valley talking nonsense again.

Jason tapped her on the shoulder and startled her.

"Mom, come on in and finish your dinner."

He picked up the pitcher of lemonade and they went back out on the porch. She made an attempt at small talk, but the kids wanted nothing to do with it. Instead, Jason and Lisa kept giving each other looks, a silent language they spoke since childhood. She finally gave up and finished her meal, then started to collect the plates.

Jason stopped her. "Lisa and I are going to do the dishes."

Katie just barely caught the shadow of a stony look he gave his sister.

Lisa hung her head and fidgeted in her chair. "We want you to go to the barbeque."

Katie looked at Jason and then at Lisa and smiled. "You two are too much. I don't need to go to any barbeque. I just want to be here with you kids. Nice and quiet like."

"That's just it, Mom. You've been nice and quiet too long," said Jason.

Lisa reached over and squeezed her hand. "I'm sorry, Mom. That was really a nasty thing for me to say. Jason's right. We want you to go."

Katie sat like a heavy stone while the two started clearing the table.

"Go on, Mom," said Jason. "Go upstairs and get dressed."

Katie showered thinking it was as if she were on a train heading for a crash at full speed, and she couldn't jump off. Her mother's frame of mind was dangerous. Look how it had affected the kids! All right. I'll make everybody happy and go. I'll eat a little, maybe have a beer, and then come home.

She thought back to the morning when Tiger pulled her so close. He hadn't touched her in nineteen years. Not even a handshake when he hired her. She could still remember that uncomfortable moment when they both started to thrust their hands forward, but for their own reasons, just said goodbye. She could still feel the firm muscles and solid frame that she had never forgotten as he stood next to her at the sink.

Suddenly her heart started to race and an urgency took hold of her. She frantically flipped through the hangers in the closet until she found the jeans she'd worn when she went to see her brother, then a pretty white blouse. She quickly dressed and ran out of the room. Jason and Lisa stood in the hallway. Lisa folded her arms and looked her over, making her feel like their roles were suddenly reversed. Lisa's head nodded in approval, then she said for Katie to wait a minute and disappeared into her room.

Lisa came back out with a yellow cotton sweater, draped it around Katie's neck and tied the arms in front, then reached for the long shock of hair trailing down her back and gently pulled it over her shoulder and fluffed it up across her chest. "There," she said, "Now, you're loaded for bear."

"Yeah, Mom," said Jason. "You rock!"

CHAPTER SEVENTEEN

*O*H, IF YOU AIN'T GOT THE *do re mi, folks, if you ain't got the do re mi…* Tiger listened and winced. He sure knew what *that* song was all about. He checked his watch. The Frasiers had said, being Sunday, they could only play until nine, and it was already going on eight and starting to get dark. If she were coming, she'd have been there by now. Charlie had already gotten the campfire ready to go and lighted the torches around the serving tables.

Sammy tapped him on the back and handed him a beer. She studied his face. "You okay, Dad?"

"Sure, honey." He gave her a broad smile and noticed her cheeks were rosy. At least this was going to be a big night for her.

Suddenly, Bob grabbed Sammy and twirled her around with everyone stomping their feet and singing and clapping. Sammy laughed as she picked up the tune and gave a fair demonstration of clogging, with Bob tripping over himself a couple beats behind.

Tiger started to take a swig of the beer, then slowly lowered the bottle. Katie stood at the edge of the circle. She was looking around at the crowd that as yet wasn't aware of her presence. Their eyes met for only an instant before people crowded around her and blocked his view.

He moved in the general direction of where she stood, smiling and stopping to chat with folks and shouting hellos over the clapping and singing. The song finished, and a soft murmur rose, then laughing and the sound of people having a good time. He bumped into Charlie, and they talked about when to start the fire as his eyes skimmed over the crowd for Katie.

The sweet squeal of a fiddle struck the first notes of *Turkey in the Straw,* and the clapping exploded again. Suddenly Bob made a swath through the crowd. Tiger stood at the edge and watched him plunge into a cluster of people in the rear and pull Katie out. She even brushed against him as they passed. Once they reached the patch of grass that had turned into a dance floor, Katie gave Bob a mock resistance as everyone urged her to dance.

She finally pulled the sweater from around her neck and handed it to someone, made her back rigid and high-stepped like she had mountain music running through her veins. Tiger smiled. The Frasiers were a good idea after all.

He made his way over to the table Euva was tending and watched Katie dance to several tunes with a couple of partners. He got an uneasy feeling Euva was watching him. He took his eyes off Katie and searched the crowd until he spotted Sammy and Patrick sitting on the lawn. Patrick had an arm around her waist, and Sammy glowed. He winked to himself. Things were looking pretty promising for both the Morrisons tonight after all.

The music finally stopped. He quickly drained the last of his beer and asked Euva for a bottle of water, knowing she knew who he wanted it for. He searched the crowd for Katie. He spied her fanning herself with her hand in a crowd a few feet away and weaved his way through, smiling and apologizing to everyone he bumped against until he stood facing her.

"I'm glad you could make it," he said, handing her the water. A shy smile spread across her face, glistening with sweat. He couldn't tear his eyes off her as she took a couple of swallows. She finished and cast her gaze at the ground, then slowly lifted her eyes and looked sideways, trying to act as if her standing there next to him was a perfectly normal event. Her hands trembled and her eyes glowed. Wisps of chestnut hair curled softly around her flushed face.

Something beyond her caught his eye and he looked around and realized they were standing alone in the middle of the dance area with everyone staring at them. Katie noticed it, too, and if it weren't so dim, he'd swear she blushed.

Just then, Mr. Frasier announced they were going to play their last song and asked everyone to hold hands around a circle. Thank you, Mr. Frasier! He took Katie's hand and held it firm as the circle formed. When Mrs. Frasier neared the end of the hymn's first stanza, her husband yelled out for everyone to join in. He felt Katie's grasp tighten around his as their voices echoed from the hillside. *Will the circle be unbroken, by and by, by and by? In a better home awaiting, in the sky, in the sky…*

After the hymn ended, it took a while for him to let go. He noticed Sammy had drifted over to a group of counselors with Patrick and kept looking over at him and Katie. From the corner of his eye he could see everyone else stealing glances in their direction. It was now official; the whole camp knew he was courting her.

He'd already paid the Frasiers, but asked Katie to go over with him so he could thank them personally.

"Haven't seen you out much these past years, Katie, but see you still got that good ol' mountain rhythm," said Mrs. Frasier.

Katie was thanking the woman for the compliment when Charlie came along and offered to help them carry the bass fiddle. They waved Charlie off saying they had it under control, and he headed off to start the fire. The Frasiers left for the parking lot.

As they talked, Tiger could see Katie was still having a hard time looking him in the eye, and instead, kept looking off in the distance, or at her hands, or whatever her eyes could snag. She seemed so vulnerable it almost broke his heart. He wanted to hold her in his arms and not let go.

She was damp with sweat, and her aroma mingled with the sweetbush and hemlocks, and he wanted her. He wished things were simpler and she wasn't still married. They weren't kids anymore. He knew what he wanted and she must too, or she wouldn't be standing there next to him a ball of nerves with everyone in the camp gawking at what was going on between them. He was suddenly thrilled; as fearful as she was, she had come to be courted.

By now everyone had settled down around the fire. Katie could feel Tiger's warm hand on her back.

"Let's go sit up on the hillside," he said. "We've been the center of attention long enough."

She laughed, nervously. They started up the gentle slope with Katie struggling to compose herself. They walked along for a while, then she felt him fold his hand around hers as they made their way to the top. They turned and looked down at the campfire. Faces glowed as sparks shot upward and eerie shadows cast by the flames writhed around the forest growth. The breeze was sweet with the scent of hemlock and the rich moist earth.

There was too much time and space separating the last time they'd stood on this hillside, and it saddened her. Too much had been left unsaid. Maybe hidden in the darkness they could somehow heal the wound. They sat down, and the way Tiger hugged a knee in silence and stared at the fire below, she knew he had the same thoughts.

Still looking straight ahead, he spoke in a somber tone. "I was going to call you and ask you to marry me at Thanksgiving, but your mother told me you were engaged. I saw you once when you came home. You were walking down Main Street in Hendersonville. I wanted to cross over and tell you, but I thought… you being engaged and all… I'd be overstepping… like I didn't have a right to talk to you about that sort of thing anymore. I…"

The revelation tore her apart. She put her hand on his arm. She had to make him stop or she was going to fall to pieces. "Please, Tiger. It was a long time ago." Tears slowly trickled down her cheeks.

He kept looking ahead, as if he were afraid to face her. "I'm really sorry things didn't go very well for you after that… I mean… with Hal."

She swiped her hand across her face to wipe the tears, making it look as if she were brushing her hair from her eyes. "I've been beating myself up for putting up with it as long as I did. I just thought if I tried hard enough, he'd get better."

She heard something, like he was cracking his knuckles.

"Have you filed for a divorce yet?"

"Yes. Hal's agreed not to contest it, and my brother thinks the whole thing will be over with by Thanksgiving."

Katie waited. It was his turn to tell her where he stood.

"I guess you've heard about me and Liz."

"Tonight. My mother told Lisa."

He threw out a soft laugh. "Oh, it's that good ol' Green River Valley network at it again."

Katie wanted to talk about something else. She was starting to hate Liz for being so beautiful and having him all to herself for so many years. She was jealous and ashamed of it. "How are things going with Jeb's land?"

He tossed a blade of grass he'd been fingering. "Katie, I could kick myself all the way down this hill. I can't believe I let that place get away from me." He looked straight at her. "I can't believe I ever let you get away either."

His candidness was overwhelming her. She knew they had to thrash this out, but she couldn't do it yet or she would fall apart. She quickly changed the subject. "You mean Jeb's land is gone?"

"Not yet... but I'm slowly coming to the realization I might have to live with it."

"What have you done so far?"

He leaned back on his arms and folded his legs at the ankle. "Oh... I've tried the banks, relatives, you name it... the trouble is there's not enough time. The conservancy in Hendersonville is trying their darnedest to come up with a person or foundation that has the money to buy it and put it into some kind of land trust; but the problem is there's too much out there about to suffer the same fate, and all the money's committed. Their best hope right now is to get the Ledges to work with them to protect the east ridge."

She touched his shoulder. "At least that's something."

"Even if they do, there's still going to be the roads." He looked over at her. "Katie, can you hear the wind rustling through those big oaks and tulip poplars right now? Sometimes when I'm working in my office, I listen to the wind in the woods and in my head I can see those Goliaths twisting and bending and clutching the mountain by their roots, and I feel I'm just like them. Holding on to this land with my bare hands. Once they start that project, the only time we'll be able to hear the wind sweeping through the woods will be after they throw in the towel for the day."

Katie listened to him talk about the camp and the kids and marveled at how little he had changed. Hearing him pour out his heart to her, she could see his love for them was still raw and powerful.

A couple of people, coming down from the hill a little way off, distracted them. They could see Euva had stopped serving, and the tables were being taken down. The fire had dwindled to embers, and people were starting to leave.

Tiger pressed the button on his watch to light it up. "I can't believe I've chewed your ear so long. Charlie and I agreed to close things off at eleven." He laughed a little. "Well, seein' we've given everyone enough to talk about for at least a week, I better get you back to your car." He rose and helped her up.

They stood there, facing each other, neither able to move. A firefly lit up a few feet away. She could feel the warmth radiating from his body and hear him breathe. He grasped her shoulders, then slid his arms around her, uttering her name. He pulled her tight against him and kissed her long and deeply. She felt his manhood, and closed her eyes and let every muscle in her body give in to him.

"I've wanted to do that since I spotted you at the edge of the crowd," he murmured as he rubbed his warm cheeks against hers. She wanted to tell him she wanted him to do that since that morning in the kitchen.

He held her in his arms, and she felt his lingering warm kisses on her face. He nuzzled her ear and made her ache for him. She closed her eyes tight, took a deep breath and gently pulled away. "I think we better go."

He laughed softly. "I'm afraid you're right about that."

They descended the hill and walked hand in hand to her car. With every step she felt an unspoken commitment pulsating through their limbs. Her breasts swelled with each breath and tenderness radiated from between her legs. Two of the kitchen staff piling into a pick-up nearby said goodnight. She opened the door to her car and slid in, knowing if he kissed her again, she wouldn't be able to go.

She pulled out of the parking space and almost went off the road watching him in the rearview mirror. Waves of joy and wonderment rippled over her on the drive home, only to be beaten back by bittersweet memories. She'd felt like this once before on that very same hill looking down on a campfire. She remembered how her pride stung when he didn't ask her to marry him after her mother told everyone in the valley he would.

There was so much talk, none of it true. They hadn't slept together like everyone assumed. Tiger would never have let that happen. Back then, she hadn't yet learned to stand up to her mother. Her father had, though, and on the nights when her mother would rail against Tiger and insist she go up to the camp and force him to make an honest woman of her, he'd holler at her and say, "Hush woman. Katie never did a wrongful act in her life."

She drove down the road with Tiger's words echoing in her brain. *I was going to ask you to marry me when you came home at Thanksgiving.* Why, God? Why didn't I swallow my pride and wait until he was ready?

CHAPTER EIGHTEEN

Gary Skinner skimmed over the Rutherfordton *Daily Courier* for the second time. Not one mention of the two women. He tossed it on the table and picked up the Hendersonville *Times-News*. The couple down the mountain sold both papers in their store, but if they noticed him getting them every day they'd start nosing around, so he drove into Hendersonville and bought them from a newspaper stand on the curb of a strip center.

The headline across the top of the *Times-News* read: *Restrictions Lifted on Downtown Public Parking Lots.* He quickly skimmed over the front page; nothing but a lot of small town political maneuverings. He flipped past the national and sports sections and landed on local and state news. All the town seemed to care about was taxes, budgets and funding cuts. Nothing about finding the body parts he'd left in the woods off Route 9, or the one in the dumpster. He laughed scornfully. They evidently had no inkling they had a serial killer sitting in their over-taxed and under-funded backyard.

He put his hand in his pocket, pulled out a wad of money and counted it. Damn! I'm not going to last long in Florida on this. All that bitch on the trail had on her was one goddamn bank card. Good thing that illegal broad was dumped in my lap.

He thought for a moment. I've got to stick to grabbing one hiker at a time. I don't know what got into me. It was just that they looked like such easy marks. He remembered the fight the Rodman woman put up when he started to strap her hands behind her back. Damn her. She made me break my golden rule: never kill anyone at the contact point, especially when the van's parked at the trailhead. I had no choice but to bludgeon the bitch right there. Dragging her heavy ass into the woods was no picnic either.

He remembered the Winslow woman turning into a basket case after that and having to slap her silly before she could remember her pin number. That last slut in Florida rattled hers right off and knew the location of every damn ATM in the county. With the slew of credit cards she had on her, he'd picked up more than a thousand dollars in one afternoon.

His expression turned into something between a smile and a sneer, recalling how she thought her cooperation was going to get her somewhere, especially when he was doing her. Then an evil grin appeared as he pictured the shocked betrayal on her face when he came at her with the tire iron.

Today he had to find a place that had more hikers to choose from and make contact at a side trail that led back to the parking lot. It would be tricky catching someone exactly at that spot, but that was the formula that worked. He decided to get on the Blue Ridge Parkway, where they allowed dogs, and drive south.

He pulled off at the Richland Balsam Mountain Trail at Marker 431 near Waynesville. Good. There weren't that many cars. He checked his watch; just past seven-thirty. A sign indicated the summit at an elevation of 6410 ft. and the hike a mile and a half round trip. He should be able to make that in less than an hour. He'd hike it and look for a way off the path that would lead him to the parking lot, or if not, lead him to a spot near the parkway where he could hide the victim until he could get back on the road and load them into the van when no one was looking. Excitement grabbed hold of him. This time he'd look for something young.

He drove to the far end of the lot and pulled in next to a big SUV with a Vermont license plate. He got out and leashed the dog; and seeing a box on a post at the trailhead, went over and took out a guide. He studied the map and could see what appeared to be a side trail that came out at the other end of the parking lot. It was marked closed. He looked up and traced the lot until he saw a small opening overgrown with saplings at the opposite end. He got the dog back in, drove over and backed up to it.

First he'd hike the main trail, then check out the abandoned path; and as usual, stow his backpack near the contact point. He could keep his victim well off the abandoned trail until it was safe to get her in the van. But right now, he had to reconnoiter the two trails, establish the contact point, then find a woman out hiking by herself who wouldn't be missed right away. Someone who looked like she had a fistful of credit cards.

THE GROUP FROM THE CAROLINA Mountain Club started rolling into the Richland Balsam Trail lot just before eight. Sammy, one of the last to arrive, spied a bunch of members at the trailhead huddled around the club president. He was standing next to a distinguished looking bearded man who had to be the famous botanist, Bobbie Whitehall. She jumped out of the Jeep with Skippy, grabbed the leash and her backpack and hurried over.

Whitehall already had his audience enraptured. "I want everyone to close their eyes and inhale. See if you can smell the Fraser fir. If you do this every ten minutes, you will find that the higher we climb the more powerful the scent becomes."

He explained how the mountain had the vegetation of a typical Canadian spruce-fir forest because of the elevation. It was evident the Fraser firs were in a battle with the balsam woolly adelgid with skeletons of the tree scattered throughout. The botanist pointed them out, saying, "Once the dead trees fall, these blowdowns decompose to create rich new soil and open spaces for fir seeds to sprout, thus beginning the cycle again. I firmly believe the Balsam fir will continue to survive here in this manner, with each new generation becoming more resistant to adelgid damage."

Sammy was standing next to Roger Wilkins, a retiree she'd hiked with many times before. She covered her mouth with her hand and whispered in his ear. "I don't agree. My dad's been fighting the woolly adelgid attacking our hemlocks for the past five years. He says for every one he sees die, he'll never live long enough to see another one take its place."

They started the climb with everyone clustering around White-hall every time he stopped. He pointed to a small tree. "This is With-erod Viburnum. The Shawnees called it 'Shonny Haw' and brewed the bark to make 'Appalachian Tea.' The settlers used the drink to control fevers. If you come back in another month, you'll see the fruit has turned dark blue, providing food for wildlife and earning it another name, 'Wild Raisin.'"

Sammy was glad she had the morning off for the trek. This is what she loved about the Blue Ridge Mountains. There was so much history and lore. She never tired of hearing Euva's Green River tales. Descendents from the first settlers before and after the Revolutionary War were still sitting on their original land grants, retelling colorful and often tragic stories along with hard-earned mountain knowledge handed down from generation to generation.

Whitehall was raised in these mountains and felt at ease spilling out his vast knowledge. He grew animated, and Sammy could tell he loved every minute of it. He pointed to a boulder. "See the white strip midway through its center. That's evidence of molten quartz forcing itself into its crevice while the rock was still deep within the earth."

They trekked another fifty yards up a steep incline, and he stopped. "Notice the difference from a few yards back? There's less sunlight and the forest has grown cooler and wetter. Now, start looking for how the plant life has changed."

After he pointed out the difference between mosses and lichens, the path got wider, and the climb sped up with the hikers spreading out more. Sammy wanted to fall back a little so she could take Skippy off the leash for a while and let him cool down. She pretty much knew everything Whitehall told them; it was just the *way* he told it that intrigued her. Besides, she could catch up easy enough in a few minutes. She found a big rock to sit on and took a dish and some water out of her pack and gave Skippy some, then took a drink herself.

Skippy slurped the water, then suddenly lifted his head and emitted a low guttural growl. Quickly, she snapped on the leash. Another dog had to be approaching. Suddenly a big yellow lab bound around the corner. Unleashed, he faced off with Skippy. The hair on both dog's rumps rose. Luckily, the two animals settled for a round of sniffing.

A man came around the corner holding a baton. His grubby appearance made Sammy uneasy, but his sudden smile helped settle her nerves somewhat.

"I'm sorry, gal. Didn't mean to upset you or your dog none." He slapped his thigh with the baton and the yellow Lab immediately went to his side with his tail between his legs.

He neared. The oddness about him made Sammy wary, and she jumped up. He raised a hand and backed up a little. "Don't aim to scare anyone, deary. Been camping for a month now..." He looked down on himself. "...and need to drop in at a Laundromat. As an ex-paratrooper from the Vietnam War, I forget that people aren't used to seein' anyone lookin' so rough."

She nodded to him, gave a tug on the leash and started up the trail, listening keenly for his footsteps. Her pace quickened. He kept right behind her. She could see the trail take a sharp turn up ahead, across from what looked like an old logging trail. She knew it was silly, but she felt like she was in danger. She tried to calm down by asking herself how an old man with a dog could do anybody any harm.

"Hey! You comin' or not!" hollered Roger Wilkins, startling her. He had just come around the bend up ahead. "Whitehall is getting ready to teach us the history of the world. Get a move on!"

Later, on the way down from the mountain, they turned the bend and Sammy noticed the man sitting on the same rock, but decided to ignore him. She pulled Skippy tight against her, and was happy she was on the far side of the crowd passing by.

Someone in the rear yelled out, "Sammy, now that camp's almost over with, are you coming with us on the Mt. Pisgah Trail? We're going to hike up to Fryingpan Mountain from there."

"When is it?"

"Two Sundays from now?"

She jutted a thumb into the air.

LT. WILLIAMS COLLECTED ALL the notes scattered around his desk, put them in a semi-neat stack, clipped them together and threw them to the side. He had to rethink everything. His whole career was hinging on catching this perp. Sheriff Wilson wasn't going to get reelected if they didn't have this solved by November. And if that happened, his chances of following in the sheriff's footsteps… which from the way he was putting on a gut might not be too far away… might go down the drain, too.

He ran through every possible angle. From the very beginning he'd asked the bank security people not to put a stop on Winslow's bank card, and to put on an alert instead. If the guy tried to use it again, there'd be a five to ten minute lag before he got the notification, but the ATM could quickly be dusted for fingerprints and the video pulled to see if an identification could be made. Also, right quick, before anyone forgot what they saw, the neighborhood could be canvassed. Someone sitting on a porch, or a couple in a car in a parking lot might see something—a car, a pick-up, a van. Anything. They could also check all the cameras in the vicinity and possibly get a car description or license plate.

But when this killer didn't use the card again, they knew they were dealing with someone who'd already had run-ins with law officials. Probably been in prison where he learned all about ATMs and how to be successful at crime. There was no way they were going to get this guy's fingerprints. He knew enough not to touch anything without gloves.

From what they found out about the women's hiking routine, they weren't on a regular schedule and kept changing their trails. That meant this was a random act and they were chance victims.

He had put the department's new rookie on getting him a rundown of who used the park, and he found out it wasn't a drug drop or lovers' lane. Too close to Ingles Grocery Plaza across the road for that kind of activity. They looked into the possibility of the killer being an Ingles employee, but so far that path had led them nowhere. Everyone there was squeaky clean. Another possibility was a truck driver who made deliveries. Maybe somebody whose route ran from Charlotte to Chattanooga. It would be easy for them to stop off at an ATM in Reedsville. For that matter, it could have been a drifter who just happened to see the two get out of their car and enter the trailhead, then went after them.

He picked up the autopsy report and studied it for the umpteenth time. The head injuries were consistent with some kind of pipe or baton. Everything pointed to someone who had been in and out of jail, or the military, and was familiar with that type of instrument. Could even have had it used on him. It didn't take four crushing blows to kill a seventy-year-old woman. One would probably have done it. From her injuries, he could tell she put up a fight. This guy evidently got emotional and flew into an uncontrollable rage.

He wondered when the second body would turn up. If the public was putting this much pressure on them now, what was going to happen when the next one hit the front page.

The national Violent Criminal Apprehension Program had the case in their data base, and he'd pulled up every kind of search in case the guy had tried this in another park. He was convinced they were looking for a career criminal, some habitual offender who had a rap sheet twenty pages thick. The familiar feeling of anger mixed with futility crept up on him. The justice system was broken. They find these guys, put them away and then have to go out and catch them again.

He turned on his computer and booted up ViCap and started to look again for any cases that exhibited similar characteristics... a similar pattern of violence. He'd done this at least five times already, but maybe he had missed something.

CHAPTER NINETEEN

The room took on a mysterious aura. As if Tiger were seeing it for the first time. Relics from years of camp life wallpapered the rustic space. Leather couches worn smooth with use anchored the mosaic of mementos. Everything from fossils and bones grabbed up from the forest floor to arrowheads and Native American pottery chards were crammed on every shelf and table. Worthless to anyone else, they told the story of his life.

Tiger picked up a picture crudely framed with twigs. Sammy in a bathing suit flashed a toothless smile at him as she proudly held up a trout. He ran his hand over the shapeless figure he had watched transform into a tall, lithe Venus and laughed remembering the slogan he must have repeated a thousand times: *It's just you and me, kid.* Soon, another generation would be grinning at him from frames fashioned in the craft cabin. There'd be kids from Lisa and Josh as well as Patrick and Sammy. He smiled. They'd give that Sullivan family a run for their money.

Yes. His world *had* changed this summer, and he was standing at its threshold. The only hurdles left were making up with Katie... and learning to live with the fact that the property across the road was about to become a beehive of construction. Damn! He should have known the Ledges would go looking elsewhere when he turned them down!

Patrick knocked on the screen door, causing it to rattle. Tiger checked his watch. Eight. "Come in, son. You're right on time."

The reality of the man who was going to marry his only child entering his home quickly expelled him from the zone he had slipped into. "Let me get you a beer," he said as he headed out to the kitchen. He came back, handed one to Patrick and raised his bottle in a toast. "Here's to you and Sammy. May God grant both of you health and happiness." He went over to the couch. "Sit down, Patrick." The familiar scent of leather drifted up as Tiger sank into his favorite chair. "When Sammy told me you two were planning on getting married in the spring, I can't say I was surprised. In fact, I had been thinking you two would make a good match for a couple of years now."

Patrick blushed. "Thank you, Sir."

"You can relax; I'm not going to press you for answers. I just wanted to get everything out in the open so we all feel comfortable." He took a swig of beer and savored it as he pulled his thoughts together. "Sammy said you have a one-year contract with Goldsboro. I've already got you down for mentoring next summer, but if the school can find a replacement, I'll put you on full time as soon as you can get here... That is, if you want the job."

"Yes, Sir! I'll come as soon as I can."

"Good. I'm glad we got that out of the way. We can talk about your salary and future here at the camp at a later date." Sammy had made him promise not to come on too strong and to just offer him the job, giving them a chance to work things out between themselves first; but he was finding it difficult. How could he put the brakes on his enthusiasm when he had the perfect candidate to eventually run the camp with Sammy sitting square in front of him?

"Son, I can't tell you how thrilled I am about you and Sammy getting married. It's about time the next generation got on board. You know as well as I do that camp ownership around here has been kept in some families for generations. It's a way of life, and you've got to love it to live it." He studied Patrick. Calm and self-assured, he sat on the edge of the couch looking back at him knowingly. Good. Patrick understood his union with Sammy would be more than a marriage, and the challenge didn't appear to bother him.

"I don't know if you're aware of it, Patrick, but the Hendersonville/Brevard area has the highest concentration of organized youth camps in the country."

"I knew it was up there. I just didn't know it was number one."

"Tom Gibbons from the conservancy in Hendersonville was telling me that collectively the fifteen youth camps in the area comprise over 10,000 acres of undisturbed mountain land. Heck, that's ten times the size of Chimney Rock State Park next door in Rutherford County. We're real players in conserving these mountains."

Patrick leaned back and folded his arms loosely, a sign he was finally starting to relax. "Speaking about the conservancy, how's everything going with the farmland across the road?"

"Not too good." Tiger shook his head. "I can't believe I was asleep at the wheel when Jeb had enough of his place. I'm going to want you and Sammy to sit in on a few meetings with the conservancy up the road." Tiger remembered his promise to Sammy. "But, let's not talk about it tonight. By the way, how's everything going with Alvin?"

"I'm glad you let him stay in my cabin again this session. He's doin' great, but I still want to keep an eye on him."

"I know. You've got to respect a kid that tries so hard to catch up." He took a swig of beer. "I'm sure you understand why I didn't let you keep Tucker. The more these kids are exposed to a wide mix of personalities, the more they grow. I was only willing to make an exception in Alvin's case."

They chatted until Sammy came downstairs at a pre-determined time. Tiger was sure she had been listening with her door open by the way she winked approval at him before the two went off to the rec room. Tiger followed them to the door and watched them stroll down the path, wondering if Patrick had any idea that ten years ago he had this same conversation about a young camper with Bob Davies who was a counselor back then. The only difference was that the boy they were talking about was Patrick.

ALVIN, STILL TRYING TO GET used to the idea that Tucker was in another cabin, made his way to his bunk and suddenly found himself on the floor. He felt around for his glasses, put them back on and saw two kids looking down on him. Alvin remembered. The one with the red hair was Billy, and the other one his friend.

"Hey, skinny, you've got to pick up your feet a little more," Billy said. The way the one kid kept looking at Billy for some kind of signal, lead Alvin to believe the tall redhead was the leader of the duo. But Alvin had been the underdog enough times in his short life to know enough not to get goaded into a fight. He got up and brushed himself off. "You guys can call me String." He forced a slight laugh. "That's short for String Bean."

Billy looked away. "*Sure.*"

Just then, Patrick poked his head in the door from the porch. "Okay, guys. Who threw this towel on the bathroom floor?"

The two boys' faces were masked in innocence as they said it wasn't them, but Alvin caught the grins on their faces as Patrick turned and went back out.

Alvin made quick work of straightening his bed and sweeping the cabin, his duty for the morning. Then he got his backpack ready for the day's hike down the Green River. He couldn't wait. Last night at dinner, Tucker had hollered over that he was in Unit Four, the same one he was in. He also told him a bunch of the kids had gotten together and renamed the group the Slithering Salamanders.

The bell rang and he raced out the door past Patrick who was helping someone sift through a pile of shoes on the porch. He was saying, "Gerry, I can see you're going to be high maintenance."

On his way through the woods to the back field, Alvin recognized Patrick's voice coming from Hemlock Hut Two. *Let's go, Gerry, let's go! Let's go, Gerry, let's go!*

Coming out of the woods, Alvin spotted Tucker and ran across the field, amazed at how fast he was moving. He'd done pretty well at the camp-wide games last night, too. Never once thought of dropping out. Other than being a little bruised, scabbed up and chigger bitten from the first session, he was in good shape.

The Slithering Salamander's mentor for the hike was standing in the middle of a cluster of kids. A sun-bleached ponytail jutted out from the back of her baseball cap, and she was wearing hiking shorts and a tee shirt that read, "I recycled my homework to save the earth."

"Okay, guys. Does everybody have their water bottle? ...*with water in it?*" That got a laugh. "It's going to be a superduper warm day, so let's make sure we all have sunscreen on. Anyone who needs some, come over here and I'll fix you up."

Alvin and Tucker piled into the Lorax. A girl in the back jumped up and waved her arms at Tucker.

"Who's that?" asked Alvin who was right behind him.

Tucker murmured over his shoulder, "Dana. Her and her folks were staying at the Sheraton, too, and we kinda hooked up. She's got a Nintendo Wii and let me play with it." They swung into an empty seat and Tucker continued. "Her cabin sits at the table next to mine, and last night she tapped me on the back and asked me if I wanted her peach pie. I figured she wanted it herself, and just offered it to be friendly."

"So, what did you tell her?"

"Heck! I took it!"

Just before the counselor closed the bus door, Billy jumped on, giving Alvin a pang of dread; then someone shouted out *Repeat after me!* and the whole gang burst out singing. Alvin was surprised to see Tucker enthusiastically clapping and giving the song his all, and wondered what brought about the change.

Walking along the trail that led to the river, he listened to him explain the Fibonacci sequence to Dana. "My father says if you add one plus one and get two, then add two to the one and get three, then keep adding the last two numbers, you get a series of numbers that make up most mathematical patterns in nature. They're called Fibonacci numbers. My dad drew out how it happens in family trees, but when I get home he's going to show me all this in veggies, leaves, flower petals, seeds… pretty much everything. He wants me to collect as many pinecones as I can so we can check them out together."

"How did you hear about this?" Dana asked.

"Oh, my old counselor, Patrick the Evil, told me about it last week. I'd never heard about it before, so I asked my dad. *Man, it's awesome!*"

Alvin laughed to himself. Only Tucker could get this excited over numbers.

CHAPTER TWENTY

A̶LL THE SONGBIRDS WERE DONE for the day and only an occasional holler from the cabins escaped from out of the woods and floated across the now-placid lake. Skippy stood by Tiger's side knowing his master was going somewhere and hoping he'd get taken along for the ride. Tiger didn't have to leave for Hendersonville just yet; besides, he felt heavily stationary like the knoll overlooking the green lawn spread out in front of him.

From the very start of the season he knew his life was going to change, and now it was a matter of riding it out. Tonight was going to be tough and he hoped neither of them cried, but he didn't want things to end with Liz the way they had. The ten years he'd had with her were good ones, and even now when he thought of her, he knew he still had feelings for her, but it wasn't good enough. Neither of them ever crossed the threshold where they were willing to give up everything for the other. And he knew the intensity of that feeling because he felt it every day of his life for the Green River Valley, Sammy, and a long time ago for Susan and now for Katie.

He reached in his pocket, pulled out a small box and looked at the ring inside. It was mounted with one of the emeralds he'd found when he and his dad went gem mining near the old gold mine at the far end of the camp when he was twelve. A few years back he had three stones from his collection cut and polished. Sammy was going to get one as a wedding present, and the largest one was being set with a diamond on each side for Katie as an engagement ring.

Liz had been good to him for a long time, and he felt the camp owed her the beautiful green jewel chiseled from its belly for coming between them. It saddened him to think they were through, and he wanted those years to remain the way he remembered them. The dinner bell rang, and Skippy looked up and started to prance. "Sorry, boy. You've got to stay," he said, and got into the truck.

A half-hour later, Tiger pulled into a parking space in front of Hendersonville's historic gold-domed County Court House on Main Street, and walked over to the Never Blue Café. All the shops downtown were closed, but a smattering of folks were strolling along the flower-laden street and meandering into restaurants and bars. He was glad he had decided to meet Liz at the restaurant, instead of picking her up.

He reached the Never Blue and could see her seated next to the window, looking beautiful in a yellow sleeveless dress, her arms firm and nicely tanned from all the tennis. He could see how easy it would be for someone to love her. He patted his pant pocket to make sure he had the ring and went in.

"You're late."

"Am I? I'm sorry."

"I was beginning to think one of those black bears had gotten you."

"That's not going to happen."

"Why? Do you feed them a camper every day?"

Here we go again, thought Tiger as he cracked his knuckles. She just can't leave that place alone. "With all the racket those rascals make, they won't come near the place." Tiger wondered if Liz had followed through on her threat. He felt a little cheesy doing it, but couldn't resist looking to see if she was wearing an engagement ring. She wasn't. He was beginning to get an inkling this little dinner might not have been such a good idea.

They'd been to the restaurant so many times, they were ready with their order when the waitress brought the drinks. Liz rattled away about what all her friends were doing, and he thought about

Katie. They were planning on getting married as soon as her divorce came through. A small affair at the lodge, with just immediate family and a few close friends. He had called her brother and he said it looked like mid-September. He also warned him about being careful not to give Hal any cause. That was going to be the hardest part of getting through the next four weeks.

Suddenly, he felt his hand being squeezed.

"Now, what are you going to do?" queried Liz.

"About what?"

"Oh for heaven's sake! You weren't listening. I said it's all over town that you couldn't raise the money for that land, and I wondered what you were going to do."

Thankfully, the waitress came with the food.

"Tiger, considering all the dire things you said were going to happen once the Ledges took that farm over, now might be a good time to start negotiating with them for your place. Roger White... you remember him... he's that big commercial broker with Re/Max... well, he said they're still interested in your...."

Tiger looked up from his meal. "That's enough, Liz. I'm not here to talk about the Ledges."

She reached over and patted his hand. "Of course not, darling. You need time to adjust to all this."

He glanced out the large window and could see the buildings on Main Street were now dark shadows against a dying sunset. Tiger finished his meal in silence searching for a way to get the conversation back on track. What was the name of the guy she was marrying? Larry? Yes, Larry. He racked his brain. Elders! Yes. Larry Elders. He'd played doubles with him a couple of times at the club. He could congratulate her, give her the ring, then tell her about Katie, and if he were lucky, make it back to camp by evening song. "How's everything going with Larry Elders?"

She threw her head back and laughed. "Oh, that's all over." She reached across the table and squeezed his hand. "He doesn't hold a candle to you."

He wished she hadn't said that. She had misinterpreted his invitation to dinner, and he had to set her straight before things went too far. He owed it to her to tell her about Katie before she heard it from someone else. He weighed the situation. She'd never make a scene in front of all these people. "Liz, we're not going to get back together again."

Her face became frighteningly distorted.

"Liz," Tiger said gently, reaching his hand out.

She smacked it away and knocked over a small vase holding a couple of daisies. He righted it and sopped up some of the water with his napkin as he looked around to see if anyone had noticed. An elderly lady sitting alone at the next table glared at him. He leaned forward and whispered, "Liz, you know I'll always have strong feelings for you, but we're just not a good fit."

"We're not?! Well, you certainly seemed to manage it well enough."

Tiger dropped his head in his hand and took a deep breath. How did he get himself into this fix? If she was already this upset, what was she going to do when he told her he was marrying Katie? He thought of the ring and quickly pulled it out. "Liz, I got you a... sort of a remembrance gift." There wasn't a trace of calm on her face. "Come on, Liz. Let me put it on."

There was a long pause as she thought it over, then when she started to extend her left hand, he reached for the other one and slipped the ring on her baby finger.

"I found that emerald in a rock right on the camp property when I was a kid, and I had Jack Saunders get it mounted for you." He noticed her look up past him and frown like she didn't understand something. He felt a sudden grip on his shoulder and looked up to see an unshaven, disheveled man standing over him, reeking of liquor.

"You no good, two-timer. I've been watching you through that window. You're doing my wife and at the same time giving this babe a ring."

"What are you talking about? Who are you?"

"Katie's husband. That's who."

Tiger was shocked at how much Hal had changed since he met him when he stopped in at the camp to talk with Katie a few years back. Tiger caught the lady at the next table slowly roll her eyes, then he reluctantly looked over at Liz.

"Who's Katie?!" she demanded.

Hal slammed a hand on the table to steady himself, and leaned close enough to Liz to cause her to fan the air with her napkin. She pulled her head back as he slurred out, "She's the camp cook."

Liz bolted up, slamming her chair against the wall. "This takes the cake!" She struggled to get the ring off and threw it at Tiger. She snatched up her purse, then shoved Hal, who was already having a hard time staying on his feet, and sent him sailing across the floor.

The manager wanted to call the police and have him arrested, but for Katie and her kids' sake, Tiger talked him out of it and wrestled Hal out and into a cab. The driver wanted seventy-five bucks to take him to Cherokee where he said he lived, so he handed him a hundred dollar bill and told him to be sure to get him home okay.

On the drive home, Tiger kept thinking at least he and Liz were now history. As unfortunate as it was, if Hal hadn't shown up, he didn't think she was going to let go all that easy. There wasn't a kid alive that he couldn't figure out, but once those little girls grew up, they sure could be bewildering.

"Take me to 127 Pearl," demanded Hal.

"Sorry, bub. The guy just paid me to take you home."

"Yeah. But I need to stop there for a minute."

The driver could see the guy was going to get violent if he didn't agree. He should have known better than to pick up a drunk. Pearl Street was only four blocks away so he said, "Calm down, buddy. I'll take you, but I'm only waiting five minutes."

The cab pulled up to a big Victorian with one light on downstairs. Grunting and groaning, Hal tumbled out of the cab mumbling, *Okay, Okay,* when the driver reminded him to hurry.

Katie was curled up in the front living room working up the energy to go up to bed, when the doorbell rang. She jumped up, pulled the curtain aside and saw the cab out front. Wondering who it could be, she made her way to the vestibule and looked through the panel next to the door.

Hal's face was pressed to the glass. "Open up. I've got something to tell you about that two-timer you're going with."

She knew she shouldn't do it, but when she heard "two-timer," a little voice told her to open the door. She stood there in an old robe and a pair of Lisa's cast off slippers that resembled bunnies. Hal looked so pathetic that for a split second she was tempted to help him in and let him stay the night, but her brother had warned her about that, and the cab was waiting. Thank God, the kids were at camp and not there to see their father like this.

"*Well?*"

"You're curious, aren't you?"

"Just say what you've come to say, and leave."

"He's doin' you dirty again, gal."

"*Who?*"

He leaned up close and breathed on her, making her flinch. "You know who. Tiger Morrison... *your lover.*"

"He's not my lover, Hal. But we are getting married."

"Then what was he doing giving some gorgeous blond a ring?"

"What are you talking about?"

"I saw them at the Never Blue Café tonight. She's a real dish. You're pretty, Katie, but you can't hold a candle to her. He called her Liz; but classy is what I'd say." He started to reel toward her, but caught himself by grabbing the casing. "He played you once before, and it looks like he's doin' it again. Where's *your* ring? I hope you haven't been dishing it out. That whole precious valley of yours is going to be laughing behind your back... if they aren't already." His face twisted into an ugly sneer. "I can't wait to see the expression on your mother's face when I tell her."

It didn't make any sense that Tiger would take Liz to dinner and give her a ring. Suddenly a jealous rage shot through Katie. She stepped back and slammed the door in Hal's face.

KATIE FLIPPED THE BACON over hard enough to splatter the hot grease on her apron. She had tossed in bed past three last night fighting with herself, and now her head ached. Once, she actually got dressed, grabbed her keys and was almost out the door on her way to the camp before she stopped herself. No matter what Tiger did, she wasn't going to make a scene in the middle of the night while he was responsible for all those kids.

It was just like Hal to come over and throw it in her face, but when her sister-in-law phoned after he left, she was glad she'd had some warning. Her brother was out of town, so Laura had gone to dinner at the Never Blue with her mother, and was surprised when she saw Tiger with Liz. She didn't know anything about a ring, but said when Hal went sprawling all over the floor, she figured Tiger had to have punched him.

There had to be some kind of explanation. But what could it be? Tiger said he and Liz were through, and since it seemed like he didn't want to talk about it, she never had an opportunity to ask him why he didn't marry her. But mostly, she didn't ask him because she was afraid of the answer.

Every time she pictured him giving Liz a ring, she thought her brain would explode. She could understand the woman calling him up and begging to see him, but why a ring? She remembered Hal's comment about him not giving *her* one, and for the umpteenth time tears streamed down her face. The thrill of starting her life anew with someone she loved morphed into insecurity and suspicion. She couldn't stand the thought of going through another disappointment like she had all those years back. There was no question he wanted her; but was he going to marry her, or just string her along like Liz?

TIGER STRODE QUICKLY ALONG the dark path to the back door of the kitchen. He was losing Jeb's land to the Ledges and things ended grimly with Liz, but he knew once he put his arms around Katie and took in the sweet scent of her he'd feel good. He struggled with whether or not to tell her about the scene Hal made. He decided not to bring it up. Her husband's reputation had embarrassed her enough over the years.

Whistling softly as he climbed the back steps, his heart sped up when he spotted her moving around in the kitchen. Thank heavens they could steal this early morning time for themselves. He threw open the door and grabbed her from behind as she passed, biting her softly on the neck.

She pulled away and went back to the stove, picked up the spatula and shoved the bacon around. In a playful mood, he put his arms around her waist and kissed her on the cheek. "Hey, darlin', think of all the money I'm going to save when I don't have to pay the cook any more."

She dropped the spatula, swung around and slapped his face with a shocking force.

"What did you do that for? I was just joking." He looked as if his feelings were hurt more than his cheek.

She turned toward the stove, picked up the spatula and said, "I talked to Hal last night."

"So… you talked to Hal. What does that have to do with slapping me?"

She turned, shoved him aside and went to the fridge. "Three people in a marriage will be a little confusing."

He shifted his weight and threw his head to the side. "Oh, man… I just wanted to say goodbye to her."

"Did you ever think of using the phone… or the U.S. Post Office?" She stacked several boxes of eggs on her arm and closed the refrigerator door. "Do you know who was in the restaurant last night?"

He groaned. "Probably half of Hendersonville."

"That's right. Including my brother's wife. I'm sure she called my mother last night and told her about you and Liz. It's going to be all over this valley today. Tiger, you don't understand the way it is. Our families have known each other for generations. One way or another, we're all somehow related to each other. They're still talking about what happened between us twenty years ago." Her voice cracked. "Even my kids."

He took the eggs, put them on the table and grabbed her up in his arms. "I'm sorry my having dinner with Liz is so upsetting for you, Katie. I just wanted to close that chapter of my life with some dignity. I want you to get all the gossip out of your head. All that matters is that I love you and you love me, and once you get the divorce, we're going to get married and live happily ever after. So let's not go overboard on this."

He took her in his arms and kissed her, then pulled her over to the switch and turned off the lights.

She snapped them back on. "Tiger, let's not forget about the one hundred and fifty hungry kids who are going to be bursting through those doors for breakfast in a couple hours." She tossed her head. "Go get yourself some coffee."

He came back holding a cup and helped himself to one of the fresh baked sweet rolls she was setting out on platters. He went up behind her and nuzzled her on the ear. "Promise you're not going to slap me again if I kiss you?"

She let him kiss her, then as she continued stacking the rolls on the platters, asked, "Why did you give her a ring?"

"Well, I thought she deserved it."

She didn't look up. "You mean for ten years of service?"

Tiger started to take a bite of the roll. "Well… I guess you could put it that way." He knew he said the wrong thing the minute she looked up at him. "What? What did I do now?"

"Nothing, Mister. I just think we better cool this relationship down until I'm free and can see *exactly* where it's headed. I'm not going to be made a fool of again."

"Oh, Katie. We can't take this old baggage with us. We both made a mistake letting each other go once before. Let's not do it again. I love you and I'm asking you to trust me."

"Trust you!?" She grabbed a potholder, went to the oven, pulled out a tin of hot rolls and slapped it on a steel table. "How can I?! While I was at home making out a list of who to invite to the wedding, you were slipping a ring on Liz's finger!"

"You don't understand. I felt I owed it to her to tell her about our getting married myself. I wanted it to end without hurting her feelings."

"How about my feelings? Everyone's talking again, and I can't stand it! And think of my kids. What are they going to say when they hear about you tossing their father across the floor?"

"Katie, it wasn't like that! You should know me well enough by now to believe I wouldn't do such a thing."

"Are you telling me my sister-in-law is blind?!"

Tiger looked as if he had been slapped in the face again. Slowly, his expression hardened. "Okay, if that's the way you want it. *Fine!*" He went over to her desk, found her purse and thrashed around in it. He pulled out her cell phone and started inputting something. Then he tossed it back in her purse. "There. I've put in my cell phone number. I've apologized, explained, practically lay down prone on the floor begging for your forgiveness for not asking you to marry me twenty years ago, and I'm done with it. When you get the divorce and can finally swallow that pride of yours... without choking on it... give me a call."

CHAPTER TWENTY-ONE

THE CROWN VIC DROVE BARELY a few miles above the speed limit along the switchbacks bordering Lake Lure. There was no need for Lt. Sam Williams to rush. He knew he was going to be at his destination for a long time and he had to be prepared. The call had come in at seven. Two hikers found a black plastic garbage bag that looked suspicious and called 911; and at eight, a deputy radioed that there was a head in it.

Williams had already called his wife and told her he wouldn't be home until late that night, if at all. She took it in stride. After living through his eighteen years as a detective on the Rutherford County force, she had learned to take the fracture of family life in stride when he was called to duty, and he loved her for it.

He could feel the adrenalin racing through his veins and guessed this one was going to add up to two or three days of intense investigation, consuming eighteen to twenty hours a day. He always felt like a quarterback running out on the field at the start of a Super Bowl every time he began an investigation of this magnitude. If he were a guessing man, he'd say the head belonged to Annie Winslow.

The remains had been found on Route 9 just above Bat Cave, and knowing that stretch of deserted mountain road, he swung into the gas station that functioned as the only convenience store in Lake

Lure and got out. He was wearing a light blue long-sleeved shirt and a red tie. Starting to bald, his brown hair was streaked with gray. At six-foot-three, the fifty-two-year-old Williams carried his two hundred and thirty pounds with subtle authority, and looked more like a doctor than a cop.

He went inside the dated cinderblock hut that had to have been built sometime in the thirties with a canopy wide enough for two cars. He used the restroom and picked up some food ... chips, soft-drinks, crackers, water... whatever he could grab to sustain him for the day, and maybe all night.

As he drove through Chimney Rock, which at nine in the morning on a Wednesday was deserted, he called the officer at the scene. He had already heard Deputy Brown on the radio talking to his supervisor, but as the lead detective, he knew he had to control the flow of information by using his cell.

The road officer was calm under the circumstances. "I put on gloves and just peeked inside. I figure it's a woman. The hair is gray and she looked to be... gee... it's hard to tell... the smell almost knocked me over."

"Have you blocked off the road frontage?"

"Yeah. One lane. I've got my vehicle on one end and some flares at the other."

"Good. We're going to be looking for tire tracks and don't want any cars pulling off the road. Did you find anything else?"

"No. Just the bag lying where it was found. The two hikers are antsy to keep on moving, but I figured you'd want to talk to them."

He hung up and put in another call to Jake Archer, the head of their forensic team.

"We're all set, Sam. We'll be on our way in a few minutes. We've all notified our families that it'll be a late night, and I got hold of the coroner in Chapel Hill and asked him how he wants us to handle the remains."

"What did he say?"

"He thought we better fingerprint the bag before we handle it."

Williams figured if it was the guy who killed Ruth Rodman, they wouldn't find any. He hung up and decided to spend the fifteen minutes it was going to take him to get to the scene clearing his head, an exercise he went through before the start of every major investigation. He couldn't give the case his full attention if he was worried about the broken water heater at their cabin or the breaking and entering case they opened yesterday.

He pulled up behind the second squad car that had arrived at the scene, grabbed his clipboard and started toward Deputy Brown who had cordoned off an area next to the road. Another deputy was directing traffic. The two hikers were sitting on the grass looking like they were about to get sick. He took their statements, got their contact information and let them go. Next, he took Deputy Brown's statement.

"What was the bag secured with?"

The deputy produced a baggie that held a twist tie.

"Forensics is going to show up any minute. Give that to them. Meanwhile, let's send a deputy to interview all the people who live on this road in both directions. Let's see if any of them saw this black plastic bag on the road, and if they did, when? We need to narrow this thing down a bit. It could be as long ago as four or five weeks."

"Do you think it might be that missing lady?"

"Yes."

"Are you going to take a look at it?"

"No. Not until forensics gets here."

A couple more cars had arrived from the sheriff's office, and he dispatched one to drive north on Route 9 and pull the video tapes from any convenience store or bank that had a surveillance camera. He didn't think they were going to have any luck with this, since the tapes were reused on a rotation schedule of anywhere from seven to thirty days.

He checked his watch. The team with the cadaver dogs wouldn't be getting there until around two, but meanwhile he'd dispatch officers to walk the road a mile in either direction to see if there was anything else on the road. He eyed the bag. It was sitting just where it would have landed if someone threw it out of a window as they drove by.

The county coroner and medical examiner had to be notified. He made the calls in the car with the air-conditioning going full blast, and watched forensics arrive and cordon off an eight-foot square around the bag. They spent a good hour vacuuming and taping the ground for evidence before they even got to the bag.

Williams felt a little guilty sitting in air-conditioned comfort as he watched Jake Archer prepare to super glue the bag for prints. The area under the arms of Jake's khaki tee shirt were already dark with sweat. He was pounding stakes into the ground and making a wall around the bag with black plastic, then he covered the top while his team duct taped all the seams together to make it as airtight as they could. Jake weighted the plastic to the ground with some bricks from his trunk. Next, he filled a couple of pie tins with super glue and slid them into the tent. It would take a few minutes for the fumes to turn any prints on the bag white, so he pulled off his gloves and slipped into the Crown Vic next to Williams.

"Got any water?"

Williams, who had already reached in the bag on the floor behind him for a bottle, handed it to him. They had worked enough cases together for him to know Jake hadn't stopped for any food.

Jake guzzled the whole thing down, then pulled out a handkerchief and wiped his face and neck. "Damn, it's muggy out there. We should have any fingerprints on that bag in a few minutes, then we'll take a look inside. The ambulance should be here any time now. The remains are going straight to Chapel Hill. Do you know which officer you're going to have ride with them?"

"Yeah. Brown."

Williams reached into the open briefcase on the back seat and pulled out a file. He thumbed through it, took out a photo and handed it to Jake. "I think this is who we're going to find in there."

Jake took a glance, handed it back and said, "Man, things are pretty bad when Gramma can't take a stroll in the woods any more." He opened the door and stepped out. "Thanks for the water. I've got to get back to work."

Williams answered a few calls, then got himself psychologically prepared to talk to Marcie Winslow. He had deliberately chiseled away at her expectations over the past weeks, but it was still going to be a shock. He didn't have the heart to ask her to ID her mother's remains. He'd do it himself.

Forensics was crawling all over the place, photographing the bag from every angle. When he saw them finally disassembling the tent, he got out of the car, and wasn't surprised when they told him there weren't any prints.

Jake snapped on a mask and peered inside the bag with a flashlight. He looked over his shoulder at Williams. "You want to put on a mask and take a look?"

Williams had seen his share of corpses, but there was something surreal about looking at a head detached from a body. "It looks like Annie Winslow," he said. "I'll make a preliminary ID based on the family photo."

The sheriff and his chief deputy arrived, and Williams brought them up to speed as the ambulance pulled away with the remains still in the bag. The sheriff had worked in homicide for twenty years and issued a standard statement when the press arrived. He told Williams to keep him informed and took off.

A NEWSWOMAN'S VOICE TRAILED into the kitchen as Tiger poured himself a glass of lemonade. No need to rush. The weather report wouldn't be on for a few more minutes. He perked up his ears when he heard the reporter mention the Winslow/Rodman case. Curious, he drifted back into the living room.

Sheriff Wilson was on the screen. "We have found what we believe to be human remains and are starting an investigation."

Sammy came running down the stairs in her pajamas. "Dad, Euva said her daughter... you know... the one who's married to a deputy... called her and said her husband's going to be home late because he's working on that case. The sheriff doesn't want to release any details, but the human remains he's talking about is the head of the missing hiker."

CHAPTER TWENTY-TWO

A SWEATY, RUMPLED BUNCH spilled out of the woods onto the deserted camp road, tired from a rugged trek down the Green River. They waited around for the stragglers to catch up before piling into the bus. A clump of black-eyed Susans on the edge of the road attracted Tucker's attention. After a few moments he yelled over to Alvin and Dana. "Look! It has thirteen petals!"

Alvin examined the flower and looked puzzled.

"You don't get it," Dana said to Alvin. "Thirteen is one of the Fibonacci numbers. Five and eight make thirteen." She clutched Tucker's shoulders and the two of them bounced up and down crying, *Awesome!*

Billy stood with his fists on his hips shaking his head. Hopefully, thought Alvin, he won't cause Tucker trouble, too. The kid called him a "freak" twice, and every time he tried to make friends with someone in the cabin, Billy pulled them away and left him out.

Last night, Billy engrossed everyone in one of his gory camping stories. Alvin tried to get involved, but Billy looked past him like he was invisible. After a while, he just climbed on his bunk and stared at the ceiling, listening to the other kids joke around.

By the time the bus arrived back at base camp, the bell had already rung for lunch. A pleasant rumble surfaced as everyone talked,

179

laughed and hollered out to kids at other tables, offering extra rolls and veggies left on serving platters. The practice reflected the camp motto: *Waste not, want not.*

After everyone pitched in to clear the tables and separate their organic recyclable trash, a few counselors put on a skit that got everyone clapping and rollicking before Sammy stood up to deliver the usual announcements.

"We've got a few changes in this afternoon's activities. Swimming and diving lessons are going to start at three instead of two, and archery's been cancelled." She waited for the booing to subside, then moved on. "Maple Hut One is setting up for dinner and Two is taking out the Ort and sweeping up the dining hall. Everyone be sure to check downstairs and take back your laundry. We've got an extra pink tee shirt and don't know who it belongs to. We left it on the table."

Someone yelled out, "It's Patrick's." Sammy checked her list as she waited for the laughing to quiet down. "Now the field trip reports." Mentors rose and told about discoveries on their hikes, everything from an angel mushroom to a large batch of late blueberries on the Ruby Falls trail.

Suddenly the Ort bell rang. A counselor ran out of the recycling niche waving a plate with a big blob of ketchup. "Look what Patrick left on his plate," he yelled. A spontaneous shout of *Waste not, want not!* rang out, followed by the ear-splitting chant of *Eat it! Eat it!* Sammy laughed as Patrick licked it clean, an antic he was willing to go along with at every session to help teach the kids to put only as much on their plates as they could consume.

Finally, she wished the campers a nice rest; and everyone, except the kids from the cabin assigned to clean up, spilled out of the lodge.

ON THE WAY TO THE CABIN, Patrick winced when he heard Billy say *geek* to someone as he threw a thumb over his shoulder toward Alvin. They'd been together for almost a week now, and he'd noticed something was wrong from the very first day. He hoped things would work themselves out, but it looked like it was getting worse. He decided to address the problem that afternoon. He looked around for Mike and asked him to handle his wood burning activity for a while after rest period so he could have a chat with Billy.

One of the kids strummed on a ukulele as the kids wrote letters home, read a little, or just lay on their bunks. Patrick noticed Alvin wasn't sleeping through the period any more. A good sign that he was starting to catch up. But he hadn't latched on to a new buddy in the cabin and didn't seem as happy; hopefully his talk with Billy would correct the situation today.

The activity bell rang, and everyone jumped up and pulled their gear together. Patrick casually mentioned to Billy that he wanted him to wait a minute before heading out. While Patrick helped someone find his trunks on the line outside, Billy stood aside with his arms folded, tapping his feet impatiently. Patrick got an unsettling impression that Billy knew why he wanted to talk, and that it had happened to the kid a lot of times before.

The last camper finally got on his way, and Patrick went over and put an arm around Billy and said, "Why don't we sit down here on the steps." Patrick hunched forward with his forearms on his knees and rubbed his hands together. "Billy, do you remember the oath you took at the respect circle the first day you were here at camp?"

Billy folded his arms, pursed his lips and said a curt "Yes."

"Good. Good. You promised to respect the earth, yourself and everyone else here at the camp, didn't you?" Patrick turned and looked him in the eye.

Billy twisted his lips and nodded.

"Billy, do you think name-calling fits into that oath?"

"No."

"Good. Good." Patrick took a moment to think. "I noticed you seem to be having a problem with Alvin. What's with that?"

Billy took a deep breath and slowly let it out, then readjusted his arms across his chest and blurted out, "He's skinny… and thinks he's better than all of us. He tries to act so cool even though I'm better than him at everything."

Patrick searched his brain trying to remember if there was anything in the kid's file about a behavior problem. "Okay, Billy. First of all, Alvin being skinny is no reason for you to be disrespectful to him… just like if someone wanted to call you names because they didn't like your red hair. Do you agree with that?"

"I guess so."

Patrick stared ahead at the path. "There's no question that you're a super athlete, Billy. And all the kids look up to you for it..." He turned toward him. "... including Alvin. On the other hand, Alvin needs a little catching up, and someone like you could really help him. Can you think of some ways you can do that?"

"I don't know. He's pretty hopeless."

"You're sharp enough, Billy, that I bet you could think of something."

"I could give him a few tips on the soccer field. He doesn't know what to do and just stands there until the ball hits him."

"Oh, that'd be good, Billy."

"Maybe I could get him to eat more. Have you seen his ribs?"

Patrick tossed his head and coughed out a laugh. "Yeah."

Billy raised an eyebrow and looked at him sideways. "Are you going to have a *little talk* with him, too?"

"Yes, Billy. I am."

The conversation ended with Billy pledging not to call anyone names and promising to include Alvin in his group. Billy ran off to fish, and Patrick strode across the back field to the craft cabin, wondering if he should discuss the situation with Tiger. Not yet. He'd give Billy another day and see if the talk worked.

By the time he got to the craft cabin to relieve Mike, Alvin was busy burning his name on a piece of wood along with a few other kids. Tucker and Dana were counting the petals on some wildflowers they'd picked, marveling at how they totaled Fibanacci numbers. Patrick suddenly realized he was looking at one of the biggest successes he'd ever had as a counselor.

The bell rang for free time. Without making a big issue of it, he coaxed Tucker and Dana to get along so he could talk with Alvin.

Alvin fell into helping him pick up all the supplies as everyone meandered away; and by the time they finished, the place was deserted. Shouts floated through the woods from the lake where kids were enjoying a free swim. Three hummingbirds flitted around the flowers on the edge of the camp garden, and a goldfinch, picking seeds off a cluster of coneflowers, teetered in the breeze.

Patrick plopped himself down on a bench. "Sit down, Alvin. I want to talk to you for a moment." Alvin sank on the seat of the picnic table across from him. "You know, Alvin, I've noticed things aren't exactly smooth between you and Billy. What do you think is going on there?"

"Oh, nothing really bad. He's called me a few names and I think his friend tripped me once, but I didn't get hurt or anything."

"How about shutting you out?"

Alvin cast his eyes downward. "I've talked to Billy and he's pledged to correct his behavior, but he might need some help from you." Alvin's eyes enlarged with expectation. "Alvin, sometimes kids get in a habit of bullying. It makes them feel better, because... maybe they don't feel very good about themselves. Actually it's pretty complicated. Do you have any idea how you can help him?"

Alvin shook his head.

"I think he's going to try to help you out a little here and there... like at soccer. And when he does, go along with him and try your best. And get back in his little group... just hang in there and don't get left out. Okay?"

"Okay."

Alvin's eyes searched around, giving Patrick the feeling that he wanted to say something. "Is there anything you want to tell me?"

"I'm worried he's going to be mean to Tucker."

Patrick thought for a moment. "Since I've had a talk with him, that probably won't happen; but if it does, just let me know. Okay, buddy?" Patrick was hoping it wouldn't, or this could lead to him having to get Billy to sign a behavioral contract. And if that didn't work, they'd have to send the kid home.

The two sauntered across the field. Patrick had to stop by the cabin, so Alvin ran to the lake to find Tucker and Dana.

THE CALL HAD COME IN just before the bell rang for free swim. Tom Gibbons hit Tiger with the news that the conservancy had started serious negotiations with the Ledges since hope for finding an angel was fading. Tom surmised they were going to be able to buy some easement rights on the edge of the main stream going into the Green River, but that was about all he held out hope for.

The conversation ended with Tiger telling Tom he was ready to sit down and talk to them about easements on his place. By now, he realized it had to be done and would take a great deal of work for everything to be put in place. There was no way he wanted to see Sammy and Patrick put under this kind of stress if anything happened to him. A conservation agreement would devalue the land and lower the estate tax they'd have to pay. Hopefully, the money from selling the easement would cover the tax when the time came.

He had a sudden yearning to be with Katie. He took out his cell and, for the hundredth time, checked to see if she had called. Nothing. Every time he stepped foot in the dining hall he had to keep from going straight to the kitchen. She was right about waiting until the divorce was finalized. He had moved too quickly. None of this would have happened if she had been free.

He found it hard to concentrate on office work these days and decided to fly fish again. A couple of times he had fished with Jason. It had to be more than a coincidence that they both gravitated to the trout pond every afternoon. Jason was a great kid and they were old friends, but mostly the boy connected him to Katie and he found comfort in it. They never said a word about her and carried on like everything was going to be just fine. The camp would be closing in a week and he'd have the ring by then. Once she had that, he was sure she'd settle down and they could work everything out.

TUCKER AND DANA SAT on the grass on the side of the lake talking and watching all the antics in the water. Someone in Dana's cabin yelled over to her from the dock deck, then grabbed the bar of the pulley and sailed across the water. Dana cheered after the girl let go and splashed in the lake. Alvin slid down on the grass next to Dana.

She turned her attention to Tucker. "I definitely think you should do it."

"I don't know." He leaned forward and looked past Dana at Alvin. "Do you think I should?"

"Do what?"

"Enter the talent show."

Alvin was stunned. "Talent show? What can *you* do?"

"Recite the first two hundred digits of Pi."

"You mean those numbers you're memorizing?"

"Uh-huh."

"First of all, Tucker, what the heck is Pi?"

"If you divide the distance around a circle by its width, you get this ratio that starts off: three point one four... but the numbers never end past the decimal point. It goes into the trillions. And the interesting part is that this ratio stays the same no matter how big the circle gets. My dad says you could measure the earth with it."

"How long will it take you to recite them?"

Tucker shrugged. "I don't know... a couple minutes." He pulled a small sheet of paper from his pocket. "See... there're only twenty lines of ten numbers each." He gave Alvin the sheet. "Let me recite them for you right now."

Alvin adjusted his glasses and focused on the first line.

"Okay... here I go... three point one, four, one, five, nine, two, six, five, three, five..."

"Stop. I know you can do it, but your counselor's going to have to want to put you in the show tomorrow night."

"Oh, he'll go along with it. He's been trying to come up with something we can do for a couple days now."

That night when the kids clustered around Billy before bedtime, Alvin glanced across the room and detected Patrick giving him a slight nudge with his head. He went over and attached himself to a group transfixed by one of Billy's card tricks. Billy looked up and casually elbowed a kid sitting on the bed next to him and said, "Move over and make room for String."

CHAPTER TWENTY-THREE

The next morning at breakfast, they had a rare treat: warm homemade cinnamon rolls. Billy grabbed a lone extra roll left on the platter and dropped it on Alvin's plate. One of the kids yelled, "Hey, I wanted that!"

Billy shot back, "Aw, shut up. String needs it more than you do." The whole table laughed, including Alvin.

The morning's field trip consisted of a strenuous hike up to Turkey Rock outlook, but the view was worth it. The enormous bald table rock afforded a view for miles in every direction, and to the west, clear across to the Pisgah range. A peregrine falcon swooped across the sky below them, and the mentor passed his field glasses around so everyone could view its nest.

Coming back down, Billy nudged Alvin and asked why Tucker kept repeating a lot of numbers to Dana. Alvin told him about the talent show and Tucker's plans. Billy snickered. "The kids are going to hate it." Alvin secretly agreed and cringed at the thought of Tucker making a fool of himself.

While Tucker and Dana practiced the Pi numbers, a couple of kids from the cabin hung out with Alvin at free swim, seeing who would last longest standing on a Styrofoam float. Once back in the cabin, his new friends showed him the spirit stones they painted for the final council fire, and he wondered what he could put on his.

He lay on his bunk listening to the kids in other cabins yelling for help in fixing their costumes and practicing for the show, and he prayed Tucker would at least make it through the numbers before the boos started. The air was so electric with excitement that dinner turned out to be controlled chaos. When Ortman ran out for the Ort report, the place almost blew apart. Everyone was having such a rollicking good time, Alvin wished he could get Tucker off his mind.

Once dinner ended, Alvin picked up a broom and joined his cabin in cleaning up the dining hall. He liked listening to the banter of the older kids who were helping the staff put up the stage, stack tables and set up the chairs for the talent show. One of them hollered out, "Some kid's going to recite the first two hundred digits of Pi tonight." Alvin blanched. Someone answered, "That's cool." Alvin's eyes shot over to see Billy make a face like he couldn't believe what he was hearing.

The Ort pail had to be taken to the compost pile next to the garden on the back field, so Alvin strained to lift it.

"Hey, String," shouted Billy. "Let me help with that."

Patrick, putting a rocker on the stage, turned and saw Billy grab the handle along with Alvin, and as the two boys passed, ruffled Billy's hair and said, "That's it, buddy."

The two boys lugged the big container past the lake, and then into the woods past the cabins, until they reached the back field. They chatted on the way back to the lodge. Mostly Billy telling Alvin that Tucker's performance would make him a laughing stock.

Kids milled around the lodge in costumes, played banjos, ukuleles, flutes. A trio of girls huddled in a corner practicing a song, and someone tinkled the piano keys. Alvin found a seat, and looking around for Tucker, spotted him talking to Tiger, who held his sheet of Pi numbers. Tiger showed Charlie Morgan the piece of paper and Alvin groaned. Billy, sitting in the row behind him, heard it and said, "Gee whiz, how bad can it be?"

A fiddle suddenly started up a reel, and two mentors shuffled onto the stage. The crowd, all revved up for a good time, went wild. Patrick, the tall one, wore a granny dress and a hideous gray wig made from a mop head, and the other one had on a pair of hole-ridden bib overalls and long-sleeved underwear. They both gripped corncob pipes between their teeth. Alvin knew their skit was hilarious by the constant roll of laughter, but he was too preoccupied with Tucker to enjoy it. He tapped his fingers nervously on his legs all through a piano piece a girl had composed.

A lull fell on the lodge.

Billy leaned forward and whispered in his ear. "I think Tucker's next."

Tiger and Charlie stood off to the side studying the paper. They took their sweet time doing it, making Alvin worry that the kids would get fidgety. Finally Tiger jumped up on the stage and said, "I don't know how many of you have already had algebra or geometry, but we have a young man here who wants to recite the first two hundred digits of Pi."

Alvin was surprised to hear everyone cheer.

"For those of you who don't know what Pi is, I'm going to try to explain it."

Alvin looked around at the faces as Tiger proceeded. Kids listened intently.

"Tucker Watson is only nine, but I understand he's got a very mathematical mind." He waved the paper in the air. "He's going to recite the first two hundred numbers past the decimal, and I'm going to make sure he's got them right. Every time he makes a mistake, I'm going to raise my hand, and Charlie over there is going to hit the drum." He glanced over at the side of the stage. "Okay, Tucker, we're ready!"

The whole place went wild as Tucker walked up the steps. Alvin was impressed with how confident he seemed.

"Okay everyone," Tiger said as he raised his arms for silence. "When I give the signal, he's going to start."

Tiger pointed to Tucker and he spoke calmly and clearly. "Three point one, four, one, five…."

The crowd sat in silence as Tucker recited the numbers in ten digit segments. Every once in a while someone would say something like, *Wow, this guy's incredible,* and the crowd would hush them. Alvin held his breath waiting for Tiger to signal for a drumbeat.

Tucker stopped and stood motionless. Silence hung in the air.

Suddenly everyone stood up and clapped and hollered until the roar became deafening. Alvin raised his arms and jumped around whooping, until he spotted a flash of anger streak across Billy's face.

At breakfast the next morning, Tucker had been elevated to celebrity status. When someone at their table said, "They'll remember this forever," Billy told him to shut up. Alvin noticed the look on Patrick's face.

Alvin was one of the last ones out of the cabin after clean-up, since it took him forever to find a dry pair of socks. Patrick yelled, "Have a good hike," after him as he ran down the path to the back field. He raced across and could see a crowd gathered around Tucker. He and Dana hustled him into the bus and squeezed into one seat, with Tucker in the middle.

Alvin had never been to Miner's Outlook, but he had heard the mentor who headed the hike knew every plant, shrub and tree on the climb and all the Indian lore and medicine cures that went along with them. They weren't on the trail five minutes before Carrie Jones started pointing out the staghorn plantain that grew in abundance all over the mountain and telling them how the Cherokee used it for snake bites and other cures.

Dana and Tucker stayed to study a cluster of Oswego Tea that Carrie had found in a sunny clearing, and Alvin reluctantly stayed behind with them. Billy made his way up the mountain from below with another kid, and they all went on together. Someone had a bad fall and the counselor who had radioed for assistance was staying back with him.

They came to a fork in the path and hesitated. Tucker shouted out from behind that Carrie had said for them to keep right as she proceeded up the mountain.

"No!" said Billy. "When the counselor told us to go on ahead, she said to turn left at the fork."

Alvin looked at the kid who came up the trail with Billy. "Did she?"

He piped right up, "Yes! I heard her!"

Alvin looked at Tucker. "Are you sure you heard Carrie say for us to go right?"

Tucker shrugged his shoulders and grimaced. "I don't know."

Alvin faced Billy. *"Are you sure?"*

"Yeah!" He spun around and ran up the trail shouting "Follow me everyone."

They all hung close together on the trail that dissolved into thicket. After a while they came to a small clearing with an open view of the valley and decided to rest. Alvin could see Tucker was uneasy. Ever since they turned left, he kept relating all the stories he had read on the internet about people being dragged off by bears and mountain lions.

"I think we're lost," he whispered to Alvin.

Alvin looked over at Billy. "You never heard her say for us to go left, did you?"

Billy came at him. "Are you calling me a liar? If that wimpy friend of yours wasn't so slow, we'd of caught up with them by now."

The kid who had come up the trail with Billy said, "We're not even on a trail any more. I think we should try to find our way back."

"No," said Alvin. "Remember what they told us in case we're lost. We're supposed to stay put, and they'll come find us."

"That is if a bear doesn't drag us off first," said Tucker.

Billy's voice suddenly sounded meeker. "Maybe I should leave you guys here and try to find the way back."

"No. We've got to stay together," Alvin insisted.

Billy looked around. "Maybe we should try to get some idea of where we are. If we find the river, we can walk back to base camp." He looked around and pointed to a huge hemlock squeezed between two giant boulders. "If one of us could climb that, we might be able to locate it."

They ran over to the tree, but no one could reach the bottom branch. Billy looked at Tucker. "Okay Einstein, you're the smallest one here. I'm gonna lean against this tree and I want you to climb up my legs and stand on my shoulders and grab on to that limb." He looked at Alvin. "You and Dana are gonna have to boost him up."

Alvin thought the whole plan was nutty. Billy was just trying to show off again. "Tucker are you going to be all right with this?"

The stories of bears snatching kids off trails had gotten to Dana. She looked at Tucker pleadingly. "You can do it, can't you?"

Tucker stared into Alvin's eyes for an instant, then took off his backpack and said he was ready. Billy quickly told the other kid to lace his hands together to give Tucker a foot up, then he put his arms up against the tree and spread his legs. "Okay, Einstein, start climbing."

One moment Tucker placed a foot in the kid's hands with Alvin and Dana braced to boost him up by the rump, and the next he teetered on Billy's shoulders and hugged the trunk. It took a couple of tries but he finally got a leg around the lower branch and pulled himself up onto it. They all backed up and watched him climb. A big gust of wind suddenly rippled through the woods, making the tree sway.

"Do you see anything, yet?" yelled Alvin, nervously. So much rain fell over the winter and spring, causing blowdowns all over the mountains, that the stability of trees growing next to granite outcroppings couldn't be trusted, and they'd been told not to climb them.

"Nothing but a big open space," he yelled. "Be careful, you guys. One false step and you'll go off a cliff. I'm going to go up a little higher so I can see the whole valley."

They watched him climb past a few more branches, then hug the trunk as a strong gust of wind started to bend the tree.

"You better come down from there," yelled Alvin.

A crack that sounded like a gunshot pierced the air, and the tree suddenly crashed down. A gapping red clay gash stood stark between the two boulders. They froze in utter silence—Alvin was afraid to look. Tucker had to have been flung over the cliff.

Alvin forced himself to turn his head. His eyes searched the tree, now almost level with the clearing with its top hanging over the cliff. His heart thumped when he spied a face buried deep in the branches. Tucker had been flung upside down, but he had managed to hang on.

"Climb out of there," screamed Dana.

"I can't! I'm too scared!"

"Don't look down and don't move," said Alvin, trying to sound calm. "They're going to figure out we took the wrong turn and find us any minute and get you out of there."

Billy was pacing and slamming a fist in his hand. "I've got to go find them!"

"No! We're to stay together. It's the rules!" insisted Alvin.

The second crack wasn't as loud as the first, but the tree now tipped downward over the cliff. The sound of rocks and dirt sliding from the gaping hole between the two boulders and the sight of roots swaying in the breeze made the hair on the back of Alvin's neck rise. Part of the tree's roots clung to the soil, but clay continued to fall away. The tree could break loose any minute and slide over the ridge.

"Oh, my God! He's got to get out of there," cried Dana.

Tucker moaned meekly, "I can't. I'm afraid."

"But you've got to!" she screamed.

"I can't. I can't move."

Alvin jumped up on the tree and started walking all hunched over, holding his arms out for balance.

"Don't!" Dana screamed.

Alvin crept steadily. By the time he reached a dozen feet out on the limb and looked down, he could see the mountain ease away below, and knew if the tree gave way it would slide down toward a granite outcrop one hundred feet beyond. He stealthily climbed over and around the shaggy limbs until he was an arm's length from Tucker. "Start crawling toward me. And don't look down," he said as he reached out.

"I can't. I'm afraid."

"Come on, Tucker. I'm right here with you. Get up and don't do anything to rattle this thing." Alvin's ears listened acutely for the wind in the woods. One strong gust could push the tree over the edge. "Come on, Tuck. Your dad's going to show you all the patterns on the plants and vegetables when you get home. Get your footing, nice and easy, and start movin.'"

Tucker's thin oval face was red and scratched and his eyes glistened as he slowly put his shaking hand on the branch above him and pulled himself up.

"That's it. Keep comin,'" said Alvin as he slowly backed up, still crouching down low. Off in the distance, he heard their names being shouted. People must be coming up the trail. Alvin looked back at Dana, careful not to lose his balance. They still had a way to go. He was only a couple feet from Tucker and could see him shake. "That's it. You're doin' good, Tuck." They neared a big branch tossed over the trunk. "Okay, this one's going to be a little harder. You're going to have to climb over, but then we'll be almost to the edge. Just wait for me to get over it first." Alvin slowly lifted a leg over the branch. The voices got louder.

"Oh my God, he's like a spider!" someone shouted.

The climb was too tricky to look back, but he let out a sigh when he heard the mentor's voice. Carrie was calm and deliberate. "Okay, guys. Keep on coming nice and easy. You're almost there."

Alvin worried about Tucker getting over the branch, so he stood ready to grab him. Tucker held on with an iron grip and swung a leg over. Alvin looked back at the mentor reaching out to him. She reminded him of his mother, and he fought off an impulse to scamper off the tree as soon as he could. It would only panic Tucker.

Alvin started to see tree tops underneath him and knew they were only a few feet from the edge of the cliff. Please, God. Don't let the tree break loose. Tucker's breathing became heavy. Too heavy. "Come on, buddy, we're almost there."

He felt Carrie's hands. He put an arm around her neck and got swept off the trunk. Three more staff erupted from the woods. Mike carefully got on the trunk and reached for Tucker and handed him to Carrie. A dizzy sensation overwhelmed Alvin. Someone handed him a bottle of water and told him to drink as much as he could.

"How did you guys get split from the group?" Mike asked as he knelt down to examine Tucker.

Billy came over. "It's my fault. I lied to them. I was just... just... trying to act like a big shot."

Mike looked up at him. "Son, we could have had a big tragedy here."

"Mike, it wasn't his fault the tree fell down. We were all warned not to climb any because of all the rain," pleaded Alvin. "We just forgot."

Alvin, still a little shaky on the way down the mountain, was surprised how fast Tucker bounced back. He laughed when he heard him tell another kid, "I figured if I crawled out of the tree, I'd have a fifty-fifty chance of making it."

A clamor rose once their bus pulled into base camp. One of the older kids asked Tucker who rescued him. "Alvin Magee," Tucker announced proudly.

"*Alvin? Alvin Magee?*" The kid shook his head. "We gotta fix that name."

Tiger checked Tucker out along with the two nurses in the infirmary. Tucker's cuts needed to be stitched up, so Mike and another mentor took him to the hospital in Hendersonville along with the kid who had twisted his ankle. Tiger wanted Alvin checked over, so he went along too. Meanwhile, the story of Alvin creeping along the tree like a spider to rescue Tucker spread through the camp like wildfire.

Alvin arrived back at his cabin from the trip into the emergency room as the rest period ended. Everyone was getting ready to leave for their afternoon activity when a couple of older kids stuck their head in the door.

"Is Spider Magee in here?"

Alvin looked around puzzled.

Billy poked him. "That's you, buddy."

CHAPTER TWENTY-FOUR

Sᴀᴍᴍʏ ʜᴏʟʟᴇʀᴇᴅ "Hᴇʟʟᴏ" to a little red-headed boy pedaling his tricycle up the driveway next door as she ran up the front porch steps. She unlocked the door to find the usual eerie quietness of a space where time had stood still. When she lived at home, she always had everything tidied and put away before leaving for camp, but now everything lay as if her father had just stepped out for the afternoon. Magazines were haphazardly piled on the ottoman, unopened mail lay on the hall table, and she could see he'd emptied the dishwasher but left everything stacked on the counter.

The house never did have a woman's touch, but since she moved out, a masculine aura had grabbed the place by the throat. Her father's golf bag stood in the corner of the vestibule with a tennis racket leaning up against it; but it was the neat row of footwear that defined the man who lived there—everything from his Wellingtons and heavy-duty high top hikers to a collection of well-worn tennis, golf and running shoes.

Sammy sped up the stairs. Sunlight streamed in the room that still looked like it belonged to a young girl, with its chintz curtains and matching bedspread sprinkled with miniature flowers. Her eyes traced the trophies sitting on the shelves. She'd left them behind because she knew how much her father liked to look at them. Not so much because she won, but because she always did her best. They brought back so many good times. Her athletic career was as much a part of their lives together during the school year as the camp was during the summer, with her father her number one fan at every swim meet.

She moved swiftly to the closet, pushed aside some clothes she'd left behind and pulled a blanket off a chest pushed up against the back wall. It was padded and covered with moiré-patterned pink rayon. She grabbed a handle on the side and dragged it out into the room. It had been some time since she was in her early teens and would race home after school and read her mother's diaries, but she was pretty sure she could find what she was looking for.

All the good parts already had markers stuck in them, so she easily found the two sections she thought might work. She put the chest back in the closet, placed the two diaries in a fancy gift bag and ran down the stairs with it. There was just enough time to get to Greenville, then back to the camp for dinner.

The swaying from side to side as the car swung around the mountain curves exhilarated Sammy. The terrain flattened out as it reached Greenville, but she could still see mountains looming to the west.

She had waited until she was at the gate to phone, so her aunt wouldn't have enough time to get all stirred up. She pulled onto Betty's circular driveway and caught a glimpse of her peeking from between the window blinds. She took a deep breath and reached over for the bag, hoping she wasn't doing the wrong thing. Betty couldn't even bear looking at her mother's photo album, much less read her innermost thoughts from her diary.

She got out of the Jeep and started up the steps. The landscaping looked different. When her uncle was alive he tended to the grounds himself instead of hiring a firm to do it. The door opened and Sammy was surprised to see how unimposing her aunt appeared in a simple cotton housecoat.

"Lord, help me. What a wonderful surprise," Betty sang out as she gave Sammy a big hug. She looked around, a little concerned that the neighbors might get a look at her without her hair all done up. "Hurry on in, girl."

Betty reached for the bag Sammy was hanging onto. "What do you have in there, darlin'?"

Sammy waved her off. "I'll show it to you later after we've had a chance to talk." She followed her aunt into the kitchen and sat down at the table while Betty shuffled around the kitchen setting up a tray. Sammy knew there'd be a half-dozen Lorna Doone shortbread cookies on a plate and a pitcher of iced tea, just like when she stayed with her aunt as a child.

Betty brought the tray to the table, spread out lace placemats and poured her a glass of tea. "Okay, sweetheart. You show me what you've got there or I'm simply going to burst."

Sammy took a deep breath, bit her lip and pulled two diaries from the bag, and then placed them on the table. Betty's hand trembled as she reached for one. She stared lovingly at it as she said, "I always wondered if you had ever read them."

"Every word. I discovered the chest under a blanket up in the attic when I was around twelve. I don't know why, but I just knew it was my mother's. The diaries were at the bottom underneath the quilts. It's funny, even though I'd seen all her pictures, I never realized how small she was until I tried on her wedding dress and it didn't fit."

Betty sank onto a chair caressing the diary. "She was tiny like our dear mother. You took after my father's side of the family. Sammy, you're the spitting image of me at twenty-four." She squeezed Sammy's hand. "Except you're sweet like your mama."

"You're sweet, too, Aunt Betty."

"Nonsense, girl. My brother used to say I was as mean as snot." She rocked back and forth. "'Prideful.' That's what my father called me. 'Betty,' he'd say, 'That pride of yours is going to bring you grief.'" She stopped to think for a moment. "Maybe I was proud because I was shamed so much. I only had two cotton skirts and two blouses the whole time I went to high school. Wore them every other day. We had no money for books, so I had to borrow my friend's and do my homework in study hall."

A self-satisfied smile crossed her face. "But your mama didn't have to carry on like that. Once I married Arthur and we both got good paying jobs at Duke Electric, I saw to it she had everything. By the time she was off to college, Arthur's construction business was doin' right good, and he told me to get her all the fixin's and not pay one ounce of heed to a price tag."

The room grew quiet as Betty, deep in thought, stared ahead and Sammy munched on a Lorna Doone, thinking there were only four days left for her father to come up with the money for Jeb's place.

Betty finally broke the silence. "Do you still have the chest?"

Sammy nodded. "I used to go up in the attic to read the diaries after school. One day my father came home early and caught me up there. I'll never forget it. He marched over to me, solemnly took the diary from my hand and put it back, then picked up the chest and said, 'This belongs in your room now.'"

"That hope chest was your mama's Christmas present when she turned four. My brother made it from some pine boards we had, and I covered it with material I got from the general store downtown. Padded it real nice, too." She sighed as if all the memories were beginning to crush her. "I suppose there's a reason you brought these over."

Sammy pushed the second diary toward her. "I stuck markers in a couple of the pages I want you to read." She looked into her aunt's eyes. "I know it's going to be hard for you, but promise you'll do this for me?"

Betty's eyes were sorrowful. "I'll try. But that's all I can promise."

SAMMY HAD BEEN GONE for a while, but Betty lingered at the table. She'd eaten a cookie, but couldn't remember what it tasted like. Finally, she picked up one of the diaries. She read the date on the cover and realized it was the year Susan got married. She opened it to a marker and was surprised to find how good it made her feel to see the familiar energetic handwriting run across the page.

The words: *I'm so happy* ignited Betty's memories. She held the page open with her heavily veined, tremor-afflicted hand and broke into a tender smile, remembering the joy of the two of them scurrying all over town making wedding arrangements.

Betty read on about the invitations and who was getting them, before turning the page. *Mama Betty has been so kind and generous and it's fun to see her so excited about all the preparations. I know she's proud of me the way she's spent hours going through her correspondence inviting anyone we can claim as a friend or relative.* A tingle ran through her. Susan still thought of her as "Mama Betty" at that age.

She shook her head and thought about Sammy. How could the tragedy of losing a mother at such a young age visit two generations in a row? Arthur had told her that was why she was put on this earth. She'd never wanted children of her own, but God intended for her to be a mother just the same.

She put the diary down, made a cup of hot tea and went back. Betty picked up an extra bookmark Sammy had laid on the table and remembered what she had said about it. "That tells the story of our spirit stones. When the kids come to camp, we tell them to keep their eyes open for a stone they like and put some kind of recognizable mark on it. On the last night we have a big ceremony, and everybody's rock gets placed in the spirit stone field forever."

Betty sighed and opened the other diary to where it was marked. The handwriting was frenetic. *No time tonight, diary. Sammy giggled today!!! Tiger keeps asking when is she going to get hair. All the lumber for the new lodge arrived. Stone is coming in too. Tiger and I have put everything we've got into this camp. Pray for us diary, we're so blessed to have this magical place, but we have to do something good for the earth with it. A thousand years from now I want it to be just exactly as it is today, and I want my spirit to be just as much a part of it as one of them big ol' moss-covered boulders looking down on the camp.*

TIGER FINISHED SHOWING TWO boys his proven trout fly pattern he named the Green River Raider when the sudden sound of the wind swooshing through the trees made him look up. The writhing poplars and hemlocks sealed his decision to call in the kids. He radioed Charlie and gave him the go ahead to start rounding everyone up, and the counselor quickly hustled everyone out of the craft hut and hurried them to the lodge.

The camp energy had buoyed Tiger's spirits all day, but alone in the hut, gathering his fly-tying materials, he was having a tough time fighting back the bitter taste of losing Jeb's property to the Ledges. The four weeks would be up in two days, the same day the session ended. He laughed at how ironic it was that, in spite of all the heroic efforts of the conservancies, in the end, the only option left was Liz's idea of buying the lots that overlooked the camp. He'd have to lock them in before he came down like a hammer on the Ledges for any environmental infraction.

While Tiger straightened up the hut, the storm gathered strength. Leaves tore from the trees and flew across the campus as a bus coming from a trip to the Pisgah National Forest came rolling in and kids spilled out. In all the rush to get under cover, no one noticed the Cadillac pull onto the camp entrance road. Campers and staff erupted from the woods and scurried to the lodge while a boy chased after a cap tumbling across the front field.

Patrick ran toward the lodge with his afternoon group. He thought he heard a horn honk. When he realized where it was coming from, he yelled for the kids to hurry up, then ran to the driver's side of the car as rain broke out of the sky.

A scratchy voice came from the window that was opened a crack. "Sonny, I want you to get Tiger over here."

"Ma'am, if you wait a minute, I'll get you an umbrella."

The woman inside glared at him over her glasses. "I have no intention of stepping one foot out of this car. Now, go get him."

Patrick started to leave, then stopped and looked back.

"Go on, git!" Her high-pitched voice had risen to a shriek.

Patrick took the steps to the lodge two at a time and rushed over to his group to make sure they were all there, then looked around for Charlie Morgan. Patrick told him that an older woman in a car demanded to see Tiger, and he quickly radioed him.

"A woman? What was she like?"

"I don't know. I just got it from Patrick. He said she was honking her horn and wouldn't get out of the car."

Tiger scooped the last of the hooks and bobbins into a satchel and started down the path in a trot. His heart thumped in his throat. Bullets of rain pelted him as he raced around a bend and caught sight of Sammy who had heard the message over the radio and was running toward him. They got tangled in each others arms and kept racing toward the lot, jabbering all the while.

"Honey, is that where you went on Wednesday?"

"It's her, Dad! She's in the driveway!"

He stopped and grabbed Sammy by the shoulders. "Are you

thinking what I'm thinking?" The excitement was taking his breath away. "This can't be happening!"

She took the satchel. "Dad, you've got to do this yourself." She watched him head for the lot. "Be nice to her, Dad," she shouted. Her voice trailed away. "She's doing it for my mother."

Sure as hell, it's her, Tiger shouted in his head as he spotted the big cream-colored Cadillac. He was breathless and soaked by the time he reached it. The window, streaming with rain, zipped down barely an inch and he peered inside. Rivulets of water streaked down his face, and he kept blinking his scrunched lids to keep it out of his eyes.

Betty barely glanced in his direction. "Get in."

Tiger pulled off his jacket and tried to squeeze some rain from his hair, but it was futile. Once inside he wiped himself as much as he could.

"Stop that!" she shouted in a shrill voice. "You're making it worse."

Tiger was afraid to say a word for fear of upsetting her even more.

She shoved two business cards in his face. "Here's my financial planner at First National and my lawyer. I've told them to make arrangements to release the four million." She turned to face him and lowered her head so she could stare directly at him over her glasses. "I told them to get a lien on *this* place."

Tiger took the business cards. "Betty, I don't know what to say." He looked at his watch and thought out loud. "It's already four and Friday afternoon, and I've only got 'til Sunday."

"Oh hogwash! Tell that old geezer to keep his britches on. The money's as good as in his pocket." She cocked her head to the side and looked him straight in the eye. "If you don't think you can handle it, brother-in-law, I'll go right up there now and tell 'em myself."

Tiger didn't hear her. His mind raced at warp speed. He had to get his lawyer to call Jeb. If he couldn't get hold of him, he'd have Betty's financial planner do it. Hell, if he had to, he'd go to their homes.

His eyes shot over to Betty. "I've got to move fast, but I'm not leaving 'til I give you a kiss."

She flicked her hand. "I'm not doin' this for you. It's for my Susan."

"Just the same, darlin," I'm not goin' without a kiss."

She rolled her eyes, stretched her neck and jutted her cheek toward him. The minute his lips touched her, she shook him off like vermin. "Well, you said you were in a hurry, so git."

CHAPTER TWENTY-FIVE

"**W**HO STOLE MY YELLOW trunks?" someone yelled out.

"Patrick did! He wants to give them to one of his girlfriends!"

A pillow went sailing across the room.

"All right, guys, get your clothes off the line and start collecting all your stuff. You need to be packed before we go to the Upper Council Ceremony." Patrick caught a kid running past him and pointed to a pair of shoes. The kid grabbed them, tossed them in his locker and kept running. "And be sure you've got your spirit stones… and everybody dress warm."

Alvin pulled the sweatshirt over his head and slipped in his arms. He checked to make sure the paint on his stone was dry. Good. He ran a finger across the spider Dana had helped him paint on it that afternoon and smiled thinking about the Pi symbol Tucker put on his. Dana's had four flowers. One with three petals, then five, eight and thirteen.

"Okay, guys. Listen up," shouted Patrick. "Once we go into the woods, you're to be still. After the council fire, we're going to file over to the lake and float our candles in silence. This is the last session for a lot of the kids who have been coming here every summer since they were your age, and it's real emotional for them, and we've got to respect that. I'll tap you on the back when it's time to go, and you're to keep silent until we reach the cabin. Get it?"

They shouted back, "Got it!"

"Good."

They trickled out of the cabin with Patrick checking to make sure everyone had their stone, and fell in behind another group silently making their way to the back field. Except for Alvin, this was the first upper council ceremony for all the kids in Hemlock Hut Two. Once settled on a bench at the fire pit, Alvin put his hand on his stone and figured he'd never forget the past four weeks as long as he lived. He wondered if some day he would come back with his kids and find his stones.

A whispered chant of, *the earth, the air, the fire, the water… return, return, return, return,* floated on the air along with the sound of a soulful flute coming from the woods. He stood up with his row and filed into the dark woods for the gentle climb up the wooded hillside. He fanned the smoke of the smoldering sage held by a counselor at the beginning of the field of stones, before finding a place to sit. Tiger Morrison rose and solemnly announced, "Let the council fire begin."

The reading of the Woodcraft Laws and Chief Seattle's letter had a deeper meaning for Alvin this time, especially Tiger's message about all things being connected. One by one, kids shuffled by the crackling fire and placed their stones around it as a soulful chant reminiscent of a Greek chorus came from out of the darkness.

Tiger stood behind the fire and said, "All these stones will be moved to the spirit stone field before we close the camp for the season. You have given your spirit and energy to them and no matter where you go, you'll always know they're here on this mountain."

He clapped his hands and rubbed them vigorously. "Now, let's all have some fun!"

While members of the camp band assembled at the fire, Alvin looked around until he spotted Tucker a couple of rows above him. Dana sat with her cabin and waved at him. Charlie Morgan brought out his five-foot-long bamboo flute called a didgeridoo, and explained it was used by Australian Aboriginals for their sacred rites and ceremonies. He blew in it and created a deep resonant drone. Next, Patrick demonstrated his Native American flute.

Alvin remembered when Patrick sat on his cot practicing one

afternoon, he told him that Native Americans believed the sound of the flute had a healing effect and carried the player's spirit. It sounded eerily sweet to him now, instantly bringing to mind Kokopelli, the hunchbacked flute player that was on some of his mother's jewelry. Patrick and Charlie played a song together, and the same haunting melody they had heard as they came up the mountain floated over the crowd.

A troupe of musicians made up of campers and counselors joined the circle with their instruments: a mandolin, four guitars, a banjo, fiddle and Patrick with a drum. Shadows cast by the light of the flames danced around their faces as they tuned up.

Someone started strumming on a guitar and Carrie's soothing voice glided into the night... *Daddy won't you take me back to Muhlenberg County... down by the Green River where Paradise lay...* A murmur of camper voices joined in, and the low, wistful, yearning tune flowed from the crowd. *Well, I'm sorry my son... you're too late in askin'... Mr. Peabody's coal train has hauled it away.*

Everyone joined in on a few mountain folksongs, then Tiger came back to the circle and announced that Bob Davies... who everyone knew was Ortman but pretended they didn't... was going to tell them one of his stories. The echo of wild cheers bounced around the woods as he made his way to the fire.

In the well-worn tradition of tales woven around a campfire, Bob told the rapt audience that this one took place a long, long time ago when he was a counselor at a camp in the deep, deep woods of Maine. He flew into a monologue that mingled fact with the kind of fiction that took everyone's imagination on a joyride. A master of the ridiculously absurd, continuous waves of laughter rolled through the crowd that had been set up for an hilarious adventure the minute he leapt in front of the campfire. The outrageous tale, featuring a hideous giant, talking rat that lived in his cabin, was illustrated with exaggerated body language and wild facial expressions bizarrely lit by the fire. And in spite of the story's insane premise, it ended with a gently delivered morality lesson that satisfied the crowd.

The sound of the didgeridoo and flute again drifted from the now pitch-black woods, setting the mood for the final phase of the ceremony. Tiger reappeared at the fireside. "We're all going to go quietly to the lake where someone will give you a piece of wood with a lit candle on it. Each of you will float your candle out onto the lake."

A song with Native American spiritual overtones sounded from the woods and blended with the flute. Everyone rose and followed the flashlight beams dancing along the path. No one made a sound as the tramping of feet and the haunting melody filled the night air.

A cluster formed around the counselors handing out the candles. After getting his, Alvin found Tucker and they joined the crowd circling the lake. They slid down on the grass and put their candles in the water, giving them a slight shove. Music coming from across the lake drifted over the water along with Carrie's lilting voice. Other than an occasional croak from a frog, no one said anything. They just listened and watched their candles float in random clusters with the gently writhing flames reflecting on the rippling water.

Alvin looked around. All he could recognize in the darkness was an endless stretch of bare legs being hugged by kids in a trance-like state as they watched the candles slowly start to melt.

Tucker leaned toward Alvin and whispered, "I love this place."

"Are you gonna come back next year?"

"You bet."

The song they ended every evening with came from across the lake, and everyone started to rise. The shadowy forms became an unbroken circle as kids put their arms around each other's shoulders and swayed side to side, softly murmuring, *Sisters, brothers, let me tell you how I am feeling...*, and Alvin knew at that moment that he and Tucker would be friends for life.

TIGER STOOD ON THE HILLSIDE watching the kids sway. He listened to them sing, and thanked God for all the good that had befallen him. He thought about the foreboding in his gut at the start of the season, and an avalanche of emotions flooded over him. When he had looked out at the kids at the council fire his eyes kept landing on Alvin and Tucker. He had to hold back tears of gratitude that nothing had happened to them. Yet he knew it was the kind of close call that would haunt him for years.

He still couldn't believe he was closing on Jeb's land next week.

He smiled to himself remembering what Betty had said to Sammy when she told her about marrying Patrick. He could almost hear her high-pitched voice. "You tell your father that I intend to go crazy on this wedding and I've got plenty of justification in doin' it."

He thought about Katie and how Sammy and Linda were urging him to hurry up and make up with her, even going so far as warning him someone else might steal her away. The events of the summer had proven to him that he didn't know much about women, but he did know he wasn't going to lose her. She had trembled like a frightened fawn when she stood next to him at the barbeque. No. She was his. She was just afraid to believe it could happen. *Katie, what did I do to you?*

SATURDAY WAS HECTIC ONCE the kids left, with everyone working feverishly all afternoon to close the camp for the season. They'd had the session wrap-up right after lunch, and a lot of the counselors and mentors had already left, with some catching planes early in the morning. Tiger chatted for a while with a counselor who had hung back to talk about being a mentor the following year, but he kept an eye on Sammy who was saying goodbye to Patrick. He had a four-hour drive to Raleigh ahead of him and should shove off before it got too late.

Dinner was a relaxed affair, mostly thrown together by Katie and Euva from things left in the pantry and cooler while they closed down the kitchen for the season. Sammy sat across from him and looked as tired as he imagined he did. "Well, kitten, we made it through another year."

Sammy reached for the last roll on the platter. "You want this, Dad?"

"No, honey. You eat it." He watched her scoop the last of the green beans onto her plate and dig in. "I guess this is the last summer it'll be *just you and me, kid.*"

She threw him a big grin. "That reminds me, Dad, I'm going on a hike tomorrow with the Carolina Mountain Club."

"Do you think that's a good idea, honey?" He measured his words. "There's a really bad dude out there and I don't think you should go hiking until he's caught."

"*Oh, Dad*. He's not going to stick around here. Besides, we can't all go and hide. There'll be at least twenty members from the club, and we're all going to stick together... and Katie's coming."

"Katie?"

"Un-huh. When I told her about the hike, I got the same reaction, and the next thing I knew she said she would meet me at the Mt. Pisgah trailhead at eight. She's got a real thing for personal security."

"Be sure to take Skippy along."

Sammy put down her fork. "Dad, are you going to say something to Katie before she leaves?"

He started clearing the table.

She reached over and grasped his arm. "Dad, her kids feel bad about all this. Especially Lisa. She thinks it's her fault."

"Aw, how can it be her fault? I hope you told her everything's going to be fine."

"I did." She fidgeted with her fork. "Jason and Lisa are really nice kids, Dad. I kinda like the idea of them being close to you... and Katie, too. Once Patrick and I get married in the spring, I won't be around that much... you know what I mean. Dad, Katie's so right for you it makes me cry to think about it."

"Honey, don't worry. It's all going to work out. Her brother says the divorce is on schedule for mid-September, and then..." He gave her a devilish grin. "*...you just watch your dad swing into action.*"

Sammy shook her head with a scoffing expression on her face. "Really, Dad. Ever since you got that land of Jeb's, you've been full of yourself."

He reached over and took both her hands in his. "It's made me happy, honey. I don't know how to thank you."

"Well, you can start by going into that kitchen and giving Katie a decent goodbye. She's probably getting ready to leave."

He stood up and picked up his plate. "That's just what I was planning on doing."

"I'll get that, Dad. You get in there."

Tiger took a deep breath and pushed open the door to the kitchen. He didn't see Katie, just Euva alternating glances between him and the plates she was stacking.

"You sure did take your sweet time comin' in here," she said.

208

"Where's Katie?"

"Where do you think? She's gone home. Expect her to wait all night?"

He stood motionless; disappointment rolled over him. Euva put the last of the dishes away, then picked up a dishtowel and began wiping pots left on the sink to dry. Tiger pitched in, hanging them on the rack, all the while listening to Euva.

"You got to be patient with Katie, Tiger. That clan of hers are proud folk. She got it bred into her since she was a kid." She turned, slowly wiping a lid with a towel and gazing off in the distance. "You should have seen her when she was a lil'un. You never seen such a prideful dancer. She would clog on tabletops when she weren't but four or five and get everyone clappin' and hollerin' with her lookin' so pleased. She's always been like that... tryin' hard, doin' good... and proud of it."

She handed Tiger the last of the pots and shook her head. "She's had to swallow a heap of pride over the years. First that business with you that her mother stirred up, then all those years with that no 'count husband of hers. She put a good face on it, but everyone knew what was goin' on."

Euva went around the kitchen wiping all the counters dry, then collected the dishcloths and picked up her purse. "I'll drop these off at the laundry and be on my way."

She looked back at him from the rear doorway. "You comin'?"

"Not yet. I'll look after the dining hall."

Josh and one of his helpers finished stacking the tables as Tiger gathered up a few things left behind... two caps, a fanny pack with nothing inside but some rocks. On the way downstairs to the lost and found, he stopped and looked out on the tranquil lake.

He realized, with all her talk about Katie's pride, Euva had been sending him a message to make the next move. He decided to trust her instincts and give Katie a call tomorrow after the hike. They had a couple of weeks to work things out, and once she got her divorce, it wouldn't take long to throw together a wedding. All they really needed was each other. He had picked out the perfect spot for the honeymoon, and knew Katie would think so, too. There was no better place on the face of the earth than Camp Green River.

CHAPTER TWENTY-SIX

The Mt. Pisgah Trail had been packed for the past four days, and that was just the way Gary Skinner liked it. The more hikers, the less you get noticed. He was just as careful when he went to the ATMs—always after dark, yet when people were still on the street. He knew police officers were by nature inquisitive, and if they saw anything that stuck out, they'd ask themselves *why*, just like the nosey cop who made him move his van out of the farmer's woods.

Before he left the trailer three days ago, he switched to his Florida plate just in case that cop put his Georgia license on some sort of alert. This meant he had to be careful with his driving. If he got pulled over and couldn't produce a Florida registration, he'd be in trouble.

That girl with the blond hair and the black Lab better show up, he thought. She looked like she had plenty of credit cards and would give up her pin number the minute she laid eyes on the baton. Just in case, I'll keep my eyes open. Something better might come along.

The group the girl hiked with had said they were trekking to Fryingpan Mountain from the Mt. Pisgah Trail. He had done the three-mile round trip every day, once with a twenty-pound backpack, and found several intersections where smaller trails led to old logging roads. He'd hiked them all and knew them like the back of his hand. The campsite was ready, too, off the dirt road in Cherokee County. Only this time, he found a better spot deeper in the woods where the farmer couldn't see him.

KATIE PULLED INTO THE PARKING lot at milepost 407.6 and spotted Sammy strapping on her backpack. She was on the fringe of a large group preparing for the hike with Skippy on a leash at her side. Katie nosed her car into a spot and grabbed her mini backpack. All she needed were a couple bottles of water, her wallet and some trail mix.

Sammy looked up, and Katie could tell by her smile that she was genuinely happy to see her. At first, when she overheard Sammy telling Euva she was going on the hike, she was reluctant to speak up. Sammy might be on her father's side and resent her, but there was no way she was going to let her go on any trail without someone who would look after her like their own. There was a real dangerous guy out there. Anyone who would hack off an old woman's head was capable of anything.

Making her way to Sammy, she ran into a couple of people in the club she had hiked with before and threw them a wave. "I've never been up the Fryingpan Lookout Tower," she told Sammy. "Someone said they put it on the National Register of Historic Places. I'm looking forward to it."

"So am I."

Sammy's cell phone rang and she pulled it out of her pocket and flipped it open. A broad grin appeared as she looked up at Katie and mouthed. "It's Patrick."

Katie crouched down and ruffled Skippy's fur while Sammy talked on the phone.

"You're kidding! Not 'til Thursday? …What do you mean, just get in my car and come over? I'm standing in the Mt. Pisgah parking lot ready to go on a hike." She seemed to melt as she listened. "Honey, I'd have to run over to my apartment and get some decent clothes and then head back to camp with Skippy… and that's after I talk my dad into letting me have the time off."

Katie stood up and waved furiously. Sammy told Patrick to hold on for a moment.

"Go," said Katie. "You guys haven't had a minute alone. I'll take Skippy back after the hike. Just call your dad and *tell* him you're going."

"Did you hear that?" Sammy said over the phone. "I'll call you right back."

Sammy reached her father on the second ring. "Dad, Patrick just called. He was all messed up with his schedule. He doesn't have to be in Goldsboro 'til Friday and wants me to come to Raleigh. Katie's here and she'll bring Skippy back after the hike. Please can I have the week off?" She scrunched up her face and crossed her fingers. "Thanks a bunch, Dad." She listened a while then pointed to the phone and mouthed *I don't believe him* to Katie. "Dad, we're both sensible people. You have nothing to worry about." She hung up and shook her head. "He still thinks I'm a kid."

After she told Patrick the good news, Katie walked with her to her car.

"I'm sorry I'm leaving you in the lurch," said Sammy. She gave Katie a dish and some food for Skippy, then tossed her things in the Jeep.

"Don't even think about it. I need some time alone. This hike will do me good."

Sammy grasped her hand. "Katie, Euva told me all about what went on with you and my dad way back and how it kind of shamed you. But, believe me, my dad would never hurt anyone. When I think about how he waited all those years for Liz to marry him, and the way she threw him out because he wouldn't sell the camp to the Ledges… *and after all that, his actually giving her a memento ring, I can't…*"

Katie looked confused. "He asked her to marry him?"

"A hundred times. But she hates the camp. She only came once in the whole time he went with her." Sammy stared at Katie for a moment before slowly shaking her head. "How could you think my dad would ever string anyone along? He hasn't got a devious bone in his body. He was like a kid when he told me you two were getting married." Sammy got in the Jeep. "Give him a chance, Katie. My father loves you… but when it comes to women… he doesn't have a clue." She noticed everyone starting up the trail. "You better get going," she yelled as she pulled out. "And stick close."

Katie hurried in a daze to catch up. She had judged Tiger from the same warped perspective as she had been judged years back. The worst part was she did it to soothe her hurt pride.

The group hadn't gone far when they turned left and started the climb. The column moved fast, evidence that this was an experienced bunch of hikers. With the extra time they'd need to enjoy the view of Cold Mountain only five miles from the tower, she figured it would be way past noon by the time they returned.

She fought a nagging urge to turn around and go back to the camp, but she hadn't beaten herself up enough. Tiger wanted to love her, and what did she do? Slapped him in the face with everything she had. But his giving Liz a ring had driven her half crazy. Was hurt pride and shame the same thing? She had buried it inside her when Tiger didn't ask her to marry him, and let it grow through all the bad years with Hal... pretending everything was all right when everyone knew it wasn't. Tiger's right. It was time she put all those things behind her.

She was suddenly torn between finishing the hike and turning around and driving straight to the camp. She needed to sit down for a few minutes and clear her head. She took out the dish and poured Skippy some water. Preoccupied with her thoughts, the yellow Lab startled her when it ran up to Skippy and started sniffing. She only half listened to the chatty old man following behind the dog, but managed a few responses so as not to be impolite as she weighed going back down.

She couldn't wait another minute to put her arms around Tiger and tell him she wanted to spend the rest of her life with him. She tossed out the water left in the dish and started down with the man at her side. His incessant conversation about Vietnam demanded she respond every once in a while, but mostly she kept her mind on what she was going to say to Tiger.

It was a relief when they got to a single-lane section and he fell behind her. She tried to speed up a bit hoping to lose him, but that didn't work, so she kept at a steady pace. Two men with heavy backpacks passed them going up the trail, but no one else. Everyone must be taking the shortcut to the tower off the Forest Service road that was half the distance.

A sudden bolt of horror pierced her brain as a strong, muscular arm grabbed her around the neck and a hand covered her mouth.

"Don't fight me, girly. I'm an ex-Marine and I can break your neck with one slam."

He forced her onto what looked like a side trail, and she instantly realized the old man was the monster everyone was looking for! It wasn't possible this was happening to her! She was always so careful! All her training told her she had to get away before he took her anywhere.

He threw her against a tree, brandished a knife and came near. "All I want is your bank cards and your pin numbers and I'm gonna let you go. Now hand them over."

As soon as he got close enough, she grabbed the knife by the blade, wrung it out of his hand and ran toward the trail. Suddenly, she was on the ground, being socked with his fist. She fought for her life. She blindly grabbed a rock and smashed it against his head, then sprang up. He grabbed her by the leg. She kicked him loose and sprinted a few steps before he tackled her again. He was on top of her, hitting her with a baton. She grabbed it with both hands. They fought over it hand-to-hand until they suddenly went rolling downward through the thicket and spiraled ten feet over a granite outcrop, slamming onto a table rock below.

She realized she'd been out for a while when she woke with her hands bound behind a tree and duct tape across her mouth. Looking around, she could see he'd taken her deep off the trail. Skippy, who was tied to a tree, looked at her with a furrowed brow. She knew her left arm was broken somewhere below the elbow and could feel two fingers were swollen twice their size. From the way her right hand throbbed, she must have gotten a deep gash between her thumb and finger when she grabbed the knife. Her head ached clear down to her toes.

The man appeared from out of the woods. "You've already caused me a lot of trouble," he said. "I had to go back and get your shoe and my baton, but I couldn't find the knife. Once your opponent gets their hands on your weapon, you've lost control of it. I should never have let that happen."

He bent down and put her shoe back on. "We've got to get going and I don't want any funny stuff." He showed her a nylon cord with a slip knot. "After I cut you loose, I'm going to put this around your neck and take off the tape, and if you make one sound, I'm going to strangle you with it. This cord tests three hundred pounds and you'll be dead in less than a minute."

She could feel her hands come free, and then his hand around her wrist. She wrung it loose and bolted. He came after her and slammed her on the back of the head with the baton, dropping her to the ground. He lifted her onto her feet and a feeling of nausea overcame her, and she slumped back down. He stood her up again and came almost close enough for her to smell the foul breath coming from a mouthful of rotten teeth. Dull gray eyes floated out from dark caverns surrounded by a gaunt, sallow face, belying the military cadence he tried to infuse in his voice. Even his hair was cut short like a Marine's.

"Don't fight me. I've got all your cards, Katie, and all I need now is your pin numbers and I'll let you go."

He suddenly froze. Some hikers were walking on a trail above them. He slammed her to the ground and crouched low. A soft plaintive cry came from Skippy. He lunged toward the dog, lifted the baton and smacked it down on his head. He did it again. Katie shot up and started to run, but he caught her and cracked her across the jaw with the baton, bringing her to her knees in pain.

Her mind raced. She had to survive! This wasn't working! She had to make him think she didn't have the strength to fight any more. She had to appear beaten, docile, and catch him off guard.

With the noose now secured tightly around her neck, he ripped off the tape and sat down on a large rock. He gave the cord some slack, but she didn't risk trying to run. The thought of the now-distant hikers brought tears streaking down her face. He pulled a small notebook from a backpack she hadn't seen him wearing on the trail and must have had hidden somewhere. He produced her bank card and two credit cards.

He retrieved a ballpoint pen from his bag. "Let's start with the bank card." Slowly flexing the fingers on his right hand, he said, "You gave me a hard time up there. I broke a few bones socking you." He opened the notebook. "What's the pin?"

What should I do? Katie screamed in her head. I've got to think

215

fast! That's it! Moan. She watched as he dug in his backpack for a bottle of aspirins and water. She had to save herself! Hal could never take care of the kids!

"Here take these," he said as he shoved two in her mouth and let her drink some water.

She'd told the kids not to expect her back until around four. No one would start worrying about her until then. She had to stall him as long as possible. "I can't think. My head is killing me."

He raised the baton. "It'll be killing you more, if you don't give me that pin right now."

Her brain was starting to lock. Should she give him the correct pin? He could only withdraw three hundred dollars in one 24-hour span. If she could convince him that no one expected her, she could tell him they could get another three hundred dollars on Monday. Jason knew where she had hidden her list of passwords. If she didn't come home, he'd be worried enough to check to see if there were any ATM withdrawals from any of her accounts. But even if they knew she'd been abducted, how were they going to find her? The only way she was going to get out of this alive was to stall long enough to escape. He raised the baton and she blurted out the wrong number, "LJ8384."

"That's better," he said as he wrote it down. He held her Master-Card in the air. "Now, how about this?"

She'd never used it to get money and didn't even know if she had a pin number, but if she did, it would be the same. Thank God she gave him the wrong pin. If he could get another three hundred today, it just might be enough, and he'd kill her.

"It's the same."

He showed her another one. "And this?"

"The same."

After witnessing the brutal way he killed Skippy, she was convinced he wasn't going to voluntarily let her go... now or ever. She had to keep stalling and eke out every possible minute until she could escape. She could feel her swollen face. Good. If anyone saw her they'd know she'd been beaten.

His manner was insidious. "I'm gonna let you go once I'm sure you gave me the right pin. We're gonna wait until dusk, before we take a ride to a couple of banks. Once I get the money, I'm gonna drop you off where someone will find you in the morning. By then, I'll be out of state. But right now, we're gonna trek deep into the brush in case all that screaming you did a while back got the law on us. Remember, if you make any noise it's gonna be curtains. You saw how fast I quieted that dog down."

He took the rope off Skippy's neck and covered him with debris, then put on his backpack and started through the forest pulling her along. "How's it you got someone else's dog?"

The question sent shock waves through her. He must have been stalking Sammy. She had to think of something fast. "It belongs to a girl I work with. She's on her way to Raleigh and I told her I'd take care of him until she comes back next week."

"You work at the camp, too?"

"Yes. But yesterday was the last day."

"Who were those kids in your wallet?"

"My niece and nephew." Thank God, she wasn't wearing her wedding bands any more. "I'm not married." She stumbled over a fallen limb and screamed from the pain shooting through her broken arm. He jerked the noose so tight she couldn't breathe.

"Damn you, bitch! You get the law down on me and I'll kill you!"

They trekked for what seemed like hours. Finally he stopped and she fell to her knees crying, "Please, I need something for my head."

He shoved four more aspirins in her mouth and let her drink down the whole bottle of water. He made her sit down against a tree and zip tied her hands behind it.

"My arm. You're hurting it," she moaned.

He covered her mouth with tape again and tied his dog to the same tree. The man disappeared into the woods, and the animal curled up against her. The image of Skippy being beaten with the baton was the last thing that flashed across her consciousness.

It had grown dusky by the time she awoke and found he had returned. Her whole body throbbed in pain, and she was pretty sure her jaw was cracked. She could tell both of her eyes were black, and could hardly see out of one of them. By now, her kids had to be calling around looking for her. He had said he couldn't find his knife. Hopefully someone had found it and given it to a park ranger.

She noticed him fumbling around in his backpack with his back to her. She stopped breathing. Was he looking for another knife? No, she told herself. Nothing's going to happen to me until he gets his money. She wondered if while she was asleep he had gone into town to get some money from an ATM and discovered the pin didn't work.

He put his backpack on and slipped the noose around her neck again. "I checked out the trail and everything is all set," he said, giving off a cynical little laugh. "Even walked and talked with a ranger for a while." He cut her hands loose from the zip tie and yanked on the noose. "Okay. We're leaving. But first I want you to go to the bathroom. I don't want you messing up my van."

She peeled off the tape and tried to stand, but almost fell over. He grabbed her and looked like he was going to slap her again. He appeared to change his mind and leaned her up against the tree instead. "Katie, I'm not going to hurt you again if you promise not to fight me. Now do as I say and take a goddammed pee!"

She could only use her right arm with its cut up hand, but managed to get her shorts down and go to the bathroom. While his back was turned, he handed her some paper to wipe herself, then dug a hole with his heel and told her to throw it in before covering it over.

It took a while to hike to the parking lot. They peered out from the woods and could see there were only a couple of cars with no one around. He grabbed the cord next to the noose and pulled it tight. "Okay, girly, we're going to get in my van nice and quiet. If you make one peep, you're dead."

"I don't want to go in the van."

He grabbed up the noose until she choked. "Shut up, bitch!"

They went swiftly to the van that he had backed up to the trail. He got her inside and told her to lie down. A chain was padlocked to the passenger seat mounting. He wrapped it tightly around her neck and padlocked it so she couldn't raise her head more than four or five inches.

"We're going to Greenville," he said as he started to drive. "I asked a couple of folks on the trail where I could find your bank, and they obligingly told me they were scattered all over the western part of the state. South Carolina, too."

The van hit a bump, and Katie moaned in pain. She expected

another punch, but he was preoccupied with getting on the parkway, giving her a chance to think. She was pretty sure she had told him the nines in her pin were eights. The LJ stood for Lisa and Jason, born in '93 and '94.

She could see that it was starting to get dark through a small space above the nape of his neck. She had to keep her head. This monster was pretty cagey, but he seemed blinded by desperation for money. She knew if she were convincing enough, he'd keep her alive until he got it.

Tiger looked at his watch again. Eight-thirty. It was getting late for Katie to be bringing Skippy back. He'd been pacing the porch since five, hoping to see her Subaru pull in. Something wasn't right. He picked up the phone and dialed.

"Hello, Jason. It's me. Tiger. How are you doing?"

"Me and Lisa are real worried. My mom's not home yet."

"Has she phoned?"

"No. We called our gramma around six, and she told us not to worry. She said Mom probably called the house a couple of times when we weren't home. But, that doesn't make sense. She could have reached Lisa on her cell phone."

"When did she say she'd be there?"

"She didn't give us an exact time, but said she was going to make us a great dinner, and it's past eight."

"Has she ever come home late like this before?"

"Never. This isn't like her. She always checks up on us and leaves notes and phone numbers all over the place. Is Sammy home yet?"

"No... she's... not home, Jason. Where's Lisa?"

"In the kitchen making us sandwiches."

"Okay. I want the two of you to stay where you are while I look into this. Take down my cell phone number and call me the minute you hear from your mother."

Tiger pushed horrible thoughts out of his brain as he dialed Sammy's cell. Come on, baby. Get on the phone. Darn! She promised me she wouldn't go any...

"Hi, Daddy! I was just about to call you. I've arrived safe and sound."

"Honey, I'm worried about Katie. She's not home yet."

"That's funny. Yesterday she told Euva she was going to make the kids a big dinner tonight."

"Where did you see her last?"

"In the parking lot around eight-thirty this morning. Didn't she bring Skippy back?"

"No. I've been expecting her all evening." He remembered hoping she would get there after she fed the kids so they could talk.

Her next words rocked him. "You know, Dad, I was thinking about something on the drive over here. I meant to tell her about this odd old guy I ran into the last time I went hiking."

He felt his pulse accelerating. "What was so odd about him?"

"Well… he was creepy. He had a yellow Lab and kept hanging on to me. It made me uncomfortable."

"Do you remember what he looked like?"

"Oh, yeah."

"Honey… I hate to ask…"

"Don't worry, Dad. We're on our way."

"Honey. Hopefully this is a false alarm and she's going to call me any minute and tell me she's home. If I hear from her, I'll call you right away." He started to hang up, then hesitated, almost unwilling to face what he was thinking. "Wait! Are you still there?"

"Yes, Daddy."

"Maybe you should call that friend of yours who trains rescue searchers… just in case."

"I already thought of that."

Tiger had every possible number he would need in a camp emergency stored in his cell phone. His mind began spinning out of control. First, he called Euva. She agreed with him. Katie would never leave the kids like this. He asked her to check all the hospitals in the area, then to call Katie's mom and get her over to the kids. Next, he dialed the Transylvania County Sheriff.

"First off," said the sheriff, "we'll see if her car's in the parking lot."

Tiger gave him Katie's name and address so he could run her plate, then Sammy's cell so she could tell him exactly where they met on the parkway.

"You say she had a dog with her?"

220

"Yes. A black Lab."

"Does it have a micro-chip?"

"Yes!"

"All right. I'll give your daughter a call and get a description of the guy on the trail, and then get this thing rolling."

CHAPTER TWENTY-SEVEN

Matt Stevenson took the turns along the Blue Ridge Parkway, hoping to give his two teenage daughters in the back and his wife, Sara, a good look at Asheville lit up at night. This was the last day of their vacation and tomorrow they had to head back to Wilmington.

"Daddy, do you think the pool at the hotel is still open?"

"I don't know. It's almost nine." He approached the Mt. Pisgah turnoff and hollered, "You guys want to get one last look at the mountains? I can pull in here if you do."

"No, Dad! We want to take a swim!"

Sara reached over and squeezed his hand. She didn't need to say anything. The touch said it all. The girls had had enough of the mountains, and she knew his heart was going to break tomorrow as he drove away with the monoliths to his back. At least he had his two weeks.

They came out of a tunnel and started down a steep incline before the road turned and began to level off. To the right, he got a glimpse of what had to be Tryon all lit up for the early evening. He saw something from the corner of his eye when he glanced over, and it nagged him as he kept on driving. It was on the edge of the road. He racked his brain, but couldn't get a clear picture of what it was. It had to have been in his peripheral vision. It was as if something were reaching out. A sad, plaintive motion.

He saw an overlook ahead and pulled onto it.

"Dad! What are you doing! We want to go back to the hotel!"

He rolled the car to the exit and was about to turn and go back.

"Girls, I saw something, and I want to check it out."

"Aw... gee, Dad. We're gonna miss our swimming."

"Okay. I'll take you girls to the hotel first and then come back."

He felt his daughter's knees pressing the back of his seat and pictured her all slumped down. "Oh, forget it, Dad. *Go on back!*"

"Why do we always gotta *check things out?*" moaned the other one.

Sara touched his shoulder. "Go on, take a look, honey." She turned to the girls. "You kids know your dad. He won't rest tonight until he figures out what he saw. It's only going to take a minute." She looked over at him. "What do you think it was?"

"I didn't get a good look, but I know it was black."

"It could have been a bear, Dad." The daughter pounded a fist on the seat. "Great! I can see the headlines now: *County Commissioner mauled in the mountains!*"

"Oh, no. You got that wrong. More like *County Commissioner's daughter mauled in the mountains!*"

"Ha. Ha. Big whoop, Dad. Nobody's getting me out of this car."

Matt swung onto the parkway. He remembered it was just after the tunnel where he had a good view to the right. No one was coming from either direction so he slowed down and crawled along with one eye on the road and the other on the strip of ground that dropped off across the lane. There was nothing unusual. He moved on and drove until he reached the Mt. Pisgah turnoff and turned around.

They came back out of the tunnel and he carefully scanned the side of the road as he slowly drove by, but there was nothing.

"Daddy! Stop!" shouted the daughter who was sitting on the right side. "There's something there, Dad. I think it's a baby bear. He reached his paw up like he was hurt."

Matt found a strip where he could pull off, then put on his emergency blinkers and reached into the glove box for a flashlight. "I'll be right back."

The cool air mingling with the sweet scent of mountain laurel hit him the minute he got out of the car. Thankfully, he didn't see any traffic as he walked along, flashing the light in the ditch. He let the beam travel up a distance, stopping at a shiny black mound. He approached it cautiously to get a closer look. A dog lay there, staring silently, its head soaked in blood. He ran the light over him. Strange. No other injuries. Must have just been hit in the head by a car. He ran back and asked Sara to press the key to open the trunk, and come and help. He spread an old blanket he had in the trunk, then she held the flashlight as he got the dog and put him in.

"Good going, baby," said Matt to his daughter as he looked in the rearview mirror and pulled back on the road. "We'll phone 911 when we get to the overlook."

Once he got in the parking lot and popped open the trunk, the girls jumped out with their mother to look after the dog while he made the call.

"What marker are you at?" the 911 operator asked.

"We're at the first overlook north of the Mt. Pisgah turn off."

"We already have a trooper up there. We'll have him meet you shortly."

While they waited, the girls tried to give the dog some water, but it didn't seem to have the strength to lift its head. Matt put him on the grass and slowly trickled water over his mouth with the dog licking it in. After a brief examination, Matt found nothing else wrong.

A black, unmarked pick-up pulled into the lot. The door opened and the sound of a dispatcher's voice trailed from within as the Trooper got out and put on his hat. He came over and crouched down by the dog, then ran his flashlight over it. "Looks like someone whacked him over the head a couple of times."

A cry of ...*aw*... rose from the two girls.

AFTER THE OFFICER JOTTED DOWN Matt Stevenson's statement, he called the dispatcher. When he ID'd the car in the Mt. Pisgah parking lot, the dispatcher had asked about a black Lab. He was pretty sure this was the dog. He put up a flare at the spot the dog was found, thanked Matt and his family, and saw them pile in the car and head north while he waited to hear from animal control.

A call on his radio surprised him. The dispatcher told him to sit tight and wait to hear from the sheriff—a sure sign something big was coming down. They were sending a forensic team to secure the car and take a look at where the dog was found.

His cell phone rang. "Tell me about the dog," said the sheriff.

"It's a black Lab."

"Is it alive?"

"Yes. But it's taken a couple of hits on the head."

"Is it conscious?

"Yes."

"See if it answers to Skippy."

Another car had pulled in and four passengers who had seen the dog in the glare of the trooper's headlights stood over it. The officer bent down and looked keenly at the dog's eyes and spoke in a natural tone. "Skippy."

"Look!" someone shouted. "His tail's wagging."

The officer spoke into the phone. "Yes, sir. He does."

"I want you to secure the area around where it was found. I'm sending an officer to take it over to the animal shelter so they can have a vet take a look at it and scan for a micro-chip. We need to get a positive ID."

Tiger was pacing when the call came in.

"We found the dog. He's alive," said the sheriff. "He was on the side of the parkway just north of Mt. Pisgah. The vet said he's been hit twice with a blunt instrument, and by the shape his paws are in, he's traveled a long distance on rough terrain. Forensics found a trail of blood going down the embankment and into the woods, so we don't believe we're going to find any evidence of someone dropping him off."

Tiger felt himself teetering. If anyone could do that to Skippy, what were they doing to Katie?

"We've got a search crew with dogs on their way to the trail right now, and we're pulling together a search and rescue team to go into the woods in the morning. We've called in helicopters, too." The Sheriff paused for a moment. "Tiger, what's this woman to you?"

He couldn't find words; just stared ahead, batting back tears.

"I hate to tell you this, but you need to prepare yourself for... what could turn out to be a bad ending. If it's the same guy who got those two women in Rutherford County... he's not gonna let her go."

Tiger snapped out of it and instantly rejected that outcome. "You don't know this woman. She's a tough mountain girl, and if he's got her, believe me, she's doing everything she can to stay alive."

"Good. I'm glad to hear that. As for us, we've pulled out all the stops. We had your daughter go to our barracks in Raleigh before she headed this way. She gave them a good description... down to his eyeballs, and we've got an all points bulletin out on him. She said he had a yellow Lab, and we've got that on the bulletin, too. He told her he was in Vietnam, so we're looking into that.

"We've called in everybody we can get our hands on, including Lt. Sam Williams, the lead detective in the Winslow/Rodman case from the Rutherford County Sheriff's office. He's on his way over here to assist. Right now, we're concentrating on the ATMs, but they're all over the place. We'll be working this case all night with everything we've got. Why don't you come on down to the barracks. Your daughter's on her way." He was silent for a moment. "Tiger, what we need more than anything right now is a description of the vehicle this guy's driving."

The satisfaction that the sheriff had harnessed all the power of the State of North Carolina to find Katie lasted for all of one minute. He knew from the start of the summer that something bad was going to happen. Why in God's name didn't he react the minute Sammy told him they were going on the hike and he got that awful feeling in his gut. He should have insisted on going along just like Katie had, or put his foot down and made them both stay.

From what Sammy had said, it looked like this guy was stalking her. What would have happened if Katie hadn't gone with her? If Sammy were alone, would she have left if Patrick phoned? He had to stop. He could drive himself crazy with all these what ifs.

He remembered the night when Susan died. Moments before the deputies walked in the lodge with Sammy, he had been thinking he and Susan had the world by the tail.

A feeling of helplessness laden with guilt began to overwhelm him. He could still feel Katie tremble as he led her up the hillside at the barbeque. In her wanting him, yet fear of trusting him, she seemed so vulnerable.

He had to get these thoughts out of his head! Half the law officers in the state were out there right now on a mission. He grabbed his keys, jumped in his truck and took off for the barracks.

THE ONE THING DEPUTY OLSEN hated most was pulling night duty. Other than the dispatcher, there were just a couple of officers in the Cherokee barracks getting ready to go on the road. He checked his watch. Time to get moving. He headed over to the vending machine and put in enough quarters to get some gum, then started for the door.

"Hey, Olsen," shouted the dispatcher. "You want to take a look at this before you leave. I just got this APB on my screen. I'll print it off for you."

Olsen moved across the room to the printer, and as he waited for the sheet to come out, unwrapped two sticks of gum, folded them up and stuck them in his mouth. He hadn't had a cigarette in two months, but every time he stepped foot in the barracks he had an uncontrollable urge to light up.

The sheet finally crawled out of the printer. He picked it up and studied the drawing. There was something about the crudely drawn face that looked familiar, but he couldn't put his finger on it. He started to read. *Wanted as a person of interest in the disappearance of Katie Warlick last seen in the Mt. Pisgah parking lot off the Blue Ridge Parkway... approximately sixty years old... approximately six feet tall... thin with military style haircut... claims he's a Vietnam veteran... travels with a yellow Labrador Retriever...*

"Hey! I know this guy!"

ON THE WAY TO BREVARD, Tiger called Katie's house. Jason answered.

"How are you guys doing?" Tiger asked.

"My gramma's here, but she and Lisa are pretty upset. They think that guy who killed those two women has my mom. Two deputies came over and wanted her picture and took her pajamas and stuff out of the hamper. They got her bank statement, credit card bills...

all kinds of things."

Tiger could smell her sweet hair. He could feel her in his arms. But this was no time to fall apart. "Hang in there, Jason, and try to get some rest."

"Tiger… I know my mom's going to come out of this okay. She's had a real hard life… with my dad and all… but she always kept her head… no matter what."

Tiger cringed at Jason's reference to Katie keeping her head. Thank God the only information the police had released about Annie Winslow was that they had found human remains. "That's what I'm counting on, son."

CHAPTER TWENTY-EIGHT

"LISTEN UP, EVERYONE. We're running the video again and I want you to take a good look at this guy." The detective waved a stack of papers in the air. "Gary Michael Skinner is a habitual offender with a rap sheet twenty-seven pages thick. Listen to this career criminal lie, and watch him smile like he doesn't have a care in the world… we gauge this was taken less than a month after he killed the two women in Rutherford County, hacking one of their heads off."

Tiger's eyes shot up to the huge screen mounted near the ceiling and stared at the gaunt, balding man with the grizzled face grinning at the camera. He never remembered feeling genuine hate before in his life, but now it consumed him. He listened to Deputy Olsen question the man on the screen.

The detective kept cutting in. "Listen to him. This drifter is one slick con artist." He stopped the tape when it came to the part where Skinner told Olsen that he had an expandable baton among his belonging. "The baton is his primary weapon. He probably straps it to his lower leg… or if he carries a backpack, he could conceal it in there." The tape started up again. They listened to Skinner tell about his training in Vietnam. The detective froze the screen at the point where he was grinning. "Olsen told me this is how he looked when he knew his rap sheet was being read over the radio. This guy has no feeling of shame or remorse. A genuine sociopath."

Just then, the Sheriff came out of his office and stepped in front of the screen. "We just finished getting a statement from the forest ranger who ran into Skinner this afternoon. He talked to him at length from around four to four-fifteen. Said he didn't have his dog with him, but he had seen him with it on the trail for the past three days. One day he was carrying a twenty-pound backpack. It's possible he stashed it on one of the side trails."

He put his hands on his hips and looked around at all the faces. "Officers, we're grateful to you for coming from all over the state to help with this manhunt. This woman has two children and she probably won't be alive this time tomorrow unless we catch this bastard. Thanks to Deputy Olsen from Cherokee County, we now know his vehicle and license plate. This is a career criminal who will know we'll have alerts set up on all her plastic once she's discovered missing, so he's out there right now looking to cash in. The bank is trying to contact their tech people, and hopefully we'll have her bank card up on alert sometime tonight. He'll keep her alive as long as she doesn't give him her pin and makes him believe he's going to get the money."

The briefing over, the officers scrambled out and Lt. Williams sat down at a desk next to a detective talking on the phone. He overheard the name Olsen, and listened.

"I don't want you sitting on that road. You need to get over to I-40 and watch for him there." He listened. "He's not going to return to a site he's been known to visit. This guy's going to find some place new."

Williams reached over and tapped the detective on the shoulder. When he turned his head, Williams said, "Let him stay there. This Olsen has good instincts. See if you can put him in an unmarked car. We can send someone else to the interchange."

THE VAN HID IN A DARK parking lot down the street from a Bank of America on the outskirts of Greenville. Katie lay on the floor throbbing in pain with the yellow Lab curled up next to her, the only compassion she'd been shown all day. This was the third ATM Skinner was attempting to get money from and he was taking his frustration out on her.

The door creaked open and she stopped breathing. "Did you get some?" she asked, trying to sound enthused.

"You lying bitch!" He turned around and punched her with his fist.

She let out a moan and managed to eke out, "Go back and try JL instead of LJ!"

"Goddamn you! I did that already!"

She had to be more convincing! "Okay! Okay! I'm just so scared I can't think! I've got the money. I just put my paycheck in yesterday. Go back and try 3848 instead of 8384."

"We've got to find another place. The machine won't let me run the card anymore."

"Maybe it's because we're out of state and it's not my bank. Why did you have to drive all the way to South Carolina?"

"I don't trust the law after the way you screamed on the trail."

She had to make him think he had plenty of time. "Didn't you say you talked with the forest ranger?"

"Yeah… but some nosey bitch might have heard you and gone home and thought about it some and called the cops. In my line of work, you can't be too careful."

"Did you try my MasterCard?"

"Yeah… got 'invalid' again."

"I can't understand why this is happening. Maybe you should go to Asheville where there's all kinds of banks."

"Okay. That's what we're gonna to do. And, dolly, you better pray one of your cards work, or I'm going to beat you so bad you're gonna *wanna* die."

His words chilled her. He was starting to talk as if her death was inevitable. Both of the women were found in the woods. If she didn't escape, that's where she was going to end up. "I've got over a thousand dollars in my checking account. If you wait til tomorrow, we can pull up to a drive-in teller, ask for a bank check and draw it out."

"Shit, no! I've got to have the money tonight!"

He pulled out of the lot and got onto Route 25 headed towards Asheville. As he waited at a light in Hendersonville, two police cars raced past on Route 64.

"Are you sure no one's expecting you? A date or somethin' like that?" he asked.

"My brother might phone, but he'll just leave a message on my answering machine."

The van made its way up Route 25. A police car sped toward them in the opposite lane. Skinner swung over to the right next to a truck waiting to make a left-hand turn.

"I don't like the looks of these goddamned cops all over the place," he said as he turned onto a side street. "Somethin's comin' down." He wove along back streets until the only way to cross Route 26 was to get back on 25. He drove a few blocks on the busy street packed with fast food joints and shopping centers. "There's a bank up ahead," he said. "This is going to be your last chance, dolly. This time you better come up with the right pin."

He turned onto a dark side street and pulled up to a curb next to a vacant lot. She could see him putting his jacket hood over his head. He waited awhile, then the door groaned open and he disappeared. Minutes stretched forever. She couldn't believe that she was able to convince him she was trying to come up with the pin; but how long could she keep this up? Suddenly the door opened and she tightened her muscles for another sock, but his tone had changed.

"Okay, Katie... let's stop playing around here. You wanna go home, and I wanna get the hell out of North Carolina. All you have to do is give me the goddamned pin number and you're home free." He turned around and grabbed her by the hair. "Now, what is it!"

She looked up at the hideous face staring down on her. "I changed it two weeks ago! Maybe they don't have the new number in their system yet. Go back and try my old number."

He took out his notebook. "Okay. What is it?"

"LJ1723."

"Are you sure that's your old pin, cause I'm tellin' you, girl, if it isn't, you're gonna be *real* sorry. Sooner or later, some nosey cop's gonna be on his beat and he's gonna wonder what the hell I'm doing at an ATM at eleven o'clock at night with a fuckin' hood over my face!"

The door slammed shut and the dog sat up, licked her face and lay back down. The kindness in the gesture broke her heart and tears streamed down her cheeks. She pictured Jason's grinning face and could almost feel Lisa cuddled up against her, and she began to sob.

Then she thought about Sammy and how she held her in her lap in front of the campfires during those heady days when she expected to marry Tiger. This ghoul mentioned seeing Sammy with Skippy. He had obviously been stalking her. If she hadn't gone to Raleigh, Sammy could have been the one chained up in this van instead of her. She was probably going to die tonight, and the only solace— better her, than the little girl without a mother who she had never stopped loving.

The door opened and she braced herself. "Did you get the money?" He didn't seem to be listening. "If you didn't get any this time, we can cash a check tomorrow." He ignored her, and it threw her into a panic. Was he giving up the hunt for money? She feared his plans were changing and this horrible nightmare was about to get worse.

"We're gonna camp out for the night so I can think a little. You broke a bunch of bones in my right hand and are gonna have to help me offload and setup." He reached under the seat and waved a gun so she could see it. "When we get to the campsite, I'm gonna untie you, but if you bust out runnin' I'm gonna shoot your ass down, and I'm as good of a shot left-handed as I am with my right. And, honey, remember if we get stopped… a roadblock or somethin' like that, if you make one sound… I'm gonna start shootin'. Everyone's gonna get killed."

DEPUTY OLSEN WAS NOSED IN between a wagon full of hay and a tractor. No one coming from either direction would notice him in the black pick-up, yet he was out far enough that he could see them coming. The engine was off and the windows down. The cacophony coming from the cicadas in the woods around him sounded like thousands of rattles filled with soft stones being shaken in endless, jerky motions.

He turned his radio down so it was just loud enough to hear. The sound might travel on the muggy air. He'd already driven up and down the dirt road and gotten out and looked around all the way to the creek that ran along one side. He discovered an opening where a vehicle had recently driven, then nosed around and found remnants from a campfire, but nothing else.

He leaned back in his seat and remembered his big moment

in the Brevard barracks when he delivered the video. The head of Cherokee County's detective squad had personally greeted him at the door and slapped him on the back like he was part of a winning team. Everyone gave him high fives. He wished he could savor the moment, but all he wanted to do was kick himself. He'd had remnants of the guy's black sweatshirt in his locker all the time they were looking for this bastard. He knew something wasn't right that day on the farmer's property. That's why he saved the stuff he pulled out of the campfire. Why in the hell hadn't he followed up on his gut feelings? If he had, maybe they wouldn't be searching for this woman right now.

He pawed through the stuff he had picked up at the convenience store on his way back from Brevard, tore open the bag of chips and stuffed a big handful in his mouth. He shook his head. Without the trans fats, they just didn't have the same kick. He finished them off and started in on a package of Little Debbies. A red Camaro zoomed by doing seventy, and it bothered him to let it go. He'd already given that Nelson kid a couple of warnings.

After two hours and just as many packs of gum, Deputy Olsen began to wonder if he shouldn't be out there, checking other known camping sites. He riffled through the wrappers on the front seat and found a packet of peanuts and tore them open with his teeth. Headlights suddenly appeared on the horizon at the opposite direction from I-40, and he let out a humph. What were the chances of it being Gary Skinner's van? He lay down the peanuts and picked up his field glasses that had a gyroscope image stabilizer to see if he could get a good look. Heck. You never know.

Christ! It's a white van! He glued his eyes to the glasses as the vehicle slowed down. Just as it passed, the headlights of an oncoming car flashed light on the driver. The hair on the back of Olsen's neck rose as he identified Skinner. Bingo! He watched the van turn onto the dirt road and disappear into the woods, barely giving him a chance to make out the Florida license plate.

He reached for his cell and was surprised how cool he was as he dialed the lead detective. "A white van just pulled onto the dirt road off Reynolds Road a half mile west of I-40, just past the Cleves Family Cemetery. I identified the driver as Gary Skinner. He's changed his plate and is now using a Florida license."

He could hear the detective holler out, "We've got him every-body. He's in Cherokee County!" A roar came over the phone. "Okay, stay right where you are and don't do anything to spook him. We're on the way."

Olsen turned up his radio and listened to the cars being called to the scene. "Approach with lights out and wait to enter the road."

This is it! thought Olsen as he started the pick-up and rolled across the road in the dark. They'd be sending a SWAT team with snipers. He hoped like hell they'd get there fast.

THE DOG JUMPED UP as the van bumped along what had to be a field. The vibrating sound of the cicadas told Katie they were now in the deep woods. She filled with so much terror she couldn't feel any pain. The van stopped moving, and she stopped breathing.

Skinner turned around waving the gun. "We're settin' up camp here, and I swear, you try to make a run for it, and I'm gonna shoot you down."

He reached over and took the padlock off the chain around her neck and got out. She sat up and stared unblinking at the door, just like the dog. One of her eyes was nothing but a narrow slit. She started to hyperventilate. This is no time to lose it! The door opened and she could see him clearly in the light of the full moon. He was smiling—as if a smile from him could put her at ease.

"Hon, don't look so scared. We're gonna have some fun tonight… and tomorrow you're gonna cash a check for me… and I'm gonna' let you go home. That's what you want, isn't it?" He motioned for the dog to get out, then said, "You're next, Katie."

Toting the gun in his left hand and a flashlight in his right, he ordered her to get two sleeping bags and a tarp from the van and spread them on the ground. Every time she moved, pain pierced her brain raw, and she only managed dragging out the bags. He nudged her along, pointing with a flashlight to sticks for her to pick up, but never let her get near enough to the woods to make a dash for it. She searched the area with her eyes as best she could without lifting her head. Somehow, she had to make a break for it.

OLSEN MADE OUT THREE SETS of headlights coming down the road before everything suddenly went dark. He walked out onto the asphalt, flagged down two squad cars and a sheriff's emergency response team vehicle and escorted them to an area off the road behind some trees where they wouldn't be seen. Two men in camouflage jumped out of the SERT van, wearing walkie-talkie headsets and flak jackets. The sniper got out his rifle and deftly mounted his night vision eyepiece onto the scope, while the spotter readied his night vision binoculars with military precision.

SKINNER THREW KATIE A LIGHTER and told her to start the fire. Her throbbing thumb wouldn't let her flick it fast enough to ignite a flame. He pointed to the back of the van and told her to get some matches from the trunk. She kept thinking she had to stall him long enough to figure out a way to escape. If only she could distract him for a moment, once she got into the woods, he'd never find her.

She got the fire going, and he motioned for her to stand by a tree. With the light from the fire she could finally see they were in a small clearing in the woods. Her eyes roamed around desperately searching for an opening. He put down the flashlight and pulled out a zip tie from his back pocket.

"Hon, I need to do some personal stuff, and I've got to secure you until it's time to go to sleep."

All her instincts told her not to let him do it. She knew he was going to rape her and then kill her. It took everything she had to act docile. "Please don't use those ties. If you pull on my arm, I'll pass out from the pain."

"Okay. I'll tie you up with cord. Later I'll get your legs."

She heard him fumbling through his backpack a few feet behind the tree and knew he had to have put the gun down. This was her last chance! She started to run, but he caught up with her, grabbed her shoulder and flung her around. Wrenching her wrist, he dragged her over to the van and slammed her against it. He picked up a tire iron and lifted it high in the air.

His face slowly twisted into a hideous mask. She felt the weight of his body against hers and the tug on her shirt as he slipped to the

236

ground. She slowly raised her eyes and looked at the faces emerging from the woods and realized the sound she had heard was a gunshot.

A surreal scene floated in front of her in slow motion. She couldn't hear anything, and just stared at all the moving lips and peering eyes. A revolving blue light, casting shadows that jumped from tree to tree, made her dizzy. Someone put a blanket over her shoulders and a cup of warm coffee to her mouth, and tears flooded her eyes. Two men carrying a stretcher emerged and gently lifted her on. A solemn figure led the dog away in silence.

The bright, sterile inside of the ambulance and the two medics working with understated efficiency sparked a feeling that she had a life again. One of them, a young black woman, knelt down next to her, filled a needle from a vial, and waited while the other one swabbed her arm.

Katie raised a hand and uttered her first word. "Wait!"

"Honey, this is going to put you out of your pain 'til we get you to the hospital."

"I know. But I want to call my kids first. Does anyone have a cell phone?"

Lt. Williams, who was on a seat across from her, motioned for the medic to hold on, then asked Katie for the number. He talked into his phone, then held it to her ear. "It's your son."

"Hi, Jason. I'm okay, honey." She listened for a moment. "Tiger did?" Tears streamed down her face. "I love you too, baby. Is your sister there? Put her on. Hi, sweetheart. Momma's okay. I love you. I'll call you guys tomorrow. Can you put Jason back on?" She looked up at Lt. Williams. "Can you please get Tiger Morrison's cell number from my boy and dial him for me?... I owe him a call."

EPILOGUE

Linda sat at her desk in the office and finally finished the last stack of files for the counselors and mentors to look over once they started arriving for orientation. This was her eighth year at it, but it hadn't gotten any easier.

She didn't have to look up to know someone was peeking at her from the corner office. She kept at her work and said, "All right, Susan, I know you're not on your cot. Your mommy's going to be mad at me if she finds out I didn't get you to take your nap." She didn't have the heart to be too strict with her. The girl who the camp had hired as a babysitter for the staff's kids would be arriving tomorrow, and she wasn't going to be seeing Susan all that much after that.

She pulled out the checkbook and started with the pile of approved bills to the drone of voices coming over the camp radio. Patrick was telling Jason to be sure to bring a box of roofing nails along with the shingles. She shook her head. For all the time they'd spent repairing that infirmary roof, they could have put on a new one.

Sammy's voice drifted in from outside. She was talking with someone downstairs.

"Susie... your mom's on her way up. You better get back on the cot."

The screen door opened, and Sammy, toting a carton of paper, waited for Skippy to get in before letting it bang shut. As old as the dog was, he still followed her around. She dropped the carton on a table, pried it open and started stacking the reams next to the copy machine. "Where's Katie and Dad?"

"Oh, you know Katie. She's gone into Asheville with Lisa to get new tablecloths for the dining hall. I told her to get blue and white check this time, but I know she's gonna' come back with red."

"How about Dad?"

"He's over at the trout pond putting in a new pump with Josh."

Linda began slipping checks into envelopes. "Are those two ever going to call it quits?"

"This place is the air they breathe."

"Yep. That just about sums it up."

Sammy put the empty carton away and meandered over to the corner office. She went inside and was greeted by her smiling five-year-old. She slid onto the cot and brushed the child's blond bangs away from her forehead. "Did you get any rest, baby?"

"I'm too excited, Mom. When is everyone coming?"

"Not for another day, honey."

Susan twirled her thumbs. "Mom, when I grow up and get married, are me and my husband going to run the camp like you and Daddy?"

"I hope so, sweetheart." She patted the child's arm. "But right now, Mommy wants you to rest." She bent down and nuzzled her. "I'll sing something for you."

Sammy's voice was raised just above a whisper. *Daddy won't you take me back to Muhlenberg County... down by the Green River where Paradise lay...* The words streamed out as she gazed in the distance. She could hear in her mind the shouts and hollers of happy kids enjoying the magic of being outdoors. Faces she could never forget swam in her head... *I'm sorry my son, you're too late in askin'... Mr. Peabody's coal train has hauled it away...* Spider was now a strapping sixteen-year-old and would be there for the second session with Tucker. She laughed thinking that those two were now part of the camp lore. But her favorite ten-year-old would always be Patrick, stepping out of a limousine in a three-piece suit.

Then she thought of her father. *Well, they dug for their coal 'til the land was forsaken... then they wrote it all down to the progress of man...* Ever since he came face to face with the Green River Valley when he was five, he knew a good thing when he saw it, and he had become a part of it.

She knew why he had put their land in a trust, preserving it from development for as long as the State of North Carolina existed. It lay in the words of Chief Seattle, whom he always quoted. "When the last red man has vanished from the earth, and his memory is only the shadow of a cloud moving across the prairie, these shores and forests will still hold the spirits of my people."

Her father truly believed the stones lying on the field above the upper council held the spirits of the thousands he had taught to love his land the way he did, and now he could promise the campers at every council ceremony that their stones would remain there forever. She thought of her father's deep respect for the land, and she knew how important it was to him, that for generations to come, campers would be able to stop for a moment, like he always did, and listen to the wind in the woods.

ACKNOWLEDGEMENTS

The Wind in the Woods is the second novel in my series that takes place in the Southern Blue Ridge Mountains. It is a privilege to be able to thank Sandy and Missy Schenck of The Green River Preserve for allowing me to loosely fashion this novel around the extraordinary summer youth camp they have created in North Carolina's Green River Valley. In fact, the main character in the novel *is* the camp. I am also grateful to members of their dedicated staff, especially Evan Small, Linda Lamphier, Paul and Beth Bockoven, Bob Davis, Pam Ritchie, Helen Hull and Ben Roe who have aided me in imbuing this story with The Green River Preserve's unforgettable character.

I want to thank Casey Thurman and Mary Bell of Camp Glen Arden, Chuck McGrady and Yates Pharr of Falling Creek Camp, and Hank Birdsong of Camp High Rocks for giving me added insight into the area's camping community.

The year 2010 marks the one hundredth anniversary of the establishment of summer youth camps in the Hendersonville/Brevard area, which contains the highest concentration of camps in the United States. The Laurel Park Summer School and Camp for Boys, the first camp in the Hendersonville-Brevard area, started in 1910. Camp Greystone started in 1920, and Camp Modamin was established two years later by the famed Frank Bell, respectfully referred to as "Chief." Camp Glen Arden for girls, formerly Camp Arrowhead, organized by Frank's brother, Joe, has been placed on the National Register of Historic Places by the U.S. Department of the Interior.

As this book is being written, fifteen camps exist in the Hendersonville/Brevard area, occupying land ranging in size from 100 to 3,500 acres. Collectively they comprise at least 10,000 acres of undisturbed mountain land—ten times the size of North Carolina's famed 1,000-acre Chimney Rock State Park located next door in Rutherford County.

Not only do campers from all over the states pour into the area every summer, but hundreds of college kids generated from the camps' alumni, or recruited from top colleges throughout the U.S., stream in to work as counselors. Talented artists, athletic coaches, naturalists and wilderness experts, most of them teachers or professors with summers off, come to share their knowledge and infuse campers, and hopefully future environmentalists, with love for the great outdoors and all that inhabit it.

The Carolina Mountain Land Conservancy, along with The Nature Conservancy and the Foothills Conservancy have been major factors in the preservation of the camp lands of Western North Carolina. I especially want to thank Kieran Roe, Executive Director; Tom Fanslow, Land Protection Director; and Aimee Baxendell, Outreach Coordinator of CMLC for their help in providing information and inspiration for this novel.

The heart-breaking tragedy of John and Irene Bryant, a couple in their eighties, who were murdered in October 2007 while hiking in North Carolina's Pisgah National Forest is still remembered by many in the area, and I wanted to underscore the dangers of hiking alone or in twos at a time when career criminals are able to slip through the criminal justice system and wreak havoc on chance victims. In deference to the Bryant family, I have replaced them with two fictitious widows in their seventies and put the scene in neighboring Rutherford County. The book opens with their disappearance, and traces in an exact timeline the sequence of the Bryants' disappearance and the subsequent murder investigation.

Gary Michael Hilton, the 61-year-old suspected serial killer who confessed to the murder of 24-year-old Meredith Emerson who went hiking with her dog in the Northern Georgia mountains on New Year's Day 2008 and never returned, is also the sole suspect in the killing of the Bryants. I used the transcript of his confession to Meredith's murder to create Gary Skinner's stalking of Sammy Morrison and the abduction of Katie Warlick, the 41-year-old camp cook in my novel.

I am grateful to Lieutenant Sam Williams, head of the Detective Department of the Rutherford County, NC, Sheriff's Office, and Bob Toomey, Deputy Chief of Operations for the Brevard Rescue Squad, for helping me with my research into their investigative and search and rescue procedures.

As in my first book in this series, one of my favorite resources is the series written by Frank L. FitzSimons Sr., 1897-1980. This local historian's three books, *From the Banks of the Oklawaha, Vol. 1, 1976, Vol. 2, 1977*, and *Vol. 3, 1979*, are filled with local lore and historical anecdotes. James T. Fain, Jr.'s, *A Partial History of Henderson County*, May 1979, included a summary of the history of camping in the Hendersonville/Brevard area. Also, the booklet, *Walking to Greenville: The Legacy of Joe Capps* by David Schenck, gave me an intimate insight into the tenacious love of the Green River Valley by the families that have lived there for generations. Quoted, are excerpts of John Prine's soulful song, *Paradise*, about a town in Western Kentucky.

I especially want to thank Wendy Dingwall, the publisher of Canterbury House Publishing, Ltd., for her guidance and efforts on behalf of myself and her other authors, many of whom are from the mountains of the Blue Ridge, and Sandy Horton, my editor, who as always, made my book better.

I'm grateful to all my friends and acquaintances who have offered their support and assistance during the year it took to write this novel: Robert Morgan, author of *Brave Enemies*, and *Boone: A Biography*, Wanda Maybin, Deborah Chalk, Saundra Nelson, Becky and Danny Holland, Charleen Bertolini, Linda Ketron, Elizabeth Dalton, Margie Warwick, Mercedes and Chuck Town, Betty Allen, Marian Lowry (who gave me a heads-up on the Fibonacci numbers that were introduced in 1202 by Leonardo Fibonacci), Lou Pfeifle, Linda Turner, Lynn Lund, Joanne Goldy, and Joselyn Watkins.

Without the love and support of my family, this book would never have been written. I especially want to thank my grandson Isaac who was the inspiration for Alvin, and whose picture appears on the cover.

Glossary

BLUE RIDGE SERIES of Stand-Alone Books

Rose Senehi

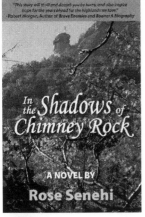

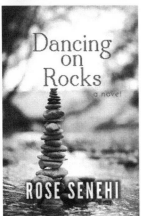

Winner of the 2012 IPPY Gold Medal Fiction-Southeast

Render Unto the Valley. Karen Godwell isn't as much ashamed of her mountain heritage as of what she once had to do to preserve it. She reinvents herself at college and doesn't look back till her clan's historic farm is threatened. She returns only to come face to face with who she was and what she did. Cousin Bruce sees life through the family's colorful two-hundred-year past; Tom Gibbons, a local conservationist, keeps one eye on the mountains and the other on Karen. Her nine-year-old daughter is on the mission her dying father sent her on.

In the Shadows of Chimney Rock. *A touching tale of Family and Place.* A Southern heiress reaches out to her mountain roots for solace after suffering a life-shattering blow, only to be drawn into a fight to save the beauty of the mountain her father loved. Hayden Taylor starts to heal in the womb of the gorge as she struggles to redeem her father's legacy, never suspecting the

Winner of the 2014 Indie-Reader Discovery Award-Popular Fiction.

Dancing on Rocks. *Georgie Haydock harbours a dark secret about her little sister's disappearance twenty-five years ago until a chance encounter forces her to uncover the mystery that's tormenting her family and keeping her from the man she loves.* This down-home story of love, family and longing unfolds against the backdrop of a North Carolina mountain village tucked in a spectacular gorge.

Other Novels by Rose Senehi

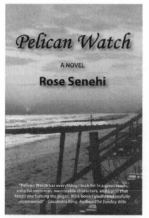

Pelican Watch. *Laced with the flavor of South Carolina's low country, this love story is told against a backdrop of murder and suspense.* Nicky Sullivan always nurses injured animals, but this time she's going to heal herself. She flees to a SC barrier island and discovers a kindred spirit in Mac Moultrie, a salty retired fisherman. From the moment she meets Trippett Alston, she's smitten, but the dark forces swirling around the island threaten to keep them apart.

Windfall. Meet Lisa Barron, a savvy marketing executive with a kid and a crazy career in the mall business. Everyone knows she's driven, but not the dark secret she's hiding. She's keeping one step ahead of the FBI and a gang of twisted peace activists who screwed up her life in the sixties, while trying not to fall in love with one of the driven men who make these massive projects rise from the ground. What will she do if her past catches up with her? Grab her daughter and run, or face disgrace and a possible murder charge?

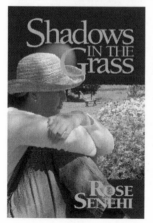

Shadows in the Grass. Striving desperately to hold onto the farm for her son, a widow comes into conflict with the handsome composer who builds a mansion on the hill overlooking her nursery, never suspecting that the man who moves into the rundown farm behind her has anything to do with the missing children.

ABOUT THE AUTHOR

The Wind in the Woods is Rose Senehi's fifth novel and the second "stand alone" book in her Blue Ridge Series. *Render Unto the Valley,* her third novel in the series, was the winner of the 2012 IPPY Gold Medal for Fiction-Southeast. *Dancing on Rocks,* the fourth stand alone in the series, was awarded the 2014 Indie-Reader Award for Popular Fiction.

"When I started developing a plot for my fourth novel in 2005, I needed to find a small town in the mountains where my heroine's father lived, so I took off from Pawleys Island, where I was actively engaged in real estate, and started my search in North Carolina. When I came upon the village of Chimney Rock I was so struck by its rustic charm that I decided to buy, as a vacation place, one of the cottages nestled in the mountainside behind the little downtown.

"That story turned out to be *In the Shadows of Chimney Rock* and the first novel of what would be my Blue Ridge Series. And when it kept breaking my heart every time I left Chimney Rock, my vacation place slowly evolved into my permanent residence. However, South Carolina's Low Country will always have a special place in my heart.

"Researching the history of the Hickory Nut Gorge and weaving stories around it, has been a wonderful experience. These four novels are part family saga, part mystery and part love story. Throughout them, I have strived to paint a portrait of the mountain culture I have fallen in love with and portray historical events as accurately as possible. I do hope you enjoy them."

P.S. I especially enjoy leading discussion groups with book clubs.

Visit Rose Senehi
www.rosesenehi.com
www.hickorynut-gorge.com
or email at:
rsenehi@earthlink.net

59168607R00148

Made in the USA
Columbia, SC
02 June 2019